TEMPTED BY MY EX-HUSBAND

PIPER RAYNE

Cover design: RBA Designs

Line Editor: Gray Ink Editing

Proofreader: Shawna Gavas, Behind The Writer

The perfect man for me is the one who broke my heart. #thanksbutnothanks

Once bitten.
Twice shy.
Yeah, I wish.

I'm on a mission to find myself a nice, solid, respectable man. The only problem is nice, solid, and respectable comes in a meh package and is B-O-R-I-N-G as hell.

It's been established. I have one type. Bad Boy. I tried the other flavors, I really did. But there's nothing like the allure of a man who takes what he wants without apology.

As if my love life isn't dramatic enough, Dean Bennett walks into my life again thinking he's going to win me back with his charm and charisma. He might come in a different package, but under that expensive suit he's still the same cocky, arrogant, pompous prick who only cares about numero uno.

I'm not that naïve young girl anymore so I have to ignore the fact that the way he looks at me practically sets my panties on fire.

Everyone deserves a second chance to right a wrong. The problem? He's not just an ex-boyfriend...

He's my ex-husband.

CHICAGO LAW: BOOK TWO

TEMPTED
BY MY EX-
HUSBAND

Chapter One

"*A*ddison and Clark." I glance up from my phone to try and give my taxi driver the directions through the rearview mirror. He nods and says something that I can't hear because he's talking into his Bluetooth instead of to me.

I shrug and continue to hammer out the message with my thumbs.

Me: *I'm going to be about ten minutes late.*

Three dots appear below my message and I envision my date sitting at the bar waiting for my arrival.

Glen: *K.*
Me: *Do you like the bar?*

The three dots appear and then disappear. I keep the phone poised in my hands for a few minutes before giving up on a response and dropping the phone in my lap.

A manila folder rests under my purse on the backseat

of the taxi that I need to drop off before I can begin my weekend. I glance out the window at everyone rushing down the streets to get to their Friday night plans. That should've been me.

When Glen reached out through Coffee Meets Bagel, I was skeptical. CMB is known to attract guys who are looking for commitment. His profile picture was a gym selfie and though it might have stirred up the lady parts, I'm working on having my brain override my vajayjay's radar these days. My brain said this guy smells like trouble —especially after the beach guy's picture who ended up being a catfish.

After I didn't respond to his message right away, another message came through. He said he knows the picture is lame, but his friends convinced him it was the way to go. I asked if the picture was him and he told me if I showed up on the date, I'd find out it was in fact him. He was playful and funny, and he hooked me. And now I'd volunteered to deliver this damn package and ruin what could very well be the story we tell our potential grandchildren with, first I had to drop off papers at a tax attorney's office for my boss.

The taxi stops, and the driver says nothing, so I hand over the cash and rush out of the car back onto the streets of Chicago.

"This tax attorney is doing pro bono work for us?" I mumble to myself staring up at the high-rise building.

Walking through the revolving door, I'm greeted by a security desk before I can access the elevators. *Shit.* I should message Glen again to say I'm going to be even later than I expected.

I approach the tall man who looks as annoyed as me for being here on a Friday night. "Hello, I need to head to"

—I glance at the envelope— "Heiberman and Lipe Law Firm."

He taps a few keys. "I think they're closed already." His face is void of any emotion.

"Can you tell me if there's a…" my eyes glance to the folder again. "Mr. Bennett?" The last name causes my stomach to gurgle.

"Let me call up." He presses some buttons on the phone, listens for a second and then hangs up. "No one is answering."

I lean over the counter, splashing on my please eat out of my hand smile. "It's Friday. You want to go home. I want to go home. I promised my boss that I'd get these on the desk of Mr. Bennett." I cough, bile rising up my throat with the mention of the name. Victoria is really going to have to take care of this in the future. "Can I please just go up to their floor and see if their door is unlocked?"

He shakes his head, giving me a look I'm way too familiar with, silently asking if I'm crazy.

"What can I do?" I ask. "Money? A date?" I look at his left hand. "No. Are you a fan of winter sports?" I'll totally pull Skylar into this. "My cousin is a Winter Classics skier and her fiancé—" A large palm lands in front of my face.

"Give me your name." His fingers position on the keyboard.

"Chelsea… Chelsea Walsh."

He types my name in, and I smile when he pulls a visitor badge out.

"Thank you, thank you, thank you." I take it from his hand and put it over my head.

"If no one is up there, they have a drop box beside their door. You can leave your package there."

I thank him again and walk steadily to the elevators, dodging people desperate to start their weekend.

I end up riding the elevator by myself to the thirty-third floor. The elevator doors ding open and I file out, my head swiveling right and then left. Spotting the door with Heiberman and Lipe Law Firm, I head over to it to find a list of the names of all the associates and thankfully there's Bennett second from the top.

Hold on Glen, I'm almost on my way.

My hand pulls on the frosted glass door and it must be my lucky day because it opens.

I step into the darkened reception area. Looking around, I find no one. Heading down a hallway, my eyes zero in on the names on the doors while peeking my head into vacant offices. Finally, after passing the conference room, I see the last name Bennett and peek my head inside to find it empty with the light on. Hopefully that means he's in the bathroom or something.

I pull out my cell phone, seeing Glen has messaged me back, but instead of responding to his I shoot one off to my boss Hannah.

Me: *Mr. Bennett isn't here. Can I drop the envelope on his desk?*

Hannah as usual, replies instantly.

Hannah: *Sure. Just leave it somewhere he'll see it first thing on Monday.*
Me: *Got it.*

I drop my cell phone back into my purse and slowly walk across the room and place the envelope on the chair. As I straighten up, I notice a baseball sitting next to the keyboard like someone had been playing with it and just set it down.

My jaw drops and my gaze scatters across every

surface, spinning around investigating each piece of art, photos, anything I can find to tell me this isn't…

Then as though I hadn't breathed the entire time I've been in this office, the smell of *him* hits my nostrils. The once familiar scent of the ocean breeze, his deodorant and fresh linen from his clothes. He never was a cologne guy.

Other than a picture of a dog on the table behind his desk, it's filled with baseball memorabilia of the Cubs. A die-hard Cub's fan certificate is framed and on display, so others know he didn't jump on the bandwagon two years ago when they won the World Series. It's proof that his family has borne the Cubbie fever for generations.

"Do you make it a habit of sneaking into people's offices?" His voice is coy and flirtatious.

I squeeze my eyes shut then grip the edge of the desk before my knees give out. Shivers run up and down my spine.

Crazy train. All aboard!

"You can at least show your face," he says, continuing his usual play. "I promise I don't bite."

"Unless I want you to." I spin around, my knuckles white as they tighten on the edge of the desk.

Now it's his jaw that slackens as he realizes his ex-wife is standing in the middle of his office.

Chapter Two

"Chelsea?" he asks, like he's not sure it's me. This isn't a twenty-five-year reunion. It's been five years. Five years since I've seen those deep chocolate eyes, the messy brown hair. He's grown even more attractive over the years. More mature. Manlier, leaving that boy next door look behind with our divorce papers.

"Dean." I'm able to cool my voice to make sure he doesn't realize how affected I am by his presence.

His gaze flows up and down my body and I swallow past the lump in my throat and heat spreads like lava over my skin.

Thank God for those spin and yoga classes and grilled chicken and vegetables. Eat your heart out asshole. Check out what you missed out on.

"You look amazing." One thing about Dean is that his eyes always tell his truth and it's clear that his compliment is genuine.

"Wish I could say the same." I cross my arms, finally finding my inner lioness.

He chuckles, rocking back on his heels and stuffing his

hands into the pockets of his suit pants. The sleeves of his white button-down shirt are rolled up to his elbows, but his tie and vest are still in place along with a silver watch adorning his wrist. The sight of him in his gray suit stirs up the lady parts something fierce. Not that I'd ever let him know it.

"I was expecting a Victoria to do the drop-off." He disregards my comment because that's the problem with two people who know each other so well. He can tell my truth just as well as I can his, and he knows I'm full of shit.

"Sorry to disappoint. Paperwork is on your chair."

I desperately want to flee this room, but he's blocking the door and there's no possible way I can get closer to him at this point. I might be able to roar like the lioness from afar, but I'll crumble like an overzealous cub if either of us move.

"So, you're working for Hannah Crowley?" He leans his shoulder on the doorframe, no intention of moving. Go figure, the man tormented me all through our relationship —just in a good way back then.

"Yes. I'm her marketing manager."

"I like the idea of the foundation…giving girls empowerment, letting them know they have a voice."

"Yes, it's a wonderful thing she's put together." I pray I look more relaxed than I feel. My heart is pounding inside my chest like a college drumline.

"You like it?" he asks, his eyes never leaving mine.

He's all cool and calm like he always was, while I sit here trying not to let my big girl image falter. He might be the only man on this planet who has the capacity to do that.

"I do." I look around his office. "So, you're a tax attorney?"

He chuckles again, his strong, broad shoulders rising

and falling. "Crazy, right? After I recovered and finally got my shit together, went to law school."

"You picked the most boring part of the legal system?" I raise an eyebrow.

A smile continues to tease his lips. "It's more interesting than you think."

"I should get going." I step forward, not interested in partaking in a where-are-you-now conversation.

He glances to my left hand for a second and a full smile creeps up his lips. "How about dinner?"

I wrinkle my forehead. He's still insane.

"I don't think so." I step away from the desk with the hopes he'll step further into the room, so we can circle around one another until I'm at the door.

"Why not? Unless your wedding ring is being repaired, doesn't look like you're committed. Did I ruin you for all other men?" He laughs to show it's a joke, but his comment only lights the fuse on my anger and resentment.

"Just because I'm not married doesn't mean I'm not committed."

Way to go, Chels. Lie.

"So, you have someone?" He stands straighter but never leaves the doorframe.

"Well..."

"I did ruin you."

"No. You. Didn't," I say through gritted teeth.

"Relax, Ches. It's a joke. Good to see you. I wanted to reach out a few times, but never knew how you'd take it."

"How I would take it?"

He shrugs. "Yeah, I mean *you* were the one who walked out on *me*."

"Excuse me?" My inner bitch has come out to play. Forget this polite crap. Hannah will understand when I kick her tax attorney in the balls.

"If memory serves, I woke up one day to an empty bed."

A cynical huff leaks out of me. "Glad to see a law degree didn't change you. You're still the arrogant jackass you've always been."

"What am I missing?" he asks, and I swear my blood runs hot enough to boil a lobster.

Forget him, I'm going to shoulder check him on my way out.

I stomp toward the door.

"No worries, Mr. Bennett, Victoria Clarke will be your contact at RISE from this point on." I bulldoze forward, thinking I can push right past him and into the freedom of the hallway.

He steps into the center of the doorframe, his broad shoulders and tall figure filling the empty space. I almost tip forward into his chest from the sudden stop.

"I'm kidding, Chels," he whispers and there's those damn chocolate eyes front and center and fixated on me again. "There's not a day that goes by that you don't cross my mind."

His smell reappears like smoke filling a room. I shouldn't inhale the toxic scent, but I do, and my body relaxes instantly.

"I have somewhere to be." I ignore his confession. A confession I've waited five years to hear. A confession I thought I'd get a day after I packed my bags and left. He never came after me. He never fought for us.

"Where?" he asks.

I look him square in the eye, hoping like hell he can't see the wetness that's been threatening behind my lids since I first heard his voice. "I have a date."

"A date?" He seems surprised.

"Is it that hard to believe?" I say with venom.

He shakes his head. "Not at all. So that means you're single then?"

I hate to admit to him that I have yet to find anyone special. "Yes."

He steps forward, our chests only millimeters apart. I crane my neck to look up at him. "Cancel and let me take you out. We can catch up."

My entire body is on fire. How did the pull to this man not die after I signed away my right to be a Bennett? The electricity is still a magnetic pull between us.

"You're dreaming if you ever think you'll lay a hand on this body again."

"I asked for dinner, not a fuck," he says, no emotion crossing his face. His eyes are cloudy now and I can't tell what exactly he wants from me.

"I see a law degree didn't erase your crass side." I tilt my head to the side, jut my hip out and wait for his comeback.

"Don't worry Chels, I can still be as crass as you need me to be to get you off while you ride me." He winks and my lady parts scream and fight, wanting to be heard. To let him show us how great he is. I refuse to give in though. I'm no longer the doe-eyed girl I once was.

"I only liked the cowgirl position because your dick was so small it was the only way I could feel it."

A slow grin warms his face. "Keep telling yourself that. We both know I wasn't even all the way in your mouth before you'd be choking during a blowjob."

He stands there all smug. I take my two hands and plant them on his apparently still muscular chest and shove him so I can escape. God help me. He falters back and I storm out of there.

"Chels," he pleads as I walk steadily out of the office.

"Fuck you, Dean." I raise my middle finger in the air

and luckily since everyone has left for the day, the elevator comes before he can chase me down. Not like he would. He didn't when it mattered, why would he now?

When the elevator doors close, I will the tears to wait. A drop trickles down my cheek. By the time I'm on the first floor, walking across the lobby to the security desk to drop my visitor badge, I'm wiping away my tears.

"Thank you again," I mumble, dropping the badge and continuing to the revolving doors. Once I'm back outside on the sidewalk of a perfect spring evening in Chicago, I flag a taxi down and slide in, finally allowing myself to crumble.

"Nearest red line L station," I say and bury my head into my hands.

The tears are hot and fast and uncontrollable. Not because of the sparing match he outwitted me in. I couldn't very well continue on the path of the small penis. Back in college, all his locker room buddies were jealous that a guy who had everything got to have a huge dick, too. Once his pro ball prospects crashed and burned, they probably said, 'at least he's got that dick going for him. He could make a killing in porn.'

Why am I even thinking about this?

I pull my cell phone out, not knowing who to talk to about this. My cousin Skylar would only warn me to stay the hell away from him. Plus, her and her fiancé Beckett are in Utah, packing their houses up for their fresh start. Her sister Zoe would likely head down to his office and beat the shit out of him.

My fingers move, and I dial the only person who would understand, even if she's in her happily ever after bubble now.

"What's up, Chelsea?" Victoria asks, the happiness

alive and well in her tone. "Did you know he bought the house next to my mom?!"

Reed Warner, the fucking prince.

"Did he? I didn't know." I really try to inflect some sort of excitement for my friend, but all I see is darkness around me.

"What's wrong?" she asks.

The phone muffles slightly and I hear a few faint kissing sounds.

"I saw the tax attorney."

"Is he hot? You've been into good guys lately and what tax attorney isn't a good guy, right?" She giggles.

"Hey now," Reed says in the background close enough for me to realize they're probably laying down in their new house getting ready to christen it or something.

"He's not a good guy, Vic." I take a deep breath, wishing I could scream at the top of my lungs right now. "He's my ex-husband!"

"Whoa," Reed interrupts again obviously hearing me through the phone.

"You're busy, I'll let you go."

"No, you won't. Meet us at Reed's in half an hour."

"What?" Reed doesn't sound too enthused about the plan. "But—" The phone muffles again.

"I'm calling Cooper to let you up in case you get there before us," Victoria says when she gets back on the line.

"Okay, thanks." I click off the phone. "I'm sorry, can you go to Michigan and Erie?" I ask the cab driver.

He nods and horns honk as he weaves all the way to the left to turn around.

It's then that I remember Glen. Opening my phone up to our thread of messages, I now have fifteen unread from him.

Glen: *It's cool. Almost here?*
Glen: *??*
Glen: *What's taking you so long?*
Glen: *Hello?*
Glen: *Earth to Mars?*
Glen: *Are you standing me up?*
Glen: *Last chance before I leave…*
Glen: *You fucking bitch.*

Whoa. What the hell?

Glen: *What is wrong with you?*
Glen: *Who doesn't tell someone they can't make it?*
Glen: *Who raised you? A pack of werewolves?*
Glen: *No wonder you can't find anyone.*
Glen: *You're such a loser that you have to be on a dating site.*
Glen: *The picture probably wasn't even you.*
Glen: *Even if it was, you weren't all that.*

Dodged that bullet.

Me: *Something came up—forever. Have a nice fucking life shithead. Go to hell.*

I tuck my phone back into my purse, searching for tissues.

By the time we pull up to Reed's condo building, Connor's friendly smile is in place as he opens the taxi door for me.

"Miss Walsh, nice to see you again." I've only met Connor once previously when I had to come and pick up Victoria for a night out.

"Thanks, Connor."

I enter the condo building and instead of going up, I

wait for the happy twosome in the lobby since I was much closer to Reed's home base than they were. It's not like I have a key to his place. Having nothing better to do, I pull up the internet on my phone and search: Dean Bennett, Attorney. Sure as shit there's my ex-husband in all his white teeth glory listed under the Associates tab on the Heiberman and Lipe Law Firm webpage.

Fucking karma, what did I do to piss you off?

Chapter Three

"Wine or beer?" Victoria asks from the kitchen.

"Or the hard stuff?" Reed glances up from his laptop at the dining room table across from me.

"You know me well."

He winks. "Get her the vodka out of the freezer, Vic."

I hear a couple of cupboard doors open and shut.

"So, you bought a house?" I ask, detouring my own issues. I'm already imposing asking to talk with his girlfriend after he just surprised her with a house. I can at least make small talk.

He shuts the laptop and smiles. "I did."

"Kind of quick, no?"

He furrows his brows for a moment, and then the perma-smile Reed's known for shines through. "Some might say that, but I don't think so."

"She said yes?"

He nods once. "She did."

"Great. I'm happy for you two."

A low chuckle flows out of his mouth. "Are you? I mean I wouldn't be if I was you."

"Just because my life seems to be in chaos doesn't mean I don't want the best for you and Victoria."

He nods again. That condescending one quick nod, like he doesn't truly believe me. *Jerk.*

"Okay I have the vodka and I found a lime. Is that okay?"

Reed shakes his head and slides out from the chair. "Do you mind?" He places his hand on my drink. "I'll make you something."

"Please." I laugh because apparently Victoria is no bartender.

"In my defense, I'm a wine drinker," she calls out to him.

"No judging baby, don't worry," he says from the kitchen.

Then we hear ice being tossed into a glass while Reed goes about making me a drink that will hopefully erase what just happened.

"I'm sorry," I say, my fingers playing with the edge of the placemat.

"Don't be. This is fine. My mom has Jade tonight and took her out for dinner. I don't want to tell her about the house yet anyway."

"Why?"

She shakes her head, understanding the question I didn't fully ask. "It's not second-guessing or anything, it's just a big step and I want her to be just as excited as I am. I want to talk to her about it without Reed first. Lay the groundwork."

I reach across and pat her hand. "You're such a good mom."

A soft smile creases her lips like she likes to think she is.

"I try." Then she pauses, waiting for me to fill her in. "So…"

I shake my head staring down at the placemat, picking at nothing because they've probably never even been eaten on. "It's him…the tax attorney."

"Is this the first time you've seen him since your divorce?"

I nod. "Yeah. Some reunion." My tone sounding sarcastically happy.

"Did you talk?"

I lift my head. "Please, you can't shut that man up."

She bites her lip like she's trying to not say something.

"What?"

Her face loses the amusement that filled it moments ago. "Nothing. I just…"

"Spit it out."

"Well, I can't imagine what a conversation between you two is like, because if he likes to talk, and everyone knows you do…" She trails off.

"We spar. Not physically, but verbally at one another and the kicker is he beat me today."

"What did you banter about?" she asks, truly intrigued.

"Why do you look so giddy?"

She shakes her head vehemently. "I'm not. I'm concerned."

I roll my eyes. "We ended up sparring about his dick size."

Reed sets down a drink in front of me. "I'm just going to leave this right here. I'll be in my office if you need me," he says more to Victoria than me.

"Thanks, Reed."

"Thanks, baby," she says and gives him those giant heart-shaped emoji eyes. Let me stick my finger down my throat now.

Reed leaves and we hear a door shut down the hall.

"Let's go back to the dick size thing." Victoria places her chin in the palm of her hand, her attention focused completely on me.

"It was nothing. I made a joke about it being small and he countered."

"So, he's not small, I take it?" she asks.

I shake my head.

"Let me get this straight." She inhales a deep breath, almost like she's gathering her thoughts. "You were face-to-face with your ex after five years and neither of you talked about anything other than his dick size?"

When she says it like that, it does sound a tad juvenile, but I wanted to hit him where it hurt.

"We said other things too," I say mulishly.

"You're still hot for him." She doesn't pose it as a question, but an accusation.

"Not at all." I shake my head.

She raises her eyebrows and sits back in her chair with her mouth twisted to the side.

"Listen, I can't deal with him. You have to be his point of contact."

"Tell Hannah, she'll gladly get rid of him." She shrugs.

"No. He's doing it pro bono although I suspect it's his firm that's making him do it. Because the Dean I knew never would've agreed to that."

"The Dean you know wouldn't have become a tax attorney."

She's right. I might know his dick size, but other than that, I know nothing about the man I saw earlier tonight.

"True. Regardless, I'm not going to mess that up for the foundation. How often will Hannah need to use his services anyway? I'll keep my distance. He's probably still a playboy anyway." I ignore the gut-churning emotion as my mind wanders to memories of him with a bunch of ladies around him, clamoring for his attention whenever we were out.

"I think the two of you should have a conversation. Hash it out and maybe you can at least have a civil relationship."

Victoria, my sweet and naive Victoria who has a daughter with her ex and still has to deal with him. But me, I don't have to.

"We don't have kids together. I can loathe him until I'm buried six feet deep which I intend to do." I take a gulp of the mule drink Reed made me. "Man, did he work his way through law school by being a bartender?"

"Reed never had to work his way through anything." She rolls her eyes.

"I resent that comment," Reed hollers from the other room.

"I thought you were hidden away in the office," I say.

"Well, you're talking dick sizes with my girlfriend. I wanted to see what might be said."

"Concerned about your length or girth?" I joke, and Reed walks in with a bag of chips in his hand, munching away.

"Wanted to make sure Vic wasn't complaining about me being too big." He winks, and his smile says he's kidding. He might be the last of the good ones.

"What do you think, Reed? Hash it out with the ex or let the bitterness burn?" I sip my drink and Victoria puts her hand out for chips. Reed tilts the bag toward her in a silent language I've only ever had with one other person my entire life.

"No kid, I say let it burn baby." He waggles his eyebrows.

"Reed!" Victoria shakes her head and leans back in her

chair popping another chip in her mouth. "That's not good for your soul."

"My soul died a long time ago." Reed and I share a laugh while Victoria rolls her eyes at us and puts her hand back out for some chips. Reed pretends to keep the bag from her, and she fights before he relents.

"I need to leave you guys alone." I push my chair out from the table and stand.

"We've barely talked about this."

"If she's gotta go, babe." Reed winks at me. "Kidding of course."

Is it national winking day or something?

"Yeah, kidding." I finish my mule and take the glass into the kitchen.

"Stick around, we can talk or veg out with ice cream. I'm sure Reed will understand if you want to go out."

"Go out?" Reed asks. "As in clubs and bars?"

Victoria glances over her shoulder, shooting him a look I can't see from my angle.

"I'm just saying, I'm not cool with you playing wing woman. I think we should clear that up." Reed places the bag of chips on his breakfast bar and opens the fridge, grabbing a pop.

"You do know women don't go out just to pick up guys, right? That we like to dance and have fun together. We're not there to try out dick-up lines on a bunch of guys."

"Yeah, we're not there to find a Vag Badger," I add.

Both their heads circle my way.

"Vag Badger?" Reed asks, quirking one eyebrow.

"You know…a guy who follows a woman around a bar, badgering her with the hopes of wearing her down and getting some vag?"

Victoria bends over and laughs, smacking the granite countertop. "I've never heard of that."

"I think most men stop being Vag Badgers at the age of eighteen," Reed says, sounding insulted.

Victoria and I wrinkle our eyebrows together.

Vic places her hand on her boyfriend's shoulder. "Babe, you have no idea what it's like out there for us."

"Let's clarify that statement, shall we? I have no idea what it's like for Chelsea out there."

Victoria rises on her tiptoes and kisses his cheek. "You make a great argument."

He turns quickly before her lips can land on his cheek a second time and captures her lips with his. His arms wrap around her waist and pretty soon I'm watching the two have an intimate moment.

"That's my cue." I place the mule cup in the sink.

"Are you sure?" Victoria breaks apart from Reed, but Reed doesn't remove his hands from his girlfriend.

"Please, we don't want to keep you from anything," Reed jokes. At least I think he's joking.

"No, I need to go buy all the cookies and ice cream Jewel has on its shelves and wallow at home by myself."

My phone dings inside my purse and I pull it out as they follow me to the front door, finding a new text message from Glen.

"At least Dean did one thing for me tonight."

"What's that?" Vic asks, looking at the phone I'm holding out.

"He kept me from going out with this asshole."

She reads the texts, her eyes widening more with each one. "Reed," she says.

"I see it." He snatches the phone away from me. Reads through them again. "Asshole." Then he types.

"Reed what are you doing?" I ask.

"I'll meet this guy in a dark alley and kick his ass for you."

I snatch the phone back before he can finish whatever he's going to say. "I'm a big girl."

They both give me a look that says, 'are you really?' I hate that look. I get it enough from my parents.

"Let me know." Reed winks yet again and then his phone rings in the other room. "See you, Chelsea." He leans forward, kisses my cheek and jogs into the other room. "Reed Warner," I hear him say when he answers.

"You really don't have to go," Victoria says.

"I do. I'll be fine. I just have to come up with a plan, which I did, so we're all set. I just need to stay far, far away from him."

"I'll be your bodyguard." She wraps her arms around me. "I'll say this one more time. It would be good for you to get everything off your chest with him. Say what you need to say so you can really move on since he obviously still has a big effect on you."

"You're too optimistic for your own good." I hug her tight and release her. "Have a good night and don't get pregnant."

She playfully smacks me, and I open the door, fleeing before she swats at me again.

"Call me if you need me," she says.

"Always. Thanks." I press the elevator and after I step in, we wave, and the doors close between us.

I'm alone and all my thoughts are of when I was Mrs. Dean Bennett. That's never a good thing.

Chapter Four

On Monday morning I'm the first one at my desk, my bag unpacked, my computer booted up, a Starbucks latte in front of me. The weekend was full of torment as my brief marriage with Dean Bennett played like a black and white flashback from the movies. Unfortunately, our reel contained more dark moments than happy. Still, even though I should have learned my lesson with my short stint of being a Mrs., the magnetism between us was alive and kicking Friday evening.

I will say, but I'll deny, deny, and deny if it's repeated… memories of my no-good ex were my mental stimulation when I was turning on my unicorn cock vibrator this weekend.

"Hello?" Hannah yells into the office.

"I'm in here," I call out, not getting up from my seat because I have the dreaded task of telling Hannah who her tax attorney is.

She steps into my office a few minutes later, minus her bags, with her coffee in her hand. "Vic is going to be late."

I nod, figuring it's Monday and ever since Reed

entered her life you'd think her Mondays would be less frazzled, but nope. I wouldn't doubt if she and Reed head to his condo after dropping off Jade and Henry for a quickie to start their week.

"Did you have a date this weekend?" Hannah asks.

"No."

Her lips tip down. "Why not? You know I'm living vicariously through you, right?" She mocks offense, all with a smile on her face.

"I had one, but it was supposed to be after I dropped off the papers to our tax attorney, Mr. Bennett, Friday afternoon."

"Oh yeah, he sent me an email that he got them. Thanks." She sips her coffee.

"Han, the tax attorney…"

She narrows her eyes and looks at me quizzically. "What am I missing, Chels? Your face is pale and that spunky side of yours didn't seem to leave your apartment with you this morning."

"Mr. Bennett is Dean Bennett."

"Yes." She smiles like a teacher to a kid who just recited their ABCs.

"I used to be Chelsea Bennett."

Her eyes bulge out. "Is it a family member of your ex?"

"Well…"

"We can totally find someone else, even if we have to pay. I won't put you through interacting with anyone from his family. God knows I wouldn't have anything to do with my ex-in-laws."

Hannah and Victoria don't know everything that happened with Dean. I may have hinted at a few things here or there, but I've never told them the entire story. It's embarrassing, and my family looks down on me enough for my whirlwind romance that led to my marriage to a douchebag. I don't want Hannah and Victoria to look at me any differently than they do now.

"Dean Bennett, attorney at law, is my ex-husband."

She places her coffee on the edge of my desk and stares at me for a second, not even blinking. "But you said he was a bum. That he was probably in jail."

"I assumed he would be. When we parted, if someone would have said he'd be a tax attorney in five years I would have bet a million dollars they were lying. Tax evasion seemed like a more likely scenario."

She sits in the chair across from my desk and crosses her legs in the elegant way only Hannah does. Her red wine silk jumpsuit is both elegant and professional all at once. Strappy black heels pull it all together. Hannah is the kind of woman who matches her purse with her outfit every day.

"Tell me about him," she says.

I blow out a breath trying to figure out where to start.

"He's gotten under your skin, Chels." She dips her head to meet my eyes. "Do you still have feelings for him?"

"No!" My head shoots up. "Not at all. It's just, it's been five years and I wasn't expecting to see him, but there are no feelings there."

"Good because I'm a firm believer that people don't change. Whoever he was before is who he still is under this new facade of a tax attorney."

"Really? You don't think people can realize something and change the way they are?" I would have agreed to that statement three days ago, but now it unnerves me. I hate to admit how upset that makes me. Maybe there was a glimmer of hope inside me I didn't realize that thought maybe things would have worked between us if he'd changed.

"I think it's a rare occurrence." She shrugs.

"Oh."

"Please Chelsea, remember these are my beliefs. Not some rule book that you have to live your life by. If there's something there and you want to explore whether he's changed, then give it a try. Just keep your hands in front of your face so he can't left hook you." She stands and takes her coffee off the edge of the desk. "We'll discuss this at lunch. I have a call in five minutes." She stops at the doorway of my office. "It's your call, Chelsea. I'll gladly thank him for his services thus far and find another tax attorney for RISE. Let me know."

"No." I stand up, my hands pressed to the hardwood top of my desk. "I'm a professional. He's doing it for free. I told him his contact is Victoria from this point forward. I can handle this."

Her face turns into a giant question mark. "Are you sure?"

"Positive. I've handled Dean Bennett at his worst. Surely, I can handle him now."

She nods. "Okay, but if you change your mind—"

"I won't."

She smiles, and I wait to hear her heels click all the way down the hallway to her office.

Let's hope this isn't added to the long list of things I've come to regret in my life.

BY MID-AFTERNOON, I'm drowning in the details of the gala RISE is having at the end of summer. Between all the marketing and finding an auctioneer, convincing my cousin, Skylar, a Winter Classics ski medalist to speak, my day has been full.

"Delivery," Victoria sing-songs as she walks into my

office and places a bouquet of tall, full, and vibrant purple flowers on the corner of my desk.

She stands there smiling.

"I don't even want to know what kind of flowers these are?" I pluck the card, not that I need to. Unless Glen somehow found out where I work and regrets being a nasty bastard the other night, this is Dean's doing. He was always good at the making up part.

Yeah, he was.

Ugh, get out of my head, dirty thoughts.

"I do." Victoria places her hands on her hips.

"Okay, brown-noser, what type of flower is it?"

"Well before I brought them in here I google image searched." A huge grin erupts out of her like she's so proud of herself.

"And?"

"They are purple hyacinth flowers. There's a Greek myth about them being named after a youth when Apollo and Zephyr caused a strong wind—"

"Okay, teacher's pet, I don't need a lesson on Greek Mythology. What does the flower mean?"

I ask even though I have an idea.

"It's an apology. Whoever sends them is asking for your forgiveness." Victoria's eyes turn all dreamy like she's witnessing a wedding where the couple writes their own vows and the groom cries.

This is just an asshole sending flowers five years too late.

I pick the bunch of them up out of the glass vase and drop them in the trash can.

"Chels!" Vic says about to bend down and pull them out. "Don't let the jerk ruin receiving some gorgeous flowers."

"Leave them." I open the card and read Dean's message.

The reality is people mess up. Don't let one mistake ruin a beautiful thing.

Love, Dean

I DISPOSE of the note with the flowers and Victoria gasps. She's all happy and lovey now, but I bet back in her Pete days she was the same as I am now.

She grabs the note from the trash can and reads it over.

"Don't get sappy, he didn't write that." I sit back down at my desk, going through my emails before I have to leave for the dress fitting for my cousin's wedding.

"How do you know?" She honestly looks disappointed. Jeez, Reed's really done a number on her. He must have a unicorn cock.

"Because that's not Dean. Not to mention, he made more than one mistake and what we had wasn't beautiful. So he's wrong on both counts."

She holds the small card in her hand. "You know what I think? Talk it out and move on with your life. It's not good for you to harbor these feelings inside."

"Gee, thanks, Mom."

"Chels," she sighs.

"What's going on in here?" Hannah looks from Victoria to me and then sees the flowers in the trash. "What a beautiful flower. I'm not sure I've ever seen an entire bouquet of them before."

"They're purple hyacinth flowers," Victoria says like the keener in the first row at school.

I roll my eyes.

Hannah pulls one out of the trash.

"Miss Horticulture over there has a whole story to go with the flower." I mindlessly scroll down my emails to double check that I haven't missed any for today. I just want to appear busy so these two will leave my office. It's bad enough I'll have to put on a brave face when I see my mother today.

"I google image searched," Vic deadpans, her disappointed eyes on me the entire time. She's really got that mother guilt thing down pat. Watch out, Jade.

"From our tax attorney, I suppose?" Hannah asks, her eyes practically sparkling.

"Why do you two keep romanticizing this?" I leave my computer and stand, retrieving my stuff off the table on the opposite wall.

"Because everyone loves the wooing of a woman," Victoria says.

"Am I the only one who remembers how I told you he'd be out all night partying, drinking too much, pretending I didn't exist, and just how bad the end our relationship was?"

Victoria shrugs because she's still in the wooing phase right now. The man bought a house right next to her mother's so she could remain close to her. Yeah, he's in that love bubble right now.

"Well, forty percent of American's make it," Hannah says matter-of-factly.

"Forty percent of American's don't *want* to divorce, and I bet only ten percent are actually happy. I mean people stay in miserable marriages for all kinds of reasons—kids, money and pure laziness." I slide my bag up on my shoulder.

"That's pretty cynical," Victoria says.

"Says someone heading toward the ten percent."

Hannah giggles. "Believe me, Chels, I'm with you. The marriage thing isn't for me either, but I don't think we should knock it entirely." She flips her head in Victoria's direction who currently has a look on her face like she just found out Santa Claus isn't real.

"I want to believe, I really do, but between the shit dates I've been on and now my ex who thinks he can woo me into giving him a second chance? Hell will have to freeze over. Now if you'll excuse me, I have an appointment to go and be criticized by my mother for the next several hours." I pump my fist up in the air. "Keep the good times coming."

I walk out, sliding between them. Neither of them says anything to stop me. It's not until I'm on the elevator that my phone dings in my purse.

Unknown: *No thank you?*
Me: *Who is this?*
Unknown: *Am I in competition? How many men do you have sending you flowers these days?*

"AHHHHHH!" I scream inside the elevator then quickly change his name in my phone. The name I choose might not be true, but I'm going to try to retrain my brain.

Me: *How did you get my number?*
Minute Man: *I have magical ways. You must remember that. ;)*

I ignore the zing between my legs.

Me: *Delete it now.*
Minute Man: *Tell me, would you delete Harry Styles number if you had it?*

Oh, this man and his knowledge of my younger self. What can I say…it was a phase.

Me: *Don't send me anything again.*
Minute Man: *Was it the quote?*
Me: *You don't send your ex-wife flowers.*
Minute Man: *I've never heard that. I think it's a myth. I'm sure plenty of guys send their ex's flowers.*
Me: *Dean, this is my final warning.*
Minute Man: *What are you going to do if I don't stop? ;)*
Me: *You don't want to know.*
Minute Man: *Ah, Chels, you've always been all bark.*

Okay, he's baiting me and I'm not going to take it.

Me: *Fine. Whatever. I don't have to answer your text messages.*
Minute Man: *Funny. Seems you can't stop yourself now.*

I press the button on my phone and drop it into my purse, noticing that I'm now outside the office building at the corner waiting to cross.

How did I even get here?

My phone continues to ding inside my purse, but I ignore it as I walk the four blocks to the dress shop. This afternoon fucking sucks and as of right now I don't see a rainbow at the end given that I'm about to meet the most critical woman on the planet who also happens to be my mother.

Chapter Five

*I*f texting with your ex-husband who you haven't seen in five years and who just sent you flowers after you masturbated to memories of him for an entire weekend doesn't put you in the mood to be in a room full of wedding dresses, I don't know what will.

And yes, that wasn't just sarcastic, but sarcaustic. You did detect an extra dose of bitterness.

I follow the loud voices of my family through the sea of white and ivory to the three-way mirror where my cousin, Skylar, stands on a pedestal, the seamstress pinning away.

She looks stunning as always—her long brown hair pinned into a bun, her girl next door vibe disappearing into the beauty of a bride.

Another damn happily ever after couple.

"Chels!" she exclaims being the first to see me in the mirror.

The row of women from my family swivels in my direction. My cousin Zoe grins, while my aunt from her seat. My mom doesn't smile and doesn't move an inch except to swivel back toward Skylar.

"Come in. Come in." My aunt waves me to come closer when really, I'd rather be practicing self-acupuncture than be here.

"Hi, Aunt Liz." I kiss her cheek and she places her hand on my upper back nudging me closer.

Zoe sits on the chair, glancing through a magazine.

"Hi, Mom." I bend down and kiss her cheek.

Her matching-my-own blonde hair is sleek and cut to her chin. Her makeup impeccable, her outfit fresh off the racks of Neiman's even if her and my dad can't really afford it. Image is everything and apparently worth going into debt for.

"Chelsea," she says. "You're late."

"I ran over from work."

My phone dings in my purse, but I ignore it.

"You look beautiful, Sky," I say, taking a seat next to Zoe, far enough away that my mother can't whisper to me.

"Thanks." Sky's voice is full of happiness and excitement all rolled up inside a confetti bomb ready to explode.

"What's up, cuz?" I ask.

Zoe drops the magazine to her lap. "Where do you want me to start? The fact that I haven't lost my baby weight yet and Caiden, he's what?"

"He's almost three, sweetie," my aunt Liz answers.

"It's called dramatic effect, Ma. I know how old my son is."

Liz laughs. "Well, you seem frazzled a lot lately."

Zoe sits up in her chair. "I have two kids and a husband who can't clean up after himself."

"Been there," Aunt Liz says, sharing a look with my mom.

"Still picking up the socks," my mom finishes, and the two women laugh.

"Beckett picks up his socks," Sky says.

"Now he does. Vin used to bring home flowers on a whim. He made me CDs, wrote me letters. Now I get a text saying he needs me to go buy him more underwear."

"No way," I say.

Although I've been married, my life never progressed to where Zoe's at.

"I bought him briefs…the ones with smiley faces and a pink pair with bananas on them."

I smack the arm of the chair, laughing uncontrollably. "What did he say?"

"Oh, he wore them. It's Vin after all, but I told him I am not his personal shopper. He argued that he buys me panties and bras, but he does that because it benefits him. I have no problem with cotton."

She drops the magazine on the table in front of us with an agitated flourish.

"Next time get him a set where they have a sleeve to put their…" I eye both our moms who are enthralled in our conversation. "Thingy."

Zoe quirks an eyebrow at me and then points. "Done." She grabs her phone. "Hello, Amazon."

"Chelsea, stop being so vulgar." My mom leans forward, shooting me her 'you know better' expression.

My phone dings again from inside my purse.

Zoe's thumbs stop moving. "Aren't you going to get that?"

"Nope."

She shrugs and dramatically presses her finger to the screen. "All ordered. I'd show you, but I don't want you envisioning Vin in all his hot glory," she says, thick with sarcasm.

"Thank you for sparing me the agony." I wink at her.

"Well?" Skylar turns and stands in front of us.

"Oh, Sky." Aunt Liz stands and looks to her daughter, tears in her eyes.

My mom gets up and hands a tissue to her.

She looks breathtaking in a strapless beaded bodice that shows off her amazing figure. Tight through the middle and flows down into multiple layers of satin and sheer fabric. The perfect dress for the perfect bride.

Thinking back to our earlier conversation at RISE about weddings, I say a small wish that Sky and Beckett are in that ten percent. She deserves it.

"Great choice," Zoe adds, her fingers feeling the fabric of the skirt. "It'll be perfect for summer."

"Definitely." My mom chimes in. "You're the most beautiful bride I've ever seen." She shoots me a fleeting glance. In five years, she's never let me forget the fact she didn't get to plan an elaborate and costly wedding that would have surely bankrupted them.

"Thanks." Sky tears up slightly. "I hope Beck loves it as much as you guys."

"He'd love you walking down in an eighties dress complete with puffy shoulders and rhinestones galore," Aunt Liz assures her daughter.

We all know she's right. Beckett might have needed a push in the right direction, but now that he's there, I've never seen a man more willing to declare his love.

"Now it's your turn." She points to me and Zoe.

"What about Demi and Mia?" I ask.

"They're getting fitted and sending their measurements."

Why didn't I do that? Because dress shopping is a rite of passage and I love my cousin and don't live out of state.

"Plus, I didn't want too many people here to make the decision on which dress you'll wear," Sky says.

I tilt my head. "You haven't chosen yet?"

"No, it's up to you girls." She smiles like she's granting a wish to us when in reality I don't have time, nor do I want to try on twenty dresses for my mother's critique.

"Great." I smack on my fake smile and head to the dressing room.

The associate brings us an array of dresses explaining the color doesn't matter because they can order our color of choice in for all of us.

I head into one of the dressing rooms, Zoe in the other. Plopping my purse on the bench, I disrobe from my work outfit and put on a mermaid style dress that's anything but flattering. My ass looks like each cheek is fighting for dominance and my tits aren't nearly big enough to fill the bodice. The only good thing is that my white Chicago winter legs are covered.

"Let's see, ladies," Sky calls out from the waiting area.

I open my door and Sky's now back in her jeans and blouse with a cute pair of flats. She smiles.

Zoe steps out of her dressing room in another mermaid dress that has capped sleeves. The dress I'm wearing is peach, while hers is pink. She looks better.

"You both look wonderful. Let's show our moms." Skylar turns and heads down the hall.

"Do we have to?" I whine, and Zoe knocks me with her shoulder.

"It's not that bad."

I roll my eyes after she steps in front of me.

"Oh, Zo, you look great. Step up so we can see all of you," my mom says.

She does, and the moms and Skylar discuss the good and the bad of the dress, not mentioning one aspect of Zoe's body. I'm crossing my fingers that the same goes for me.

"Now you, Chelsea," Sky says, and I share a look with Zoe like when is this going to be over.

I stand on the pedestal and look at myself in the mirror. Yep, now I just look horrendous times three.

"I love it. I think it accentuates your figure," Aunt Liz says. "Would all the girls be able to pull this off like Chelsea?"

Sky tilts her head inspecting it. "Are you comfortable?"

"I am if you like it."

All the women laugh except my mom. "I think we should look at something more A-line. Not so tight around her middle."

There she is in all her glory. Be jealous ladies, she's all mine.

"Why?" Aunt Liz asks, her forehead crinkled.

I step down from the pedestal.

"I just think it'd be more flattering," she continues to appraise me.

"Let's try on another style I guess," Sky says, following us back into the dressing area.

My phone is ringing inside my purse, so I pull it out.

Minute Man flashes on the screen, so I press ignore and drop it back into my purse.

"You can get it if you have to Chels," Sky hollers from outside my fitting room.

"Nope. I'm good."

For the next hour, I try on six different dresses and stand in front of a mirror to be judged like I'm on that old reality show Swan where they'd look you over and decide what parts weren't good enough and what needed to be improved upon. I might not have black marker all over my imperfections, but I now know exactly what my mother thinks needs fixing.

"I love the high neckline with the draped back and how

it's tight around the hips and flares out farther down," Sky says. "Did you like the gold? I think it's an elegant summer color."

"Love it all." I'm heading back to the changing room when my phone rings again.

"Why are you so popular tonight?" Zoe asks, darting across from her dressing room to mine in only her jeans and bra. "What are you hiding?"

"Nothing." I push my way through the hallway, knocking Sky into the wall.

"She's definitely hiding something." Skylar runs after me, but by the time I reach the fitting room, Zoe's on the bench staring at my phone.

"Who's the new guy?" Skylar asks, joining us in the four by four changing room.

Zoe turns the screen for Skylar to see. "Minute Man?"

My shoulders sag. "Just a date."

"Good or bad?" Zoe asks.

"Bad. Definitely bad."

"Let's see why he's so anxious to speak to you then." Zoe scrolls through, the smile on her face dipping with every swipe. Her head snaps up in my direction. "Is Minute Man, Dean?" Zoe whisper-yells.

"Shh." I bring my index finger over my mouth and glance behind me as if Zoe saying Dean's name could conjure my mother up.

"Chels." Skylar takes the phone from her sister's hands. "He's called you four times since you've been here." She hands me over the phone. They really aren't ones to snoop, but Dean's number in my phone is not going to go unquestioned.

I glance down the hall again. "I was going to tell you."

Zoe slides over on the bench to make room for me. "How does he have your number?" she asks.

I shrug. "He's the tax attorney for the foundation I'm working at. I just found out on Friday."

"Wait." Zoe puts her hand in the air. "Dean Bennett is an *attorney* and at that, he's a *tax* attorney?" Her eyes are swimming in doubt.

"I saw the license on his wall."

She crosses her legs and places her chin in her palm waiting for more.

"He wants to take me out and I refuse to let him."

"Good girl, you do not need him in your life." Skylar's always a nut breaker when it comes to anyone but Beckett.

"What do you *want* to do?" Zoe asks.

You'd think when I went through my brief marriage that Skylar would've been the shoulder I cried on, but it was Zoe. Skylar was busy in the circuit trying to become a Winter Classics skier, so she had no understanding of how I felt for Dean. Zoe did and helped me through one of the hardest times of my life. Who am I kidding? *The* hardest time of my life.

"I can't," I say in a low voice, shaking my head.

"Good. Keep that train of thought and don't let him railroad you like he did before." Skylar hangs up the rest of the dresses.

"Sky!" Aunt Liz calls out and as much as I love my cousin, I'm happy at this moment that her presence has been requested elsewhere.

Once Sky's gone, Zoe pats my leg. "Maybe you should. Let him know how much he hurt you. Let him know your own regrets. You guys were so young, and I'm sure over the years things have changed. Maybe he's on the right path now."

"But?"

"What if you still have feelings?" Her lips tip down.

"Yeah." I hate the way my voice sounds so small, so weak.

"Then you deal with it. But maybe it'll just let you put him behind you once and for all."

No way I'll ever let myself get to where I was five years ago. I use my knuckle to dab at the tears in the corners of my eyes. "Nope. I'm hiding out. Now if I could get him to lose my phone number."

She taps the phone in my lap. "You could block him." Then she stands and exits the dressing room.

Skylar would've stood overhead and watched me do it. If I didn't, she probably would've blocked him herself.

I'm not sure what's best as I sit in a bridesmaid dress in a place where most people who enter are giddy with happiness at the prospect of what lies ahead.

I tuck my phone inside my purse.

I'll do it when I get home.

Even I know that's a lie.

Chapter Six

"Now I can totally see why delivery people are so happy." Victoria enters my office and places a bouquet of chocolate candy on my desk. "I do wish the recipient was happier though, but I was smiling the whole way down the hall."

"You can pick them up, turn around and head right back down that hallway. Give them to Jade."

"I'm sorry, but I don't let Jade have this much sugar." She turns on her heels, leaving the bouquet on the corner of my desk.

I tossed and turned last night, hoping to find sleep, but only saw Dean and imagined where we'd be if we'd stayed together. Would he have become a lawyer, or would I have been supporting him? Would we be scraping by, would he have been faithful, would he have ever been able to be the man he promised to be when he proposed to me?

"Victoria," I warn, sliding the chair out from my desk, stalking after her down the hall with the bouquet in my hand.

"I told you, the dentist said Jade couldn't have sugar

anymore."

"That's bullshit and we both know it." I drop it on her desk.

"I don't want it, Chelsea." Victoria's words have lost their amusement.

"Whose is that?" Hannah comes out from her office, appraising all the chocolate.

I give it to Dean, he's got the memory of a dolphin.

"It's another special delivery for Ms. Walsh." Victoria leans back in her chair, rocking it back and forth.

"I don't know which one I like better. I mean the fact he sent a specific flower that meant forgiveness or the fact that, well wait." She points to the bouquet. "Are these your favorites?"

I inspect the 100 Grands, Butterfingers, Snickers and Whatchamacallits. "Yeah." I shrug.

"Then my vote is for this one. I mean anyone can look up what flower means forgiveness. Not my asshole ex, of course, but it doesn't take memory."

"Thanks for the support guys," I deadpan.

"What's the meaning of the tin?" Victoria asks.

I look down to see a tin with the logo of the restaurant we used to go to in college to eat wings and drink beer. The same place he met me.

"It's the place we met."

"Do tell." Hannah slides into one of the chairs in front of Victoria, waiting.

"Don't we all have work to do?" I ask, exasperated.

"Nope," Hannah answers for both of them.

I sit in the adjacent chair. "I was with my friends. He was with his. He approached me, and I turned him down. See, Dean was the big man on campus. He was the star pitcher for the baseball team and a senior to boot. I was a freshman who thought her shit didn't stink. I knew Dean had his pick of women, and I thought that if I resisted him, even for a little while, he'd chase, and I'd become the girl he wanted."

"And did you?" Hannah asks.

"Well, we got married."

"And you weren't pregnant?" Victoria asks.

We all chuckle because we know that's what led to Vic's walk down the aisle with her ex, Pete.

"No." I shake my head still remembering the impromptu proposal only months after we met. "I dared him to eat the hottest wing the restaurant made. I told him if he did it without drinking anything for five minutes afterward, I'd go out with him."

"And he did it?"

"I might've caved after four minutes and let him drink a glass of milk."

They both laugh and retelling the story is the lightbulb that's been dim for the past five years. It just needed screwing in all the way and now it sheds a new light on our whole relationship.

"See, this is why he thinks he can walk all over me." I pluck the note off the bouquet.

See me for your chocolate milk.
    Love, Dean.

"IF I WOULD'VE HELD out the whole five minutes, he would've known he couldn't walk all over me." I point my finger like I'm making a case to a jury.

They both stare at me like I just took acid and I'm tripping while they're sober.

"I mean, think about it." I stand, pacing back and forth as I work it out in my head. "I never thought about it until now. I gave him the instructions to get a date with me but didn't make him adhere to them. That's why he thinks I'll always roll over for him." I shake my head. "I'm such an idiot." I jog back to my office, grab my purse from the desk chair and head back to Victoria's desk. "I'm going to tell him I'm not going to roll over like some obedient dog. There's no chance for us. It's over."

Neither of them says anything as I grab one of the Snickers bars. "Shut up, I need the energy."

Hannah holds her hands up in the air. "No judging."

I open the door to our office and press the button on the elevator.

Watch out Dean Bennett because here comes the ass kicking I should've given you five years ago.

I ROUND THE REVOLVING DOORS, my eyes locked on the security desk.

"Dean Bennett with Heiberman and Lipe Law Firm." I stand in front of the man I had to beg days earlier to let me up.

"Back again?" the big guy asks, not moving to get me a badge.

"It's obviously still working hours, so why don't you grab one of these badges, type my name in the computer, and send me on my way."

His bushy eyebrows furrow. "You seem a little upset. Is he expecting you?"

"Yes," I answer because I know if that man calls up to him, Dean will allow me up thinking he's won me over.

He picks up the receiver to the phone, dials the

number. "You can ask to be put on a guest list if you're a weekly visitor," he says while he waits for someone to pick up.

"This will be my last time here."

He tips his head down. "Yes, it's Justin down in security. There's a Chelsea Walsh here to see Dean Bennett."

How does he remember my name in a building this size?

"She wasn't on the list." He pauses. "Thanks." He drops the receiver from his mouth. "She's checking."

I roll my eyes and turn my attention to the groups of people returning from lunch.

My fingers tap along the top of the security desk, and I sigh like I have much more important things to do. Well, I kind of do, but it's not like I'm the mayor or Oprah or anything.

"Yes," Chucks says.

I perk up and turn to face him.

"Great, I'll send her up." He hangs up the phone, looks at me. "Lucky day again." His fingers type in my name and soon he's handing me over the badge. "I feel like I should warn Mr. Bennett or something."

I snatch it from his grasp. "Believe me, he can handle himself."

Getting on an elevator is much harder this time of day, but I manage to squeeze through since a nice man held the door open for me.

By the time I'm on the thirty-third floor, I'm happy we work in such a small building. The mixture of perfume, cologne, body odor, and takeout food is enough to nauseate a bear that's just woken up from hibernation.

This time when I push open the frosted glass door, there's a woman sitting at the reception desk, poised and ready for me. "Ms. Walsh?" she asks.

Of course, she's young. Blonde and beautiful. Not that Dean had anything to do with hiring her, but she fits his mold to a tee.

"Yes." I wait at the edge of her desk.

"It will be a moment, he's in a meeting." She signals for me to sit and I look back at the chairs.

"Can I wait in his office?"

It's bold and ballsy seeing she has no idea who I am, but I'd rather get this over with and not have to be polite while he escorts me down the hall.

"I'm sorry, he said he'd be out to get you in a few minutes."

I grit my teeth then huff, rolling my eyes like a thirteen-year-old girl before plopping myself into one of the uncomfortable seats. Not interested in my phone, I grab a magazine from the side table and nosily flip through the pages.

Minutes later, I hear his voice talking with someone else. The closer it grows, the more it feels like there's a rocket zooming around in my stomach.

I place the magazine down, wanting to be armed and ready for him.

He walks right into the reception area.

"Good meeting with you, David. We'll get it all straightened out."

A male probably in his fifties shakes Dean's hand, gives me a friendly smile and opens up the glass doors to leave.

"Thank you, Kylie, for being so accommodating to my unplanned visitor," Dean says to the receptionist.

She smiles up at him like he's Bradley Cooper. Give me a break. "No problem, Mr. Bennett."

I stand. "Charming. Can we go to your office now?"

His smile grows and his eyes heat which only pisses me

off more. He steps out of the way and holds his arm out for me to go first. "You know the way."

I narrow my eyes as I walk past him.

"Kylie, hold all calls."

"Will do, Mr. Bennett."

I walk fast so he doesn't have long to stare at my ass. Back in the day, he wouldn't have been able to stop himself from grabbing it.

Not wanting to stay long, I stay on the visitor side of the desk, assuming he'll go to his chair. He shuts the door behind him and flicks the lock.

"That's not necessary, I assure you." I cross my arms over my chest.

"Oh, no? My bad." He shrugs, not unlocking the door and sits down on the couch against the back wall.

"You can sit in your desk chair."

He shakes his head. "Nah."

Of course, he'll do anything to infuriate me.

"Are you here for the chocolate milk?" A coy smile appears on his lips.

"No. But feel free to pour it over your head."

He tsks me. "Now is that any way to thank someone?"

Leaning back, I rest my ass on the edge of his desk.

"Why don't you come over here?" he asks, that seductive tone of his coming out as though he thinks it's an on/off switch to turn me on.

"I'm good. Listen, I'm done with this chase of yours. I know you think it's funny. You're probably at home thinking of ways to torment me, but I'm done. What we had ended five years ago. It's over. Now, I've told Hannah if you're willing to work pro bono to keep you on, but you have to deal with Victoria. As far as this," I waggle a finger between the two of us, "it's done. The coffin is closed, sealed, and buried."

His eyes dip to my lips and a sputtering sensation trips up my heart. He stands without an ounce of effort and saunters my way. I need to step away. My eyes flicker to the door until they're drawn to his again.

"Now, Chelsea, you know how turned on I get when you're mad." He approaches me, the lust in his dark pupils slicing away my icy exterior. Before I can catch my breath, he's in front of me. Dangerously close.

"Dean." I put my hand on his chest and my eyes flutter shut from the surge of want that's channeling between us.

"You feel it. I know you do. It was stupid of us to think it would fade." His long fingers reach out and he tucks my hair behind my ear. "I can't stop beating off at the image of you laying on my desk and my head tucked between your thighs." He steps closer and I feel how hard he's already becoming.

"We can't. We already failed at this," I continue to fight against the need coursing through my veins as my voice loses all its conviction.

"You're telling me you can walk away right now and not lock yourself in a bathroom stall, pull up your skirt, dip your hand below the elastic of your soaked panties and finger yourself to visions of me grinding in and out of you over…" his voice lowers to a whisper. "And over," he softly continues, "and over again."

He always did have the filthiest mouth and I'm woman enough to admit that I loved it.

His fingers move from my ear to the back of my head and his strong thigh separates my legs, pushing my skirt up and placing pressure on my clit.

"We can't." He'd be a moron to think I mean it as my head falls back with a sigh. Talk about a guy who has the secret map to my treasure trove.

I raise my head to meet his gaze and we each lick our

lips. Our mouths descend, hesitant at first, as though we're feeling each other out, but it only takes one taste before we're ravishing each other.

His tongue dives in, my hands grip his strong shoulders and his thigh rises higher between my legs. He swallows down my moan as I lose all sanity.

Somewhere between his tongue down my throat and my hand venturing down to his rock-hard dick, my sanity returns with the impact of a freight train. Instead of pumping his dick, I place my hand on his chest and push him off.

"What?" he asks.

"No, Dean." I wipe my mouth and straighten my skirt.

"I don't think you mean it." He approaches me again, his cocky smile on display.

I smack him.

"Fuck," he says, his hand covering his now red cheek. "Did you really have to do that?"

"Yes. Jesus, Dean. I'm your ex-wife. You hate me, remember?" I step a good distance away from him, out of the bubble of arousal we were in.

"I'm kind of remembering now." He holds his cheek.

"That's it. We're through. Please respect that."

He stands straight, and I want him to watch me leave this time around, instead of the cowardly way I did it five years ago after he was passed out.

"You have your wish. If you change your mind, you know where to find me."

I open the door and pause for a moment, looking back over my shoulder. "I won't."

Shutting the door behind me, I vow to leave him in the past where he belongs.

Chapter Seven

That Friday, I shut my apartment door after saying goodbye to another dud of a date after dinner. Stepping out of my heels, I pick them up and retreat to my bedroom.

"Tonight, I need pajamas, popcorn, and a movie."

Opening my closet doors, I place my heels next to my other ones and strip out of my dress, thinking back on the date that can only be described with one word—boring.

I've been determined to find a straight-laced guy but give me a break. The guy visits his mom every Sunday and keeps a gratitude journal. Sweet yes, but I'm not signing on for that. He volunteers at three different places during the week after he's done at work. You know when people say you date or marry up? To this guy, I would've seemed like the used gum at the bottom of his shoe. He had a damn halo over his head.

Five minutes later, I'm in my silk pajamas, sitting on my couch with a bowl of popcorn in my lap.

"This is the life." Again, I'm talking to myself since I'm alone.

I click through the movies. Nada, Zip. Screw this.

Since I refuse to get rid of my DVD player because contrary to popular opinion Netflix does *not* have every movie available, I open up the media cabinet under my television to dig for a movie.

As I go through them, nothing sounds interesting. A romantic comedy won't work since my romantic life sucks right now. I pull out a few other cases, but nothing sparks my interest. When my hand clenches around the Rambo case, a shiver wracks my body.

It's our DVD. The one Dean and I made. God, that man can convince me of almost anything.

I'd hidden our recording in the back of the cabinet so no one coming to my apartment would stumble upon it. I should've taken a lighter to it years ago. There's no use in denying that my feelings for Dean haven't exactly waned over the years. Do I hate him? Hell yes. Do I ever want to go down that road again? No way. That doesn't mean he's not hot as hell and seems to still have some magical pull on me.

I hold the DVD in my hand, the contents of what's inside causing my desire to burn even more.

"Fuck this." I shove the DVD back into the pile of movies underneath all the other ones, shut the glass doors to my entertainment center and head to the kitchen. "Ice cream solves all."

I abandon my bowl of popcorn and instead dish myself up a bowl of strawberry ice cream.

Sitting back down on the couch, I channel surf for a good ten minutes.

"AHH." I click the television off.

I grab the newest Cosmo magazine on my end table and scour through it to see if I missed any articles when I read through it last week. I toss it back on the end table once I see that I even did the quiz.

Replacing the magazine with my phone, I thumb through Instagram and Snapchat. Blah, blah, blah. Nothing new.

Since when did I become so boring?

I decide to text Zoe.

Me: *Hey, game night still on for tomorrow night?*

The phone rings immediately with her name on the screen.

"Hey," I answer.

"You know I have two kids. That means one hand for each one, plus it's bath time." I hear splashing in the background. "To answer your question though, yes, our house. Are you bringing someone?" She laughs, and I roll my eyes.

"Shut up." I rise from the couch and rinse out my bowl, placing it in the dishwasher.

"You ready to talk yet?" she asks. "CAIDEN!" she screams, and I pull my phone away from my ear for a second.

I hear his laughter a second later.

"Stop it. You're scaring Mommy. Do you want me to have a heart attack?"

"What's a heart attack?" he asks.

"What's he doing?" I ask.

"The kid thinks it's funny to see how long he can hold his breath."

"A Houdini in the making." I walk back over to my living room and sit down on the couch.

"No. He's a doctor in the making. Isn't that right?"

"I want to be like Daddy when I grow up," Caiden says followed by more splashing.

"What about Mommy?" Zoe questions and I can't believe the best entertainment for me on a Friday night is listening to my cousin and her young son.

"Mommies are boring. Daddy plays with tools."

"His own tool," Zoe mumbles.

I laugh.

"If you played with it I wouldn't have to." Vin's voice comes through the line, obviously having joined their little party.

"Now you come up when he's almost done," Zoe says sounding annoyed and then taking me off speakerphone.

"You're so much better at it than I am."

I know without being there that Zoe is rolling her eyes at him.

Then again, like with Victoria and Reed, I'm forced to wait while they make-up or at least whisper to one another while kissing noises sound through the phone.

"Your son is in the room," I say.

"Chelsea," Zoe answers to Vin when he asks who she's speaking to.

"Hey, Chels, game on tomorrow. Want me to fix you up tomorrow night?"

"Tell Vin, I'm good."

"She's good. Her ex is back in the picture." Zoe's tone is one of amusement. Like this is all a big joke, but she's not sitting here trying to keep herself cooled down enough not to get herself off while watching a DVD of her and her ex.

"What? She isn't bringing him, is she?" Vin asks.

"No," I say.

"Maybe," Zoe overrides my answer.

"Shit babe, hurry this up, we need to practice. That

guy and his sports trivia knowledge used to beat us every time."

I smile remembering when I used to win game night for that brief moment Dean was in my life.

"Um, Vin, you're missing a few key elements there. I think you're killing brain cells from playing with your tool so much," Zoe quips.

"I know, I know. I'm supposed to put him on the cross and burn him, but I have some empathy for the guy. What happened couldn't have been easy for him."

"That didn't mean he had the right to treat Chelsea the way he did," Zoe fights my battle for me.

"Hey," I try to interrupt.

"He was going through a hard time," Vin argues.

"Seriously? You're going to take his side?" Zoe's playful tone has turned serious.

"Hey, Zo," I interrupt again.

"There are no sides. They're divorced," Vin says. "Come on bud, out of the bath."

"One more time," Caiden says.

"No. Do not let him keep going under and holding his breath," Zoe says using her mom voice.

Nothing good can come from this. Mark my words. Nothing.

"What's the big deal? I'm right here," Vin says.

"Hey, Zoe, I'm going to let you go," I say, fiddling with the seam on my pajamas.

"No, no, Chels. Hold on a second."

"Oookkkaaayy." I sigh.

"See look, he's still down there. Are his eyes open? They are. He's challenging us." Zoe is none too pleased.

"He's playing," Vin says with a chuckle. His voice seems to hold a little bit of pride.

"Playing my ass."

Then I hear a big tumble, Caiden wailing, and their arguing voices.

"See, I told you," Zoe snaps.

Click.

I hang up. I'm not going to make my Friday night worse by listening to two married people argue about their child.

Read. I can totally pick up a book. I rise from the couch once more and pull out my iPad, scanning through the new release charts for a book.

"No romance," I murmur to myself, my finger scrolling down past all the covers with abs and couples hugging and almost kissing. "Fiction," I sing-song, clicking on horror. I like horror.

I read a few blurbs and finally settle on one. After downloading it, I open the first page and start reading, trying to lose myself in a story about a killer of women. Single women that no one will miss. *Huh.*

I plop my iPad on the couch beside me and zero in on the glass doors under my television.

"Bad idea," I say to myself, shaking my head hoping some sense will fall into it. My feet land on my warm rug. "The hell with it."

My hand is poised on the handle of the glass door when my phone rings. I glance down, intending to ignore Zoe, but it's my other cousin, her brother, Mikey. He's always good for a laugh and a good time.

"Hey cuz." I flop back down on the couch, hoping this call will improve my mood.

All I hear is loud music pumping and screaming in the background.

"Get dressed, I'm sending a car to you."

"I'm in my pajamas. Why don't you afterparty here? And bring some Mickey D's with you."

"Hell no. I got a 911 call from Zoe that entails getting you out of your pajamas, preferably into a dress, and out of your place. The car will be there in ten minutes."

"Where are you?" I ask, already heading toward my bedroom.

"The driver knows where I am. The doorman has your name. Stop sulking because I'm gonna be really pissed if I have to leave this bar and the girl I've been warming up all night to come get your ass."

He hangs up.

I pause in the doorway of my bedroom, my gaze moving to the glass doors once more.

"Yep, I'm not going to destroy it, so I might as well ignore it."

I head into my bedroom to forget Dean and dance my ass off. The best way to get over someone is to get under someone else, right?

Chapter Eight

I fall into the booth, sweaty and exhausted and in desperate need of another drink.

"Are you working on your moves at home or something?" Mikey falls in right next to me, waving his hand to his friend who's ventured to the bar instead of our booth. "Grab two."

His friend nods. A friend who's gotten handsy with me a few times on the dance floor, but he's not bad looking. If I would just stop thinking about that DVD and Dean, I'd probably take him home with me.

"Who's your friend?" I ask Mikey, sitting up straighter.

"Nope. Hands off." He shakes his head.

"What? Why?"

"Because I'm not listening to another friend whine about you blowing them off."

"Who me?" I act offended although he only speaks the truth.

"Yeah, you." He laughs and sits up straighter, playing with the triangular advertisement in the center of the table. "So?"

"What's with everybody's so's?" I grumble.

"Because you make us draw things out of you like a prisoner of war." He looks up at me through his thick eyelashes.

"What does everyone want? In a city of millions, he happens to be the one tax attorney who volunteers to do pro bono work for the foundation I'm working at. End of story."

His eyebrows lift.

"What?"

"Nothing." He raises his hands up in front of him.

"That look isn't good on you. I'd lose it for the ladies."

He chuckles. "It's a bit of a coincidence, no?"

I shrug. "Coincidences happen all the time." His eyebrows lift again. I pluck the advertisement out of his hands. "You're not one to hold back your thoughts."

"You don't want to know my thoughts." He chuckles and leans back into the booth.

"Well, from tonight's conversation, there's Vin's side and Zoe's side."

"Vin has a side? Usually that man is either on Zoe's side or right down the middle." He pauses for a second. "Strike that, he's always on Zo's side."

He smiles, and I laugh. Truth is, I don't want to know what side he's on because there is no side to take.

"Seems Vin sees Dean's side."

Mikey shrugs, his gaze diverting to the packed dance floor.

"You, too?" I stare at him slack-jawed.

Mikey glances back at me. "I'm a guy, Chels." He shrugs. "Don't get me wrong, I mean, how it all went down was horrible and I hated seeing you so heartbroken afterward, but the guy's hopes and dreams were shattered."

"And that grants him permission to ruin our marriage?"

He places his palm up in the air. "I'm not saying what he did was okay, I'm just saying that I get the self-destruction. I think what you need to figure out is if it really is a coincidence, or if he knew you worked at RISE."

I sit there blinking at him for a second, unnerved with what he's suggesting. "No way. Why would he purposely seek me out?"

A smile lifts his serious lips. This is not why I came out tonight, but like any big family, mine doesn't understand what privacy is very well.

"Maybe he has regrets? Maybe he wants you back? Maybe he wants to make things, right? I'm not him, I can't say. But when Zoe called me tonight and gave me the low down, it all just seemed a little too coincidental to me." He shrugs again and shoots me a look like, 'hey, but what do I know.' Obviously, a shit-ton more than me.

Why didn't I suspect foul play from him? Because I'm too busy being enamored with him.

"Well fuck a duck."

Mikey laughs and his friend slides into the booth, bringing along two girls, all their hands full of beers.

The girls instantly cozy up to Mikey and his friend. Feeling like a fifth wheel, I figure I'll call it a night.

"I'm heading home."

Mikey sits up to attention. "I'll get you home. It's late."

I stop outside the booth and shake my head. "I'm the older cousin, remember? I can get home myself."

"You sure?" he asks as the girl's hand rubs along his stomach.

"Yeah, stay put." I tuck my purse under my arm.

He slides out of the booth giving me a kiss on the cheek. "You have your pepper spray?"

I giggle at his assumption that I can't handle myself. "I'm good. See you tomorrow night." I kiss his cheek. "Don't bring her," I whisper in his ear.

He just shakes his head at me.

"Have a good night." I wave and then walk off while his friend eyes me one more time like he's committing my body to memory.

Then I vanish into the throngs of people and head back to my place that suddenly feels very lonely.

I'M NOT HOME for more than five minutes before I'm back to where I was hours before. My time out of the house was a nice reprieve from the burning desire to watch the DVD.

"Fuck it." I plop down, grab the Rambo DVD, the plastic creaking in protest when I open it. Before thinking twice, I put it in the DVD player, head to the couch with the remote and press play.

The music starts, and I roll my eyes as a smile crosses my lips remembering how much work Dean put into it. Lights of the Las Vegas Strip shine out the window of our hotel room.

There's me naked on a bed with a sheet over me, holding my hand out with my ring on it for his viewing.

"Say your name," he jokes.

"Chelsea Bennett," I say, my voice innocent and lovesick.

"Wrong."

He yanks me by my ankle down the bed and I giggle not protesting one bit. "Do you need me to spank you?"

The camera shakes from him laughter.

"Please," I pretend to beg.

"Say your name," he repeats, and I hold my arms out.

"Mrs. Dean Bennett," I say on the video.

I inhale a deep breath and suddenly I'm that girl again. Naive and pure and a true believer that my forever just got etched into some imaginary book of destinies. That Dean and Chelsea Bennett would live happily ever after.

Maybe that's why the crash back down to earth was so painful.

"What do I get for saying it?" I tilted my head to the side into a sex kitten look with hooded eyes.

The sheet slides over my lower half and there's my much younger pussy on display, freshly waxed. Ah, the good old days.

His hand comes into view, his middle finger running up my folds, his thumb pressing lightly against my clit. My gasp audible.

"Already wet." Although he's behind the camera, I can still remember his satisfied smile.

"Am I the best husband?" he asks.

"You are." I'm panting as his fingers manipulate me.

"Are you going to come for your husband?"

"That depends." I squirm on the bed, my body growing hotter.

"Oh, I gotta hear this." He chuckles, pushing a finger into me and my body stiffens, then relaxes.

"Put that phone down and join me." Again, I hold my arms out, practically begging for his body against mine.

The picture moves off me and to the ceiling for a moment. A small patch of Dean's dark strands and half his eye show before the camera shows the entire bed with me lying on it.

Damn, I looked good. Not trying to be conceited but Jesus, where did that body disappear to?

The camera shows Dean's tall, muscular body climbing

up the bed as I inch up toward the headboard. His hands slide up my legs, parting them while his mouth teases me with kisses along the sensitive flesh of my inner thighs.

My head falls to the side, my eyes closing and just like that, I'm in that too-expensive-for-college-kids-hotel room after coming back from eloping at a chapel in Vegas. Our two duffle bags sit on the chairs by the table. My fanciest dress balled up on the floor, my panties on the side table. My bra hangs from the headboard. The floral scent mixed with citrus and cedarwood fill the room and I'm with Dean all over again.

His five o'clock shadow prickles my skin, his thumbs opening me for his viewing pleasure. His dark eyes promising an orgasm that will have me tearing up the sheets. His tongue searches out my most sensitive area and I rock my hips to his rhythm, but his strong arm holds my pelvis down to the bed.

I always loved him walking the tightrope between being loving and firm with me. He knew what I wanted and made sure I ended up completely spent.

His tongue torments me and he shoves two fingers inside of me, arching them to hit my G-spot. My body protests, my hips grinding out of control, wiggling to match the speed of his fingers.

He moans, and I become greedier and greedier to have him. His fingers aren't enough. I want his body on top of me. As though realizing it, his fingers slide out of me, his thumb continuing to play with my clit as he uses one muscular arm to hover above me until his cock rests at my opening.

"Protection?" he asks.

I remember being scared. Up until then, we'd used condoms. I'd gotten on the pill three weeks prior. At that moment, I didn't want anything between us. It was just a piece of latex, but I thought I'd made it to heaven as Dean looked down at me, hope sprung in his eyes.

"No. We're good," I say, opening my thighs up more. "I need to feel you."

He smiles that genuine one he reserves for me.

I always felt like we were sharing something special between us when he did that.

As he pushes inside, I feel myself stretch from his girth. Inch by inch he eases inside of me. *It wasn't our first time together, but something felt unique and rare that time around.*

His eyes swim with mine as we move from lust to love, the camera long forgotten.

He rolls over onto his back and his hands mold to my hips. "Ride me like you want to." His voice holds pride and a promise—that I will always be his number one.

My hand plants on his firm pecs and I rock back and forth, up and down. Our breathing grows faster, our moans hammering out a melody between us, the bed protesting our movements.

Eventually, his hands hold my breasts, his thumb and finger tweaking my nipples until I fall slightly forward because I might die without his lips on mine.

He lifts his hips to get as deep as he can while our tongues mesh together in a frantic and chaotic dance.

My body begs for release, becoming unnerved and chasing my orgasm that's right there.

Dean holds my face to his and rolls us so I'm on my back, pumping into me over and over again, never letting up until my hands fist the sheets. My legs tighten around his waist to make sure he doesn't stop.

My breath hitches and my climax hits me like a bull-dozer. Hard, heavy and leaving me dazed as he slows our kiss, his tongue exploring rather than conquering. A few more pumps and he moans out his own orgasm, coming inside me. The beads of sweat slide off our bodies to the wrinkled sheets as we lay there catching our breath.

"I love you, Chels," he says and kisses my forehead. "Always will."

Dean picks me up, and carries me into the bathroom, leaving the camera on. Light laughter echoes until the video ends. He edited out the last fifteen minutes of just listening to the two of us talking in the shower.

As I lay on my couch remembering one of the best nights of my life, my phone flashes next to me. Speak of the devil.

I press ignore.

A minute later a text comes through.

Minute Man: *I'm sorry. You know for what.*

I hold the phone in my hand, staring down at the words that never came out of his mouth years ago when they would have mattered.

Minute Man: *That's all. Have a great life, Chelsea. You deserve it.*

My heart thumps. My hands itch.

The damn video is giving me a soft spot. A soft spot that's taken over my common sense.

Me: *Do you want to meet?*

Chapter Nine

*I*t takes all of one second before his answer comes through.

Minute Man: *Name the time and place.*
Me: *Lunch tomorrow.*
Minute Man: *I'd prefer earlier. Breakfast?*
Me: *I'm extending an olive branch and you're playing tug of war with it.*

A few minutes go by and my thoughts drift to what he could be doing. Changing for bed? Is he out drinking with his buddies? Who are his buddies now? Is he home alone? Did he just watch his copy of our sex tape?

"UGH!" I scream from wanting to know more than I should about his life.

Minute Man: *I'm an impatient man.*
Me: *I'm aware.*
Minute Man: *Do you ever wonder how we know each other so well from such a short time together?*

Me: *I try not to think about our time together.*

Again, there's a long pause. Again, my mind wanders to wondering what his apartment looks like. How well is he doing as a tax attorney? Is his family still in that small Indiana town? What made him come to Chicago?

Minute Man: *That's below the belt.*
Me: *Maybe, but it's true.*
Minute Man: *Let me make it right.*

I drop the phone to my chest, clutching it like his words can speak directly to my heart.

Me: *You're asking for a lot.*
Minute Man: *I'm a desperate man.*

Never in my time as Mrs. Bennett was I ever privileged enough to see this side of Dean. Maybe he's just different over text because he rarely ever let his cocky and arrogant facade fall. Even with me. Up until the end, he held on to it.

Me: *I'm not a desperate woman. I have many options to choose from.*

There you go, Chels, act like you've got great guys waiting outside your door.

Minute Man: *Give me one breakfast. After that, if you want me out of your life, I'll walk.*

My thumbs hover over the phone and then I put it on the coffee table, and put my head in my hands, pulling at my blonde strands. I shouldn't be so surprised that he wants so much from me.

Me: *Fine. Ann Sathers at 8.*
Minute Man: *I had other plans.*

I drop the phone, my hands rising in the air like I'm asking for Jesus Christ to save me. This guy never changes. Picking up the phone off my coffee table, my thumbs press hard on my screen.

Me: *Of course you do. Name it hotshot.*

A knock hits my door and I look around like there's someone else who will share my bewildered expression.

Oh no.

That son of a bitch.

I stomp to the door, rising on my tiptoes to look through the peephole. Already hearing me, he lifts a box of donuts, a gallon of chocolate milk, and a bag of McDonald's.

"Breakfast," he says casually as if I should expect my ex-husband at my door when I never gave him my address.

"Why are you here?"

"You agreed to breakfast."

"Dean." I shake my head, my body wanting to disobey my brain's strict instructions.

"Come on Chels. You're awake, I'm awake, let's talk face-to-face."

"I told you tomorrow at eight."

I hear a noise, so I glance out the peephole again, and all I can see are his long legs. His feet tucked into a pair of slider sandals. Same Dean.

"What are you doing?"

"Just getting comfy. The floor could have more cushion, but I'll manage. I wouldn't object to a pillow though."

I fall back down to the heels of my feet. My hand on the doorknob, my teeth biting my lip.

"Do you really think I should let you in?"

He chuckles. "In my opinion, yes, but I get your hesitation. I'll be here at eight."

I slide down the opposite side of the door and I'd swear the smell of him permeates through the small sliver of space at the bottom. Like he's freshly showered.

"Dean?"

"Yeah." His voice is nearer than I expected, as though he's right next to me.

"Is this all a coincidence?"

"What?" There's shuffling on the other side of the door.

"You being the tax attorney for RISE?"

Silence grows between us and as if that wasn't already my answer, he eventually talks.

"Chels," he sighs.

"I take that as a no."

"Just listen."

"Why?" My voice is curt. How could he purposely seek me out just to hurt me all over again?

"Just relax."

"Explain, Dean," I bark out.

"Stop talking and I will."

I thump the back of my head lightly against the door. "You sure are taking your sweet time."

"You're the best thing that ever happened to me."

There's silence between us again and it takes me a minute to gather my thoughts after that declaration.

"If I was, you wouldn't have done what you did," I say.

"I was a dick." His playful tone has disappeared.

"Yeah, you were."

"Let me apologize face-to-face." His large hand lands on the door and it jiggles against the lock.

"I'm not sure I can handle that," I say honestly.

He chuckles. "Just some donuts and a conversation. That's all I want."

I pull my knees up to my chest, my mind a jumbled mess. Like a word search puzzle and I'm struggling to find the right words on a sheet full of letters.

"Fifteen minutes," I finally say.

There's movement on the other side and I expect he's on his feet.

"Do I get brownie points if I'm under?"

I inhale the deepest breath I have since the moment I stared at him on our wedded bed five years prior. My shaking hands slide the lock and I open the door to a smiling Dean.

Bad idea.

Such a fucking bad idea, Chels.

YOU'D EXPECT someone begging for forgiveness to walk into my apartment, dragging his feet and with his head down. Not Dean. His back is straight, and a smile plays on his lips.

"Nice place." His eyes scour my apartment.

"You mean your search didn't come with pictures?" I shut the door and flick the lock. I live in a safe apartment complex, but I don't want any drunken guys or girls getting confused about where they live.

"Just an address."

"And a phone number."

His smirk grows wider and he shrugs. "Yeah, and a phone number."

"Great to know that anyone can find out anything about me."

"If only we could figure out how to report feelings and moods with an internet search. We'd be filthy rich." He smiles, signaling to the couch.

I nod.

His large frame sits, placing the donuts, milk, and McDonald's on the coffee table in front of him. He doesn't lean back into the sofa but sits on the edge, his hands clasped together between his muscular thighs hidden under a pair of gray sweatpants. I'd forgotten how good he looks when he's dressed comfortably like this.

"Do you want me to fall to my knees?" he asks.

"If you're going to continue making jokes, you can walk back out the door." I sit down in the chair, pulling my legs to my chest. I need a barrier between him and my heart.

"Donut?" He opens the box and holds it out as an offering.

I roll my eyes at the same time my heart drums. All chocolate Bavarian cream. My favorite. I should have expected nothing less.

"What did you do order them special?"

"I make friends easily." He sets the open box in front of me. "Mind if I grab some cups?"

Not waiting for an answer, he rises to his feet. I'm not used to having anyone over and he eats up the minimal space.

"You're not even going to wait for an answer?"

"I figure you want the chocolate milk?" He leans over the edge of the chair. "Am I wrong?"

I scoff. I can't go letting him think he can read minds

70

or something. Needing him away from me, I nudge him in the shoulder with my foot.

He backs up and disappears into my galley style kitchen.

"Cabinet next to the fridge."

"I figured."

He acts like we were married for twenty years or something. How does he know I didn't have them above the stove, or on the other side next to the pantry? Damn know-it-all.

The clanking of glasses alerts me that he's returning. I straighten in the chair, crossing my legs. The smell of the donuts is driving me crazy with want.

He sits back down, except this time he takes the opposite side of the couch. The one closest to me. Setting the cups down he smiles like this is an everyday occurrence. Him in my apartment, eating donuts and drinking chocolate milk. Live in fantasy land much, Dean?

I try to ignore the pull toward him as the muscles in his forearm flex when he picks up the gallon of milk. I let it roll off me how neatly manicured his nails are, wondering where the boy with dirt under his fingernails from hours on a ballfield went.

"Here." He hands me the cup and I almost spill it so that our fingers don't brush. "Got it?" he asks.

"Thank you." I sip it, placing it on the end table.

He leans back on the couch, his long legs parted as he drinks out of his own glass, smiling at me after he swallows.

"Dean…"

His smile only grows.

"Time's a-tickin'," I say.

He tips his head and sits up, placing his cup on the coffee table and resting his forearms on his thighs. "You're right."

His eyes dip to the rug on the floor. His fingers clasp together. Then having pieced the words together his eyes lock with mine.

"I know sorry isn't enough, but I am. I could give you some excuse, but I'm not going to because no matter the shit I was going through you should've been my number one priority."

"I know what you were going through. I tried to help." I can't help it. I sound bitter.

He shakes his head. "You couldn't have. It wasn't you, it was me. Besides you were dealing with your own shit and I wasn't there for you."

He better not want to talk about *that* because I'm not going there with him.

"Chels, I fucked this up and I know it's a shit-ton to ask, but will you give me a second chance?"

My heart rises in my throat and lodges there. It begs me to let it do the speaking for us. Fuck that. I push it back down, rise to my feet and disappear into the kitchen.

"Should I not follow you?" he asks without an ounce of sarcasm.

"Just give me one minute." My hands grip the counter edge, I lean forward, shutting my eyes, trying to compose myself.

Why did I let him in? That DVD is getting destroyed as soon as he leaves.

"Chels?" he calls out after a minute. "I'm coming in." He's already at the small opening into my kitchen. That's how small my place is, but it's cozy and homey and I love it despite the size. It's mine and I paid for it. "I'm not trying to upset you," he says in a soft voice.

I circle around, my back on the edge of the counter. "I don't know if I can answer you."

"Fair enough." He steps in and the room shrinks. His

one hand lands next to my hip, but he doesn't break the distance further. Instead, he hovers over me. "Being indecisive is a maybe, right?"

The one corner of his lips tick up.

I say nothing because I'm conflicted, but unlike him, I'm not going to give him hope if there really is none.

"What are you thinking? That we just head to Vegas and get married again? Give this a go around once more?" I break away from him, walking into my family room. "Do you honestly expect me to say yes? It's been five years. Where the hell have you been?"

There was a time I would've died to hear him say those words to me.

He follows but stays against the wall to keep his distance. "I had to get myself right."

"Why me? Go find some new girl." I wrap my arms around myself.

"You're kidding, right? It's always been you, Chels. Always. I don't want anyone else. Never have."

"I'm a bitch."

"You are." There's not one ounce of humor in his tone.

My head whips around.

He shrugs. "I'm not gonna lie. You can be difficult sometimes, but it's something I love about you. I don't want some woman who's going to have my favorite dinner on the table at five o'clock when I get home. Someone who lets me watch whatever I want on television without a fight. I want someone with their own dreams, their own thoughts and opinions. Because you're not really a bitch, Chels, you're a fighter."

I swallow down the words that wanted to go after him.

"I love our banter, I love the way you don't let me get away with jack shit."

"You didn't like it once upon a time." I cock my hip and put a hand on my waist.

"Once upon a time I was an asshole."

"And that's changed now?"

He chuckles to himself like he's living his fucking dream life right now. "It hasn't. I'm not making a promise of lifting the toilet seat, washing my dishes, and doing laundry. Truth is, I might just let a t-shirt miss the hamper just to piss you off, because when you fight with me Chelsea, it means you care, that you love me."

The room grows quiet, me remembering when I lost the will to fight. When I didn't care about unmade beds or dirty dishes. When I was so mentally exhausted, I gave up. But he's wrong, the love was still there. Maybe buried really, really deep, but the part of me that would never admit to it was there.

"I'll tell you what?" he asks, pushing off the wall. "Hannah's party next weekend...let me take you."

Hannah's hosting a get together for all the people who are involved, even indirectly, in RISE. As a thank you of sorts.

When I don't say anything, he continues to talk. "Just as an escort. Nothing more."

"You can meet me there." I cross my arms again and realize I have no bra on, so I quickly let them hang back down at my sides.

"Not a chance. You'll have your friends there, but I want to pick you up and bring you home. You gotta see that's a small start. I'm not asking for dinner or drinks. Just a car ride together in an Uber."

He approaches me, and I step back, needing space to think this through.

Hannah's party is at her penthouse in the city and it shouldn't take long to get there.

"Fine," I say.

"Not exactly the enthusiasm I was hoping for, but I'll take it. Pick you up at six." He steps toward me one more time, but I place my hand out in front of me.

"Not happening."

He nods. "What about Ann Sathers tomorrow?"

"We already hashed this out."

"I kind of wanted the cinnamon rolls and you know I hate dining alone."

"Order it and pick it up." I walk to my door opening it for him.

"My time is up I see."

"You got more time than you deserve." Truth is I don't want him to go, but I can't let him think he can walk all over me.

"Kiss?"

"NO!" I screech.

He laughs and his hand slides over my hip as he leans in and places his lips on my cheek. Shivers run along my body.

"Goodnight, Dean."

He winks and steps out the door. "Oh, Chels?"

"Yeah?"

"Did you enjoy Rambo?" he winks.

Shit. I forgot the movie case was sitting on my table.

I slam the door in his face before he sees how pink mine is.

Sitting back down on the couch, I pull the box of donuts onto my lap and take a big bite of one, then gulp down the chocolate milk, leaving the McDonalds alone.

He's already under my skin. I *cannot* let him get under my panties.

Chapter Ten

"*I*'m sorry, what?" Victoria asks, sitting next to me at Torrio's Table, the speakeasy Hannah is a member of.

"We talked."

"In other words, you hashed your shit out?" She's looking at me like she's waiting for me to tell her she may have been right.

"Yeah, and now the bastard wants a second chance." I run my finger across the condensation on the outside of my drink while Victoria and Hannah exchange a look.

This is our regular Monday night at Torrio's that Hannah now insists we have. Usually it keeps me going through the Monday morning gloom, but not when the subject of our conversation is me. Especially when it's me *and* Dean.

"Stop it." I sip my vesper. "What am I supposed to do?"

"So, you agreed to a second chance?" Hannah asks, her words poised and elegant. A few men walk by and wave to her.

She could have her pick of any of these successful men and sometimes I wonder if she comes here by herself and hooks up on nights when we're not with her. She doesn't seem the type, but I would if I were her.

"I agreed to let him take me to your party." I point a finger in her direction. "Which, by the way, thanks a lot for inviting him."

"He's our tax attorney." She holds her hands up in the air. "You told me to keep him on. So turn that finger back around and point at yourself."

Victoria laughs, sipping her drink, then pulls out her phone and checks it—again.

"I'm going to take that phone and drop it in your drink," I say.

She crinkles her eyes at me. "Reed was getting Jade after school. I just want to make sure everything is all right."

"You're worried that Reed, Mr. Responsible, is going to forget your daughter or what...let her take up knife throwing as a hobby?" My sarcasm is thick. "That's the least of your worries."

She shrugs. "Hey, I've been a single mom for a long time, it's hard to put trust into people where Jade is concerned." Her voice has an edge. A mama bear edge I'm not going to poke around for fear of getting cut.

"Fair enough."

She straightens her shoulders, leaving her phone in her lap, seemingly pleased with herself for putting me in my place.

"Don't try to detour this conversation. You're in the hot seat, Chelsea." Hannah smiles, sipping her drink as her gaze slides around the room.

"I think we should talk about the fact you're searching for the silver fox," I say smugly.

Hannah coughs, almost spitting out her drink. Almost, but she doesn't. I can't help but think Hannah attended an etiquette school when she was younger and would never let such a thing happen. She's always the epitome of poised perfection—unless we're talking about her ex-husband's divorce attorney.

"I just don't want him to ruin my night." Flush warms her cheeks and now it's me and Victoria sharing the look.

"Don't you dare." She waggles her finger between the two of us. "I loathe Roarke Baldwin. He got my husband way more than that cheating asshole deserved."

We nod because it's hard to argue with Hannah, she's stubborn and defiant and even if she ever sleeps with the silver fox, she'd probably deny it.

"We know." Victoria takes on the mother role, patting Hannah's hand with her own. "That brings us back around to you." She whips her head in my direction and smiles.

I narrow my eyes to slits and then roll them to the back of my head.

"Come on. If you still want him, admit it," Victoria pries.

With a sigh, I decide to lay my cards on the table. "Truth is, I do want him. I want him over me and under me and behind me until he's out of my system. But I do not want a husband, especially the one I threw back into the proverbial sea five years ago."

While I sip my drink, I glance over to the men in this place rather than take in the expressions on my friend's faces. They're probably sharing that 'she's lying to herself' look, but they don't understand. How could they when I've never told them everything that went down between us?

"Listen. Our marriage was hot, spontaneous, and reckless. Why do you think I love bad boys? He's the king of them, but I never wanted to change him. I loved his ragged edges. I loved his sexual thirst that had me in more positions than I knew existed as a college freshman. I loved that every girl wanted him, but he was mine. I loved how protective he was over me. But I was naive. I was young and stupid. I actually believed that I met the man I was destined for at eighteen. The problem with bad boys, they might be protective of you and piss around you like you're their property, but they don't put you first. Not really." I swallow down my emotions that are now a hard lump in my throat before I finish. "The reason this is so hard is because even though a part of me does want him, I will *never* let him hurt me again, which means I'll never open up to him and we don't really stand a chance."

Hannah reaches over, placing her hand on mine. Victoria puts hers on top of Hannah's.

"Honey, I hate to say this, but I think you still love him. And I think that if you let him in, you'll fall harder. He could very well have changed. I mean, he sought you out. That's romantic. He found a way that you'd have to interact with him because he knows you, and he knew it wouldn't be easy. We don't know everything you went through and even if you told us we wouldn't truly understand. It wasn't us who experienced it, so it's unfair for us to tell you to put your heart on the line again for a man who hurt you so deeply." She glances over to Victoria. "Victoria knows how hard it is to trust another man, let alone the same man who caused the damage in the first place."

Victoria nods, her eyes telling me it will all be okay, look at how things turned out for her. Hello, am I the only one who realizes she scored the one in a million jackpot in this world?

Hannah continues, "Don't fool yourself into thinking

that hope hasn't already sprung inside you. Just protect yourself. Have your eyes wide open."

"Protect yourself but try to be optimistic. People do change, Chels," Victoria adds.

Where was Miss Optimistic when Reed was trying time and time again to get her to date him? I never told her to give him a chance. Or did I? I don't remember.

"Thanks for the therapy session girls, I'll go home and write in my diary now." I down the rest of my Vesper.

Their hands leave mine and they slide their backs to the booth once more.

Hannah raises her hand to the cute waiter who is probably no more than twenty-one years old.

"You know I'm surprised they don't have women as the waitresses. I mean all the patrons are mostly men," I say.

Victoria looks around and nods in agreement with me. "Maybe they keep him especially for us." She smiles, looking him up and down as he approaches the table with a round of shots.

"Ladies," he says in that flirtatious tone he's probably trained to use.

We thank him, and he places the shots on the table and leaves. Probably something else he was trained to do. Not linger. Women usually like a challenge.

"Hannah, I think I need Tad's help again," I say, referring to her best friend/personal trainer who whipped us into shape when Victoria started seeing Reed.

She laughs.

"Are you sure? Remember what happened to me?" Victoria asks.

Yeah, yeah, but she's a weakling.

"I'll give him a call," Hannah says. "Do you want to cleanse again or are you going to work out?"

"Probably a little of both," I say.

"Consider it done."

I smile. "Thanks."

"We're really not going to say anything about her getting in shape for Dean to see her naked?" Victoria asks. "I was open about my insecurity."

Victoria sounds offended and so I laugh.

"I'm getting in shape for me." I pick up my shot.

"Chelsea, you work out five days a week. It's all we could do to get you out here." Victoria raises her newly done eyebrows.

"There's nothing wrong with a little tender loving care," I say with a smirk.

They each pick up their glasses and we raise them.

"To Chelsea finally getting some." Hannah smiles and they push their glasses to mine to clink.

They down their shots while I'm still holding mine out.

"Oh, just drink it." Hannah shakes her head. "Who the hell cares? I'm not getting any on the regular, but my pussy is waxed in case the opportunity presents itself."

A man who was walking by stops and looks over his shoulder at Hannah.

"Keep walking. Not interested," she says, and he does what she instructs and continues to the other side of the bar.

I'm still getting over the fact that Hannah just said the word pussy out loud.

"Nothing wrong with looking your best on the off chance," Victoria says.

"Off chance there's a silver fox around?" I ask.

"Hey now, I'm being nice. If you want to see me angry, keep talking about that man." Hannah is kind of scary when we bring up the silver fox.

"Nope. I'm good." I raise my hands in a placating gesture.

"Thought so." She goes back to drinking her Vesper.

For the rest of the night, we talk about RISE and the gala, Hannah's party and how she hired a planner to take care of most of the details. I swear the woman must roll around in cash. I can't even imagine living her life.

It isn't until my phone chimes that I realize it's so late.

Minute Man: *Can I swindle lunch with you tomorrow?*

Hannah and Victoria are chatting about the renovations her and Reed are planning for their Barbie dream house.

Me: *No.*
Minute Man: *Promise to keep my hands to myself.*
Me: *No.*
Minute Man: *I remember you being much more accommodating.*
Me: *And I remember you being much less irritating.*
Minute Man: *Want to make a new Rambo DVD and see how much endurance I really have?*
Me: *I have no idea what you're talking about.*
Minute Man: *I'll keep your secret if you go to lunch with me.*
Me: *It's your secret, too.*
Minute Man: *It's some of my finest work…I'd be happy to show it off.*
Me: *You're bluffing.*
Minute Man: *Try me. I keep my copy in a Steel Magnolias case.*

I laugh.

"Who is that?" Hannah asks.

I lift my head and they both smile, again sharing that damn look, so I return my attention to my phone.

Me: *When was the last time you watched it?*

Minute Man: *Last night.*

An eruption of butterflies fills my stomach.

Minute Man: *I must say, I'm an awesome partner.*
Me: *Excuse me?*
Minute Man: *Oh, you stole the show, baby. No doubt about that.*

The butterflies slow like they're flitting through molasses and a wave of warmth runs from my head to my toes.

Me: *I'm not sure I like you having a copy.*
Minute Man: *Technically, it's mine. You have the copy.*

He's kind of got me there.

Me: *I thought you turned off the camera?*
Minute Man: *Aren't you glad I didn't ;) Then you would've forgotten how I rock your world.*
Me: *You're okay.*
Minute Man: *Care for a refresher course? I'm sitting alone in my apartment, you can swing by.*

My body is screaming yes, yes, oh God what is wrong with you? YES! But I cannot allow my body to make the decisions where Dean's concerned.

Me: *It's girl's night. Gotta go. Have fun.*
Minute Man: *Okay, I'll just pop in Steel Magnolias. I can never get enough of the female star.*

I swallow, cross my legs and uncross them. God, why am I this aroused just knowing he's watching the same

DVD I watched a few nights ago? The one I almost took a lighter to last night because my willpower was waning.

Me: *Have fun because that will never happen again.*
Minute Man: *Oh, sweet Chelsea, I'll be under you again. I guarantee that.*

My mind blanks. I have no smart comments to hammer back at him. I sit there staring at the text he sent because as much as I hate it, I'm woman enough to admit that this is the one time I hope I'm wrong and he's right.

Chapter Eleven

A knock lands on my door at six o'clock on Saturday.

I twist the cap back on the mascara, examine myself in the mirror, and take a deep breath, silently telling myself that I've got this. I only have to be alone with him on the way there and back. A nice goodbye at the end of the evening and I'm done.

A knock hits my door again.

"Always impatient," I murmur, leaving the bathroom and heading to the door. "You got this," I remind myself.

I open the door and my pep talks from the past hour were all for naught. Dean stands there in a pair of black jeans, a black V-neck shirt with a black leather jacket over the top. His hair is styled messier than during his work day. He really is trying to torture me. Did he put on Chapstick? His lips are a light pink, his dark eyes even more mysterious when paired with an all-black wardrobe.

"I'm game if you want to stay in." He walks past me into my apartment.

Uninvited I may add.

The only good thing about his entrance is that I get a view of his ass. Don't worry, it matches the ensemble perfectly.

"The polite thing to do is wait to be invited in."

He circles around, hands in his pockets. "You know I ain't got no manners."

I giggle. Giggle. Like a damn school girl! At least I stopped it quickly.

"Let me grab my coat and we can get this over with." I breeze past him toward the hallway.

"Usually my dates beg for more."

I ignore the stab of pain in my chest at his comment while he follows me down the hall to the closet. When the two of us are in the darkened small space, it feels like I'm suffocating. I should've turned the light on.

His cologne. Wait, cologne? Dean never used to wear cologne.

He leans forward to look into my bedroom. "What are you doing?" I step back. "Excuse me." I place my hand on his chest to push him back. Wrong move. The hard muscles tense under my touch.

"Just getting the lay of the land so we don't bump into any walls tonight." It's too dark to see his expression, but I'd bet his eyes are lit up like Michigan Avenue at Christmas.

"You're incorrigible."

"After you doubted my skills the other night, I have to do some legwork. You know I'm not a young buck anymore."

"Yeah, need a cane yet, twenty-six?" I shake my head.

"Twenty-seven," he corrects, and my shoulders falter a little. "It's okay, I forgive you."

His birthday is in February, so he's already turned

twenty-seven. Fuck me. Why do I feel so bad for not remembering? I bet he doesn't remember mine.

"You forgive me?" I grab the coat off the hanger because I need to escape this area. It's like a sexual trifecta with him, me and a bed five-feet away.

"You could make it up to me...give me a belated birthday gift," he says from behind me.

"I can only imagine what you had in mind." I stop in the family room and push one arm into my coat when suddenly the back of the coat is held up for me.

"Nah, you never were the birthday blow job kinda girl, were you?"

I say nothing because there's currently a fire igniting between my thighs and I know it's only going to spread.

"I think you loved my cock more than I did," he says in a low, gravelly voice.

There it goes, a full five-alarm fire between my thighs.

I slide my arm through my other sleeve. His fingers brush the nape of my neck as he straightens the collar.

"November third," he whispers my birthday into my ear. "Figured you were wondering."

"You figured wrong." I move to the table to grab my clutch, my eyes never meeting his. "I don't like to be late." I yank open the door, but he grabs the edge, motioning for me to go first.

I was so wrong about this only being a ride. I'm not sure myself or my panties are going to survive.

SOMEHOW, I did just that—survive. Mostly because I made sure to stay on my side of the Uber car. Thankfully, Dean took the signal and stayed on the opposite side. We discussed RISE mostly, he wanted more information on the charity he only volunteered his services to help so that he could have a "casual" run-in with me.

I admit, Hannah's right, I like the fact that he sought me out way more than I should.

We make our way into the building and one of the three doormen direct us to the elevator and steps in with us.

"Why did Hannah start RISE again?" Dean asks, dangerously close to me.

"Because her ex was an asshole."

The doorman glances over his shoulder with a smirk.

"Those damn ex-husbands," Dean jokes. "Can't live with them, can't live without them."

Giggle number two. I'm going to count them the entire evening, so if you'd like to grab a piece of scrap paper, you'd be doing me a service.

"I could live without mine."

His hand lands on my hip. It doesn't mold, just stays there and the heat between us makes it feel like he's branding me.

The elevator dings and the doorman holds his hand on the doors so they don't close on us. Dean's hand finds the small of my back to lead me out.

"Have a good night." The gentleman nods to us.

"You as well. Thank you." Dean puts out his hand, shakes it with what I assume is money.

"Where did the farm boy go?" I ask.

"I told you I've changed." He shrugs.

We stop in front of a woman dressed in black and white who's holding her hands out. "May I?"

Dean helps me with my coat and hands it over to the woman, and then sheds his leather jacket. For some reason, I have a momentary lapse of judgment. Before he hands it over, I twirl around and place a hand on his chest. "Don't go stripping away the old you completely."

He smiles down at me, his hand covers mine and we stare into each other's eyes for a moment. I want to look away. I *need* to look away.

"Chelsea!"

Thank God.

"I'll be keeping that." Dean keeps his jacket, sliding his arms back through the sleeves, leaving his cool persona intact.

"You look gorgeous." Victoria approaches, Reed at her side. "Spin."

"No."

"Come on, spin." Victoria's eyes are expectant. Are they handing out crack at this party? What the hell is wrong with her?

"No."

Dean steps up beside me and links his fingers through mine and holds our hands up in the air between us. For some reason that I can't fathom, I don't pull away.

"Oh, I'm not supposed to like you," Victoria says with dreamy eyes.

"You're Victoria?" Dean asks.

Reed steps closer, putting his arm around his woman and planting his hand on her hip. "And I'm Reed."

"Down dog," I joke. "This is Dean."

"Dean?" Reed questions and then he removes his hand from Victoria and extends it out to Dean. "The ex-husband?"

"The one and only." Dean shakes his hand while still holding my arm up with his free hand. I fight to lower my hand, but he's stronger and wins out.

I spin quickly to get it over with. Victoria claps. "Just gorgeous. Love the dress."

I swear she's transformed into Mary Poppins since Reed came into her life.

"I couldn't agree more, Victoria." Dean's hand extends to Victoria.

She stares at it and then glances to me, hesitantly letting Dean's big hand swallow her petite one.

"You look beautiful. Spin," I say back to her with a shit-eating grin.

She laughs, spinning without the assistance of Reed. Even does a curtsey.

"Reed, are you giving her drugs?" I ask.

He chuckles and kisses her temple. "If happiness is a drug, then she's overdosed."

I roll my eyes. "They're newly together." I point to the happy couple and look at Dean.

He nods. "Hopefully they'll rub off on you."

I roll my eyes and glance around the room, trying to spot Hannah's German Shepard, Lucy. When I don't spot her trying to climb up anyone's leg, I turn to Victoria.

"Where's Lucy?" I ask.

"Hannah said things did not go well when the caterers came to start setting up, so she begged Tad to take her for the evening.

I chuckle. "She's going to owe him big time."

"Who's Lucy?" Dean asks.

Before I can respond, Reed spots someone behind me. "Raegan!" Reed raises his hand and Victoria slides to the side to see past Dean.

"Oh. My. God." Victoria's face pales.

"I told you, she doesn't like me. See, she brought a date with her." Reed argues against Victoria's jealousy of a lawyer who did some intellectual property work for us pro bono. He introduced us to her and she helped us out of a jam.

Victoria's hand smacks Reed in the stomach. "Give me some credit." Her eyes find mine and her voice lowers. "It's the silver fox."

"What?" I spin around and sure as shit, the silver fox is helping Raegan with her coat and handing it to the lady who just took mine.

I spin back around to Victoria, my gaze scanning the immediate area for Hannah.

"Last we saw her, she was on her way to the kitchen to make sure everything was going smoothly." Victoria bites her lip.

"What am I missing?" Reed asks. "Is that Hannah's boyfriend?"

"NO!" we both screech.

"It's her ex-husband's attorney," Victoria says.

"Divorce attorney," I clarify.

"So, he might be more hated than me at this party?" Dean asks.

Reed and Victoria laugh.

"I don't hate you," Reed chimes in.

"I don't…" I narrow my eyes at Victoria. "Let's find Hannah," she suggests.

Whose side is she on?

"I'll be back." I eye the silver fox and then Dean.

"I make friends easily." He slips his hands into his pockets and shrugs.

"I'll show you to the bar." Reed nods in the direction of the other room.

Dean's smile dims slightly for the first time tonight and my stomach flips. His smile returns after a moment and he leans forward so his lips are at my ear. "Relax. As I think you remember, I'm a big boy."

I suck in a breath and he winks, nodding his head in the direction I need to head in.

Go Chels. Move your feet. Up and down. You've been doing it since you were eleven months old.

His hand lands on my back and he nudges me forward.

"Come on." Victoria's already ten steps ahead of me, her expression telling me we don't have time to waste. There's a bomb we have to diffuse, and it's set to go off soon.

Victoria and I meet Hannah as she's coming out of the kitchen. She's elegant in a conservative yet sexy champagne colored dress. Her long chestnut hair flowing down over her exposed shoulders, her smile bright and welcoming.

"Chelsea, hi. Is Dean here?" She pulls me into a light embrace and we half attempt to kiss each other's cheek without messing up our makeup. "I bet he lost his voice when he saw how gorgeous you look."

"Dean never loses his voice."

"Where is he?" She looks at Victoria. "Are him and Reed doing shots at the bar?" She laughs softly.

"Um, Hannah?" Victoria places her hand on Hannah's forearm.

"Is there a problem with food or drinks? This is why I hire party planners. I don't want to be in charge. Let me go find her." She steps forward to slide between Victoria and me.

"Don't go in there." My hand lands on Hannah's forearm, but a lot firmer than Victoria's touch.

Hannah stops, stares at me in bewilderment. "What am I missing?"

"Raegan's here," Victoria says and cringes at me from behind Hannah's back.

"Oh, great."

"She brought a date," Victoria continues.

Hannah smiles and looks from me to Victoria.

"She brought the guy from Torrio's."

Hannah says nothing, her smile still in place on her face. Maybe she doesn't understand.

"The silver fox," I say.

"I understand. Okay, thanks for telling me." Her smile widens and glows if that's even possible.

"I don't think you did," I said, glancing at Victoria for a quick second.

"No, I did. Roarke Baldwin is here. I heard you." Turning to both of us, she seems too calm and put together. Like the eye of a hurricane or the calm before the storm. "Let's go greet them, shall we?"

She steps forward first, Victoria and I following like the two other Charlie Angels in our clique, exchanging a 'what-the-fuck' look. I can't help the feeling that this is either going to go very, very well or very, very bad.

Chapter Twelve

*R*eed and Dean step away from the bar when they see us approach. My head might be somewhere else, but my eyes focus in on Dean's left hand. To say the glass with ice and dark liquid with a lime doesn't scare me would be a grave understatement. Tonight is the real test to see if he really has changed.

Victoria shakes her head to Reed who halts in his footsteps, watching from afar. Dean follows suit, bringing the drink to his lips, eyes intent on the scene that's about to unfold.

"Raegan," Hannah coos with a fakeness I've never heard from her mouth.

"Hannah."

The two lightly hug, kissing cheeks like I did with Hannah moments ago.

Victoria and I stand in the wings like the pink ladies.

"I love the dress," Hannah compliments her. "The color brings out your sparkling green eyes."

I glance to my side at Victoria. Never in the time I've

known Hannah have I seen her have such a Valley of the Dolls/Stepford Wife vibe.

"Thank you. You look stunning as always."

Hannah waves off the compliment. "I've owned this forever. Glad it's still in style. After my divorce and his lawyer taking me to the cleaners, I rarely shop anymore. I've had to get inventive, you know?"

Raegan's timid smile suggests she's uncomfortable with Hannah's forthcoming. "Well, it's a great dress."

Roarke is talking to someone just a few feet away and as I wait for him to notice Hannah, my heart starts racing.

"Thanks. I thought you were bringing a date?"

"Yes." Raegan glances back behind her. "He's right there."

Hannah pretends she didn't know, exaggerating her movements as she leans to the side to spot the silver fox. "Oh, you brought Roarke Baldwin?"

It's like watching a master, ladies and gentlemen. I want to be Hannah Crowley someday.

"You know him?" Raegan asks.

"Not personally. Not in a friendly way. Just from the courtroom."

Raegan being the smart girl she is, puts all the pieces together now.

"No way," she says, her eyes wide.

Roarke Baldwin's reputation is well known. He's the man you hire to stick it to your ex.

"Yes, he was my ex's lawyer, but hey, no hard feelings."

If we were anywhere else, I'd cough out bullshit, but this is Hannah's fight.

"I'm so sorry, I wouldn't have brought him," Raegan says in a hushed voice.

Hannah smiles. "Of course. How would you know?"

Roarke breaks apart from his conversation and all four of us women stare at him as his attention flickers our way.

He's a man who seems to have it all together, but for the briefest moment, I see fear flash in his eyes. But instead of running, he proves his reputation of a damn pit bull, approaching with a swagger that would suggest he expected this all along. Like he knew this was Hannah's condo.

"Ms. Crowley," he extends his hand, a large, expensive watch peeking out from under his suit sleeve.

"Why Mr. Baldwin, I have to say, I never thought I would host you in my home."

Raegan's eyes are volleying between the two and I think we all probably look like a pack of kids watching their parents argue.

"It's a great place. Family owned?" he asks with a smirk.

"Is that your assumption because you weren't able to take it from me?"

"It was just a question," he says in a lazy way.

"Questions, questions." Hannah's smile hasn't faltered and I'm wondering how long until she loses that high society etiquette and punches the guy square in the nose.

Dean and Reed approach and at this point I'm grateful.

"Hi," I say, and Dean hands me a glass of wine while he watches on, his eyes on the couple.

"We were thinking we'd go out on the terrace," Reed suggests.

Victoria nuzzles up to him and accepts the glass of wine he has for her. "Perfect."

"Hannah, you're good?" I lower my voice and lean into the back of her head.

She nods.

"Please enjoy yourself, Mr. Baldwin, and hands where I can see them. Maybe there's a silver fork somewhere you think my ex deserves."

Roarke's eyes sparkle with mischief and I think there's a high probability he's envisioning her naked right now.

These two have some sort of weird chemistry.

Two men walk into the room and Hannah excuses herself to greet them. Roarke's eyes watch her leave. I really hope Raegan isn't invested in Roarke because I'm sure he has eyes for someone else.

"IN THE MOOD FOR TACO BELL?" Dean asks when we climb in the Uber.

"I'm in the mood for my bed." I slip off my one heel, running my barefoot along my leg.

I'm not trying to be sexy, these new heels are killing me.

"Perfect. We're still in sync." He opens up his arms then pats his lap for me to put my foot there.

"Alone," I add.

He continues to pat his leg. "Let me cop a feel before I drop you off?"

Reluctantly, I allow him to massage my feet. Maybe then he'll realize he's not into relationship stuff and he'll skip along.

The minute his hands land on my foot though, my head falls to the glass window and my eyes close and a moan squeaks out of me.

"If you want me to act like a gentleman, stop with the noises." He shifts my foot so I'm closer to his knee than his crotch and I wish the tingling sensation in my core would go away.

"You still a Sox fan?" he asks.

"Still a Cubs fan?"

"You mean the World Series champs? Hell yeah." The smirk on his face invites me to bring on my best comeback.

"Yeah, that was two years ago."

"This is their year again, I feel it."

I roll my eyes. Whether it's because of the foot rub or his words I'm not sure. "Rumor has it that the Sox are more likely to go farther."

The Uber driver glances through the rearview mirror at us.

"Who are you listening to? WGN-AM?"

"Silly Cubs fans, baseball is for Sox fans." I lean forward and pat his shoulder. It's a nice shoulder.

He chuckles. "My company is having a party. Crosstown Classic. Would you like to join me?"

"Are you asking for another date?" His thumb digs into the arch of my foot and I swallow down the long moan that wants to roar out of me.

I hadn't really thought this was it with us. I mean I only agreed to tonight, but the thought that our time was over did sadden me. Even though it shouldn't. I forgot how easygoing Dean can be. No pressure, easy conversation, like not much can get under his skin. The entire night he mingled all while staying at my side. If I ventured off, he found someone to talk to. He didn't spend the entire night hovering around the bar, he didn't rush me out, and he didn't brag about himself to anyone. Maybe Dean has turned over a new leaf. Or more likely he just had a good night.

"Think of it like a favor," he says.

"A favor?"

"I don't want to show up solo."

He motions for my other foot and I oblige because I

like to torture myself. He slips the heel from my foot, placing it down and goes to work on my other foot.

"You expect me to go to Wrigley Field?" I screw up my face.

"Technically, it's rooftop. You don't have to go in. If it helps, my boss is a ChiSox fan."

"He knows you're a Cubs fan?"

The conversation sounds juvenile, but honestly, jobs have been claimed, jobs have been lost, by what color you wear. In Chicago, if you're a baseball fan, there's no such thing as liking both teams. It's one or the other. End of discussion.

"Yeah."

"You think bringing a Sox fan will give you brownie points. Hence the favor?"

His gaze shifts off my feet to my eyes and it's too dark to truly read his face, but his silence is deafening. "Yeah."

It's one simple word, but there's a weight to it I don't understand. I'm not even sure what made the shift in the conversation. Where did our usual banter go? I can't help but think there's another reason he wants me there and as usual, my curiosity gets the better of me.

"Okay. I'll go," I say.

"I'll take you to the game at Cellular."

"Well, how can I refuse then?"

He tickles my foot and I slide it back my way trying to get free.

The car slows, and I start to pull my legs toward me to put my heels back on, but Dean locks his arm across my shins, picking up each heel and sliding it on like he's a shoe salesman and has done it millions of times.

Again, the energy shifts when he finishes and our eyes lock.

I turn away, grabbing my clutch and opening the door.

"Thank you," I say to the driver and step to the concrete sidewalk in front of my apartment.

Dean slides to come out my side, but I hold my hand out in front of my chest. "I got it from here."

A sly smile crosses his lips and he doesn't stop, his foot landing between my legs as he pulls himself out of the car, leaving us chest to chest.

"You think you can get rid of me that easily?"

His hands grip my hips and he shuffles forward pushing me away from the car. While he's busy shutting the door and telling the Uber guy to leave, I fiddle with my keys to get in my apartment complex.

In the small glass foyer, his chest hits my back and I'm not going to lie, a small part of me wants to turn around and smash my lips to his. My nipples peak in my bra and I suppress a shiver.

Willpower, Chels. You have a few minutes and then you can pop in Rambo and relive what it's like to sleep with Dean Bennett.

The key finally fits, and I unlock the door, stepping toward the elevator.

"I can let you go here." I look behind me.

He raises his hand up in the air, pointing to the ground and does a spinning motion. "Turn back around."

"Really, Dean, I got it."

"I'm walking you to your door." He reaches past me, pressing the elevator button.

Someone has it out for me. Now I have to survive an elevator ride with him. Please, there are hundreds of people who live in this apartment complex, someone has to be coming home at the same time as us.

It arrives quickly because it's late at night and most residents are probably asleep.

I step in, pressing my floor. Dean stands shoulder to shoulder with me.

When I spot a woman coming through the glass doors, she turns her key in the lock and smiles. I smile back.

My savior.

Dean reaches across the elevator and presses the close door button. For once it actually does what it should, and the doors slowly come together. The woman's smile turns into a look of disgust and she flips Dean off.

My head swivels in his direction. "That wasn't nice."

"I don't care." His chest pushes into mine, his hands locking me on either side.

I have no idea how he did it, but my back is against the wall, his body looming over mine with lust filled eyes and lickable lips. I want to open my arms and tell him to take me.

"She's—"

His hips slide forward. "I'm done sharing you tonight."

"Dean," I sigh.

"One kiss?" he asks. "Please?"

His voice so desperate like he's pleading for a drop of water after running a marathon.

"Shouldn't you see me to the door first?"

His lips turn up, his perfect row of teeth making an appearance. "You don't want to make-out in the elevator?"

"One, I agreed to a kiss. Two, kind of cliché, don't you think?"

He leans forward, his nose running along my cheek, gliding down to my neck and back up to my ear. Goose bumps prick my skin. "I wish I could oblige with your wishes, but if my lips don't land on yours in the next ten seconds, I'm going to die."

"That's a little dramatic, don't you think?" My voice doesn't hold the tone of reproach it should. Instead, it's breathy and inviting.

"Come on. I've been a good boy, can't I get a treat?"

The elevator dings and the doors are about to open, but Dean presses and holds the door open button, leaning into me.

His lips hover over mine and he waits. "I won't do it unless you agree."

He runs his tongue over his bottom lip, his eyes devouring me like he's a starved man and I'm the innocent prey he's caught.

"One kiss," I whisper, unable to deny him any longer.

No sooner do the words get out of my mouth, then his lips are on mine. One of his hands slide around my waist, pulling me into him, his erection poking at my stomach. My hands landing on his cheeks, keeping his lips on mine.

Dean takes what he wants. There's no gentleness when his tongue thrashes with mine, there's no slow going as our heated kiss turns frantic. Our heads weave from side to side, unable to get enough of each other.

The elevator alarm buzzes from Dean holding the button so long and we finally break apart as quickly as we came together.

Needing air, I race out of the elevator and down the hall to my apartment, him following me the entire way.

Turning around when I reach my door, I stare up at him. "This is where we say goodbye and you already got your goodnight kiss."

"Pushing my luck for a second?"

I nod.

"Say it."

"Say what?"

"Say I can't have a second taste."

"You can't have a second taste."

His gaze dips down to my chest, probably noticing my uneven breathing. He leans forward, his head descending.

"Dean," I say, losing any fight inside of me.

His lips never touch mine this time. His hands are in his pockets, but his breath tickles my ear. "Sweet dreams, Chelsea. Thank you for a great night." He backs away. "I want to make sure you get in." He nods to the door.

"Goodnight, Dean." I fiddle with my keys somehow losing all sense of what key I'm supposed to be using. Finally, someone is looking down on me because I find it, stick it in the lock and click the door open.

I flick on the light of my apartment and circle around. "Thank you."

"Enjoy Rambo," he snickers and heads toward the elevator again.

"Enjoy Steel Magnolias," I call out as he heads down the hall.

Circling around, he shakes his head. "Didn't I ever tell you? I have the memory of an elephant." He taps the side of his head with his finger. "There's enough in my arsenal, I don't need a video of you to relive it."

I don't bother mentioning that dolphins have a better memory than elephants according to science.

"Now, get in there and lock yourself in. We'll talk tomorrow," he says.

He stops and waits in the middle of the hallway of my apartment floor.

Not knowing what else to say, I shut the door and flip the lock wishing like hell he was on this side with me.

Chapter Thirteen

*O*ne week later, I'm all decked out in my black and white, wearing jeans and a White Sox shirt, sweatshirt tied around my waist. The only thing I'm leaving behind is my hat. Since this is an office thing, I don't want to appear too grungy.

A knock lands on my door at the exact time Dean said he'd be here. As usual, my stomach erupts into its own little firework show inside. It's been a common occurrence every time he texts me. He's tried to call, but I'm not ready just yet.

I open the door.

"Oh, excuse me, I have to go throw up." I pretend to choke, taking in his head to toe blue and red ensemble.

"Damn, even in White Sox crap you look hot." He steps in.

"Please come in," I say sarcastically, and he shrugs. "Why is it you never have to press the buzzer?"

There's a buzzer to get into the apartment building, but he always seems to find his own way in.

"Did you swindle a key from my landlord?"

"Believe me, it's scary how easy it is to get into this place. I'm half tempted to move you out."

His jeans are slightly worn but still have that new look to them. His Cubs shirt and jersey pull at his shoulders and I realize that he opted to skip the hat, too. Though his hair is messier than when I was at his office. Must be his casual Saturday look.

"Is this okay? Since it's a work thing." I motion to what I'm wearing.

He looks me over. "I don't know. Spin."

I glare at him and he chuckles.

"Worth a try."

I grab my cell phone, tucking it into my crossbody purse and get set to leave.

"Ready?" I ask.

"Let's go see the Cubs kick the Sox ass."

I roll my eyes. We clear the doorway and I lock my door, Dean waiting for me the entire time.

As we make our way to the elevator, his hand finds mine and he entwines our fingers. "I figure we should get used to it. They think you're my girlfriend." He presses the elevator button.

"Not your ex-wife."

"I don't like them knowing too much about me."

I raise both eyebrows at him. "So, you want me to pretend I'm your girlfriend?"

"Are you seeing anyone else?" he asks and I'm half-tempted to lie.

"Technically, I'm not seeing *anyone*."

"Do you swallow every one of your date's tongues?"

The elevator arrives, we step in and I purposely leave space between us. "You swallowed mine, for the record."

He chuckles. "I'd swallow a hell of a lot more if you'd let me."

There goes the hot flash like I'm a menopausal fifty-year-old woman.

"I think I'd be the one swallowing." Tit for tat.

"You always were a gamer when it came to that. Then again, it's probably because you didn't want a mess." He winks.

Thankfully, the elevator doors open, and we exit the apartment building.

"It's so sunny," I exclaim.

"Like a true summer day." He captures my hand again and leads me down the street.

"Public transportation today?" I ask as he weaves me through the crowded weekend streets.

"Nope."

"Are we walking?"

If we are, I'm going to be really pissed. I'm not wearing my running shoes.

"Nope."

"Then how are we getting there?"

He stops and stares down at the two-wheel vehicle parked under the train line.

My eyes widen, and I look over at him. "I'm going to look like shit when we get there."

"No, you won't. Come on."

I stare down at the motorcycle while Dean bends down, grabbing the two helmets out of the side compartments.

"You do remember how to ride, right?"

I snatch the helmet from his grasp. "Of course, I do." I place it over my head cringing to myself over the amount of time I spent on my hair this morning. "You're buying me a hat when we get there."

"Done." He puts on his helmet which feels odd to see on him. He never wore one in college and his bike was nothing like this one. Obviously, tax attorneys do well for themselves.

He hops on first, kicking up the stand and straightening it out for me. I get on and straddle him, my arms locked around his middle until we get started.

He eases out into Chicago traffic and I assume this is going to be a nightmare of a ride because traffic on the weekend is a constant stop and go. But I should've known better.

The true Dean comes out a minute into the ride. He doesn't wait behind the cars stopped in front of him. Instead, he zooms ahead and beats the next car off the line and veers into that lane before almost running into the back of the bus.

"I'm not interested in dying today," I say loud enough for him to hear. My hands are wrapped tightly around his middle and my helmet is pressed against his back for fear of watching what is surely going to be a crazy ride.

"You're always safe with me."

He stops at a light, his feet landing on the cement, and my body relaxes a little. We're only blocks away from the field and as much as I shouldn't, I'm hoping he brought the bike so that we can go somewhere after. Like an open road like we used to do.

Just as I'm adjusting to his way of riding, Wrigley comes into view. He stops at the curb of the place where we head up to the rooftops. Lifting up the flap of his helmet, him and the valet guy talk—Dean not about to let him ride the bike, so the guy directs him to an alley.

"You get off here," Dean says, and I ease myself away from his body which is like prying a baby from their mama. I might act like I'm okay with it, but every part of me wants to wrap itself back around him.

Dean's forearms flex as he roars the bike back to life

and speeds down an alley.

"Nice bike," the valet guy says.

I nod.

"This ain't Comiskey." He eyes my shirt and since he uses the original name for the White Sox Park, I'm guessing he must be in his thirties.

"It's crosstown." I shrug.

"You should save that for your side of town."

He's joking, I see it in his smirk, but still, how Dean convinced me to go to Wrigley is beyond me.

"You'll be first in line once we win the World Series this year."

The guy exaggerates a laugh. "First, if the White Sox reach the playoffs I'd be looking for hundred dollar bills falling from the sky. Second, I'm not a fair-weather fan."

At that same time, we see a group of women all decked out in their Cubs gear. One of them even has shoes with baseballs and Rizzo's face painted on one and Bryant's face on the other. Total fair-weather fans.

"Wish I could say the same for all of us," he says.

I giggle, watching the ladies glance around wondering where they're supposed to go.

"Wrigley is that way ladies." He points to the gigantic metal structure and we share a look of annoyance.

"At least we don't have that where I'm from," I say.

"Because you guys can't win."

The razzing is fun and takes up the time while I'm waiting for Dean who finally rounds the corner.

"See your boyfriend, he's a good guy." He points in Dean's direction.

"Let me guess he got the special parking spot because he's a Cubs fan?"

"You should be happy you came with him. I sent a Sox guy a mile down."

Dean wraps his arm around my shoulders as soon as he reaches us.

Protective much?

"Thanks a lot." He slips the valet guy some cash.

"No problem." The professional he is, he tucks it into his pocket without ever looking. "Go Cubbies." The guy winks at me.

"Yeah." Dean's tone holds not even half the enthusiasm as the valet guys.

Once we're inside and climbing the stairs, Dean shakes his head and says, "I leave you alone for a few minutes."

"He was innocent."

I shouldn't like the protectiveness, but I do. Maybe it's the schoolgirl inside of me, but the fact he's scared to lose me says something. Of course, does he even really have me is the question?

No, I have to be firm on that. This is a work thing. That's all it can be. Right?

"DEAN!" A half-lit man yells, followed by everyone's heads turning in our direction.

Are we back in college again where the party doesn't start until Dean arrives?

The man approaches us the minute we walk into the bar area. I look at the sun shining down on Wrigley ahead and my attention wants to veer that way.

"Mr. Heiberman." Dean's hand extends immediately.

The man glances my way, shakes Dean's hand and then places his large and hairy-knuckled hand in front of me.

"This is my girlfriend, Chelsea Walsh," Dean says.

I shake his hand. "Pleasure to meet you, Mr.

Heiberman."

"Gary, please." His eyes don't leave mine. "We didn't even know Dean had someone until he asked for a plus one." He leans in. "Good for you to show all the women he's taken."

"Um. Women?" I plaster a fake smile on my face.

"Dean is quite the catch. From what my daughter tells me, a lot of the women have been scoping him out for some time. Makes sense why he showed them no interest now."

Stop stomach, just because he wasn't interested in the advances of women in his office doesn't mean jack. They may not be his type.

"Oh, Mr. Heiberman." Dean looks over at me. "He's being kind."

Gary smacks Dean in the stomach. "He's being modest. But now that we've met you, we know why. You two make a stunning couple."

Instinctively my hands go to my hair wondering how bad it looks after the helmet.

"Well, enjoy yourself. God knows Dean doesn't get out of the office enough. Then again, that's why we love him so much."

The whole exchange is odd and if he wasn't wearing a triple XL Sox jersey, I'm not sure I'd care for the man. I mean who tells someone there's a long line of women waiting for the man you showed up with. What the hell is wrong with people?

"Come on, I'll grab you a beer," Dean says, pulling me from my thoughts.

We head to the bar, Dean's hand on the small of my back, but we're quickly stopped by a brunette who wants to say hi, openly eye fucking Dean right in front of me.

Am I really going to have to kick some ass tonight?

Chapter Fourteen

"*Hillary*, this is Chelsea," Dean introduces me to the brunette whose eyes are throwing invisible daggers at me through her fake-ass smile.

"Nice to meet you." She daintily shakes my hand.

"Pleasure."

"How come you never mentioned a girlfriend?" Her entire body shifts to face Dean, like I'm not even there.

I roll my eyes.

"It's a new thing."

"Or an old thing," I chime in with an insincere smile.

Judge me if you want, but I hate when girls think it's some sort of pissing contest. Can't we just allow another girl to get a guy and be happy? If she's been setting the hints down and he didn't pick them up, he's not interested. Move on. Why do you want a man who's not interested in you? You're worth more than that.

Dean chuckles lightly, glancing over at me with a sparkle in his dark eyes.

"So, you're an on again off again hook up?" Hillary asks.

"You can't be serious," slips out of my mouth before I can stop myself.

Dean's hand lands on my side, applying a little pressure.

"Excuse me?" Only her head swivels my way.

"Nothing." I bite my tongue. Dean owes me big for this one. I circle around, place my hand on Dean's chest, my fingers running up and down. "I'm going to go get that drink." I lift on my tiptoes, plant a kiss on his cheek and then set my eyes on Hillary. "Nice to meet you."

She smiles, and I walk away before any voices or fists are raised.

The bartender sets a napkin in front of me, another woman but thankfully not an admirer of Dean. At least not yet. "What can I get you?" she asks.

"Just a Miller Lite."

I keep my eyes poised on the televisions and not once do I allow them to linger toward Dean and Hillary. He isn't mine. I'm here as a favor. Yes, he says he wants me back, but it's yet to be established whether he really has changed.

I continue to stare at the television, feigning interest. Sometimes I'm so good at acting like I don't care it scares me.

"I like you." The bartender washes a glass and I'm surprised how few people are here. Surely this isn't his entire office. "Ballsy to wear the black and white."

"I'm not going to pretend I'm a Cubs fan."

She smiles, lifting another glass. She's probably in her late thirties, a modest wedding ring on her left finger.

"Good for you. Nothing good comes from pretending to be someone you're not."

"That's for sure." I sip my beer, sitting down on a stool and watching another televised game in a different city.

Her sentence causes a lump to lodge in my throat. Is

that what Dean is doing? Is he pretending? My insecurity wins over my pride and my gaze veers to Dean who's now talking to a group of two men. Relief hits me fast and hard. I take in the rest of the room and find Hillary by the opening to the bar, talking with a group of women who look like they're currently rating me on a scale of one to worthy of dating Dean Bennett.

It doesn't take long for Dean to join me, his hand going up to get the attention of the friendly bartender whose name tag reads Noelle. "Just a water please."

"Are you bleeding?" I ask, and his large frame sits down on the stool next to me.

"What?"

"From her claws digging into you."

He chuckles. "I always did love you jealous."

"And you went to great lengths to make me jealous."

Noelle opens the bottle of water for him, placing it on the napkin and sliding it in front of him.

"She's Heiberman's daughter." He confesses and it all clicks together.

"And she wants you?"

"I'm not available." He gulps down half his water, setting it back down.

"Yes, you are." I swivel my stool in his direction, noticing the ladies still trying to figure it all out. I can hear them now, "Why is Dean wasting his time with her?" I could list a whole spreadsheet of my great qualities, but they'd probably still be confused.

"Even if you don't agree to be my girlfriend, it doesn't make me available. My heart only belongs to you. That hasn't changed." He says this all with a straight face.

Words that would never have come out of Dean's mouth five years ago.

I reach up, the back of my hand touching his forehead. "You feeling okay there?"

He snatches my hand, bringing it down to his lap. "I've never been better." He stands up upon hearing the national anthem. "I think we're here to see a ballgame."

"That we are." I allow him to guide me to the opening, sitting us on the opposite side of the woman who shall not be named.

We mingle with another tax attorney and his wife. Although they're a little older, they enjoy razzing me about being a Sox fan and they're cool with me hammering it back as the Sox score against the Cubs.

"Do you want another beer?" Dean leans over, his lips dangerously close to my earlobe.

"Maybe just a water."

He nods, stands and heads to the bar.

A minute later Hillary takes his seat.

"Hi, I just wanted you to know I meant no offense, it's just usually when a guy doesn't mention a girlfriend it's because she's really just a booty call."

I stare at what I assume is a Long Island Ice Tea and then look into her eyes. I really hope she's acting like this because she's drunk.

"I'm not even close to a booty call for Dean." My attention moves to the field as they let the new pitcher warm up.

"There's nothing bad about that. Like I said, no offense."

Do yourself a favor, Hillary, stop drinking and head back over to your side.

"Listen." I swivel in my chair. The nice couple behind us is polite enough not to stop me. "You're the one he doesn't want. I'm sorry to tell you this and I know you're probably a little inebriated, but Dean would marry me if I asked him right now. He sought me out because he wants me back. I can tell that you've probably liked him for some time and I get it, I've been single for five years. You have to dig hard for a good, available guy and Dean is a great catch." I place my hand on her leg and she stares at it like it's bird shit that just landed on her. "You deserve someone who wants you. Who chases you. A guy who is available. Don't go around trying to break another woman's self-esteem because you think you deserve her man."

She picks up my hand with her thumb and forefinger, disposing it back in my lap.

"Get a clue. He might like you now, but I give it two weeks."

She stands and heads to the other side of the seating area. After she's gone, the woman in the row behind me pats me on the back. Dean's large frame slides by me to his seat. He sits down without saying anything and hands me my cold bottle of water.

"Thank you."

"Well, I gotta keep up the appearance of being a good catch." I elbow him in the ribs and he fakes injury. "I did like the way you kind of claimed me."

"You heard wrong," I say.

"I don't think I did."

"I said *you* claimed *me*." I focus my attention on the field. Anything other than give in to the pull toward Dean.

"One day you will." He lifts one leg and rests his ankle on his knee. He's nothing but casual as he puts his arm around my shoulders.

"Nice move," I murmur.

"Well, I've got no shot at Hillary now that you went all girl power on her." I elbow him again. "Okay, that one hurt."

"Good," I deadpan.

"Now we just sit and wait for the kiss cam."

I glance over and his usual smirk rests on his face. "Pushing it."

"Oh, come on. I'm not looking for the hard on inducer one from the elevator the other night, but a little peck never hurt anyone."

"Sorry to tell you but the kiss cam doesn't do rooftops."

"Damn it. No nachos and no kiss cam. What kind of baseball game is this?"

I giggle and somehow our bodies end up closer together.

The couple behind us heads to the bar, leaving us by ourselves. Mr. Heiberman is regaling the rest of Dean's co-workers with some story near the area where the food is laid out. I'm not sure he's seen much of the game at all.

Hillary and her friends finally descend on a table. Other than a few scattered other employees it's just the two of us who are concentrating on the game.

"Does it bother you?" I ask the question that's been at the back of my mind most of the day. Hell, from the moment he brought up taking me to the game.

"What? Being at a baseball game?" His mood shifts and I regret bringing up the subject, but if he truly changed, this is where I'll find the answer and I need to know.

"Yeah. That you could have been out there," I say in a soft voice.

He shrugs. "I might not have. I mean people assumed I'd make the bigs, but there was never any guarantee. I could be on a bus right now off to play in the minors."

"You think about it a lot?"

"Of course. It was my dream."

Dean was already in talks about being drafted before his chirping another guy at the bar one night got him involved in a bar fight that tore up his shoulder. No team wants a pitcher with a bad shoulder and suddenly team scouts stopped showing up or calling and Dean fell into a depression. A depression that cost us our marriage.

"But do you…"

"No, I don't wallow in it." He looks me straight in the eye as if he's willing me to see the truth there. "I'm happy being a tax attorney, believe it or not. Do I ever think what if? All the time, but there's a helluva lot more to life than playing professional ball."

"You didn't think that once upon a time." Even I can hear the hurt in my tone and so I sip my water to push down the lump forming in my throat.

"I told you I've changed. I'm not lying, Chelsea. I know what destroyed us and I'm here to tell you it won't this time."

The saying 'a leopard doesn't change its spots' pops into my head.

"So, you'd rather deal with taxes than be out there." I point to the field.

"If it means I have you with me, then right here, every time."

"Man, you're heavy on the lines tonight." I shake my head at him with a smile.

He winks, the one that makes my stomach flip. "Are they working?"

I hold up my finger and thumb, opening a small space between them.

"How about a bet?" He glances over to the scoreboard and I do the same.

Cubs, nine. White Sox, eight. Close game.

"Let me guess, sexual?"

"Is there any other?" he asks, arching a brow.

"With you? No." I chuckle.

He swivels in my direction, the game no longer on his radar. "It's my way to get you to do things you really want to do but are too stubborn to admit." He takes my hand and squeezes it.

"Maybe I don't want to play your game then?" I cross my arms over my chest.

"Oh, you'll play. How's this? Whoever wins gets a double after the game."

"A double cheeseburger? Deal." I hold out my hand.

He stares down at it and then back up to my eyes. "Let me be clearer, whoever wins, gets to second base."

"Are we skipping first?"

"I'd never skip first with you, Chels."

I ignore the way his words heat the blood in my veins.

"How come I feel like I'm getting the raw end of this deal? I get to feel your nipples. Yippee."

He widens his legs. "You're welcome to steal third."

A flash of heat invades my face. "Well, you're not."

We shake on it and from that point on, the game gets a whole lot more interesting.

Chapter Fifteen

The sun is descending, and I smile to myself when Dean turns the handlebars of his motorcycle down Lake Shore Drive.

My arms are securely wrapped around his waist, my cheek on his back. I can't help but wish I didn't have to wear this helmet so that I could feel the heat of his skin on my face. His muscles flex under my hands as he maneuvers the bike past cars. The breeze off the lake makes me happy that I chose to put my sweatshirt on before we left.

The ride ends way too quickly for my liking when he slows the bike, parking it along the curb, Lake Michigan on our left and Grant Park on our right.

He puts down the kickstand, gets up and holds out his hand for me.

After securing our helmets in the side pockets, his fingers wind with mine as we walk along the sidewalk. Buckingham Fountain comes into view with its lights glowing under the streaming water sprouting out of the concrete fixture.

"You know when you asked me about baseball earlier?"

In the five-minute trip from the stadium, his mood has shifted from playful to serious, causing a nervous weight to press on my chest.

"Yeah."

"I didn't say something I should have."

The gravel around the fountain crunches under our feet and I admire the beautiful scene in front of me—the fountain spray with the skyline of Chicago in the backdrop. The scene seems contrary to the conversation we're about to have. I've pushed it away as long as I could, but from the look on Dean's face he's not going to let it slide any longer. Still, I don't know if I'm ready to discuss…everything.

"What?"

"I only have one regret."

"You shouldn't have any regrets."

He stops me and sits me on a bench on the outside perimeter the fountain. "Will you let me talk?"

I face him, hearing the frustration in his tone.

"I only have one regret," he says again, his gaze intense.

"The fight? I know. It sucks."

"Jesus, Chelsea." He sounds mad and I don't really understand why.

"What?"

"Listen to me." He takes my shoulders in his hands, squeezing lightly. "It's not the fight. Not my finest moment, but that's not it."

I keep my mouth shut, purposely staring him in the eye to let him know I won't interrupt him again.

"It's you. Losing you is my regret." His voice breaks on the last word and he takes my hands in his. "I'm trying to take this slow. I'm trying not to push you, but please tell me we're moving forward?" The desperation in his voice sounds like he's pleading with a higher power on his deathbed for just one more minute on this Earth.

"Dean," I sigh, sliding my hands from under his and standing and stepping toward the fountain.

"Why can't you answer me?" He comes up alongside me.

Thankfully, most people aren't lingering around and the people who are aren't paying us any attention.

I sigh. "You're asking a lot of me."

I admire the water shooting, the colors, again trying not to feel the pull to Dean.

"What else do I have to do to prove to you before you'll give us an honest chance?" he asks.

"I've let you take me out twice, you've kissed me, and if I make good on the bet, you get to feel me up tonight." I turn his way and a smile graces his lips.

Of course, it does. What guy doesn't want to feel up a pair of titties?

"I'm not doing that unless you want me to. You do want me to though, right?" he chuckles, his arms wrapping around my waist and pulling me close. "I know you feel it." He brushes a stray hair off my cheek and tucks it behind my ear. "When are you going to start being honest with yourself?"

Question of the century.

Can't people want someone but never act on it if they know it's bad for them?

"I can't deny it, Dean. That's not my hesitation."

For some reason, rather than stepping away, I move closer, needing to feel him. Needing to let him shelter me and loving the safety of his arms.

"I'm afraid." I rest my chin on his chest, staring up at him. "I won't make it through another heartbreak from you." A single tear slips from my eye. "You didn't see me after."

"And you didn't see me." He wipes the tear with his thumb before it falls down my cheek. "I might've been the cause of our divorce, but it was no easier on me. It took me a long time to get my shit together, but I did. I'm an impatient man. I waited a long time to come for you, but I'm here, and I'll wait until you're ready, Chelsea. Just tell me I'm on the right path. Tell me I'm winning this battle and I'll continue to fight to win the war."

I stare into his chocolate eyes, and without thinking nearly enough about my decision, I let my heart speak for me.

Stretching up on my tiptoes, I place my hands on his shoulders to steady myself and press my lips to his. Warmth spreads through my body and I fall back down to my heels. "You're winning."

His hand slowly moves to my neck and he pulls me into his chest, one arm tight around my waist, the other one cupping the back of my head.

"Here." He lets me go and digs into his pocket, retrieving two pennies. He places one in my palm. "Make a wish."

I take it from his hand, walking the distance to the edge of the fountain. Closing my eyes, I wish for something I've wished for before at a fountain located a thousand miles away on the Vegas Strip. This time I hope whoever grants fountain wishes hears me.

Dean kisses his penny and tosses it in.

"What did you wish for?" I ask.

"I'm hoping the same thing you did." He takes my hand in his again. "Now I want you to fill me in on everything I missed over the past five years." He guides me down the path farther into Grant Park.

I chuckle. "In a nutshell, I got my degree and had a string of jobs until I landed this one."

"Come on. I want all the details. I want it to be like I missed no time in your life."

"Well, I walked out of our apartment and sat in my car for an hour…"

He frowns for a second and then says, "Let's skip to a few months after you left me." There's no anger in his voice, just a calm acceptance.

"I transferred to the city."

For the next hour, I tell him about going to school in the city versus the country town where we met. We discuss the reason I couldn't seem to find a job I liked, about how I ended up at RISE. My parents, Skylar and Beckett, Zoe and Vin. Lastly, he admits he saw Mikey at a club three years ago. When he asked about me, Mikey punched him in the face.

"He did not!" I cover my mouth with my hand, aghast as we approach his bike.

"I told him I missed you and wanted your number." He hands me the helmet.

"I guess he didn't like that?" I strap it on.

"I had to tell my boss I got elbowed in a basketball game."

"Why did you wait so long? You could have looked me up."

"It wasn't the right time, I'm glad Mikey knew that." He puts on his own helmet. "How about a ride for old time's sake?"

I smile. "Thought you'd never ask."

"The sun's heading down pretty fast, so just a quick one up Lake Shore and then back to your place."

I nod, climbing on the bike ready to assume my koala bear position. "Dean?"

"Yeah?" He waits to start the bike.

"Go to your place after the ride."

He doesn't turn around, but he places his hands over mine where they rest around his stomach.

"Are you sure?"

My arms tighten around him and I nuzzle my head. "I'm positive."

"You sure you still want the ride?"

I giggle. "A romantic ride down the lakefront sounds like great foreplay."

"Screw the bike, I've got other foreplay moves."

He turns the ignition, the bike roaring to life. Doing a u-turn, we head the other way.

I take one giant step to the edge of the cliff praying it's deep water below and not just a bunch of jagged rocks.

FORTY-FIVE MINUTES LATER, the sun has slipped beneath the horizon. When I come out of my dazed state, we're pulling into a garage. He parks the bike and for once, Dean says nothing, leading me to the elevator, and pressing the button.

My hand is in his and my body is hyper-aware of our proximity, my thoughts focused on what we're about to do.

He presses floor nineteen and we ride up in silence. Is this weighing on both of us? We're about to make a decision that we can't take back.

The doors slide open, and he holds his hand out in front of him for me to step out first. Then his hand is tucked around mine again. My heart pounds as we bypass door after door until we reach the one at the end of the hall. Apartment nineteen twenty-one.

Dean lives in apartment nineteen twenty-one.

There's something weird about not knowing where he lived until this moment. I can't help but wonder what's on the other side of the door.

I lived with Dean for four short months. I knew his bad habits of toothpaste all over the sink, of leaving empty shampoo bottles in the shower, not rinsing dishes before putting them in the dishwasher. I knew what he smelled like in the morning, or how he couldn't sleep without his hand on my ass.

Now, I know nothing. For a man I thought I knew everything about, I'm just now realizing I no longer know anything about the man beside me.

"You don't have to," he says, noticing my eyes fixated on the door.

"I want to." I glance over to him.

A soft smile wraps around his face. He's happy I want to take this next step.

"Welcome to your future home." He pushes and holds the door open for me.

I smack his stomach and try to tamp down my expectations as I walk over the threshold.

"You've got to be kidding me." I bend down to the floor. "Are you trying to bribe me?"

Chapter Sixteen

"Meet Grover," Dean says from behind me, shutting the door. "I have to take him out real quick." He scrambles to a table by the front door and grabs a long black leash.

The dog rolls over on his back, letting me pet him, but when Dean clicks the leash, he's up and panting with his tail swinging back and forth.

"I never thought my dog would cockblock me. Don't leave, okay?"

I chuckle. "I'll go with you."

"Really?" Dean seems shocked and I don't understand why, I'm a dog person.

"I guess I could stay here and snoop."

"Come on, it's a great night for a walk." He swings his arm around my shoulders pretending like he wouldn't want me here without him.

Truth is I do pry, it's in my nature, and I don't want to do that to Dean.

We leave the apartment and head to the elevators. "What kind of dog is Grover?"

"Bulldog."

"He looks like he might be a drooler. Does he shed?"

Dean chuckles. "Wondering how you'll clean up after him already?"

"You're way too hopeful."

"Optimistic. There's a difference."

The elevator dings and the doors open. We file in, Grover panting a musical melody as the elevator descends.

I look down at the drool dripping from his tongue and watch a long strand of saliva stretch to the floor.

Please don't shake. Please don't move.

Like he heard the worries running through my head, his head twists and he stares up at me with intrigued eyes. The long gross strip of drool drips and lands on the carpet.

"Is there something wrong with Labradors or golden retrievers? Or how about a small poodle?"

The elevator doors open, and we step into a large foyer decorated with brass and marble. "A doorman? Fancy."

"Well, I am an attorney after all." He straightens his back like it's a big deal, but I know it's an act.

When I walked out on him five years ago, he was passed out on a mattress that had no frame or box spring. Our eatery set included paper plates and not the name brand ones. The ones where you grab ten plates instead of just one because it's near impossible to peel one away from the other. No metal silverware or glass cups. It wasn't exactly like we were eating steak and needed a heavy-duty knife anyway. We were college students and the only thing we had between us was love—but that hadn't proved to be enough.

Now he lives in a condo with a man who opens doors for him. The foyer here is bigger than our apartment back then. I shouldn't be so surprised. He sacrificed every part of his life for baseball, including me. Why would he not do the same for whatever he wanted after his dream to go to the big leagues was over?

A thought flashes through my brain like a light bulb that was just turned on and I realize that he's going to use that same drive to get me. Which means, I'm in way over my head.

"Clark, this is Chelsea. Chelsea this is Clark."

A tall man stands from behind the desk. "Nice to meet you, Miss…"

"Walsh, but please call me—"

"Good evening Miss Walsh. What a great night for a walk." He rounds the desk, staring down at Grover. "What's the word, Grover? Looks like you got some company tonight." He flashes Dean a smile.

"Hopefully he can stay on his best behavior and not scare her away," Dean jokes, walking to the door.

Clark walks a little faster.

"I got it, Clark." Dean opens the door, but Clark takes it from his hold.

"Don't go putting me out of a job." He smiles as we walk through the door.

"Thank you," I say.

Clark nods. "My pleasure. Have a good walk, Grover."

The door shuts and the three of us fall in line. Grover seems pretty well trained on a leash, or it's taking enough energy to get his four legs to hold up his chubby little body.

"There's a dog park up here a little ways. He'll do his business and then we'll head upstairs. Grover doesn't care for much exercise."

"Sure thing."

We walk along the street, Dean positioning Grover's leash in his left hand, enabling him to be in the middle now. His right hand seeks out mine and goose bumps run up my arm when our fingers entwine. I've grown used to this stage of our affection and although my body craves more—we never had this type of loving affection before.

"What do you think went wrong?" I ask under the dark sky with scattered stars you can barely see between high-rises on either side.

"Me. I'm what went wrong."

"No, it takes two. I didn't exactly fight for us."

"Chels." He stops in the middle of the sidewalk. Grover panting next to him like we just ran the Chicago marathon. "You did the right thing."

My gaze diverts to a couple walking hand in hand, laughing as they pass us by. The man nods and the woman smiles our way. We politely do the same.

Fear that I'll never have that pricks my chest. Dean and I always seem to be so hot we burn out or so cold we get stuck in the same spot. We can never seem to find that happy middle ground.

"Sometimes I think that if I would've—"

"Don't," he says. "Don't second guess one thing." We reach a black iron rod fence and Dean opens up the gate to the dog park and we step through, shutting it behind us.

"Good evening," Dean says to a woman in her fifties with a small poodle.

She smiles down at Grover and then up to us. "Great night."

"A perfect spring night. Summer is coming," I say.

Dean leads us to a white stone wall and sits down, unhooking Grover. He waddles around, sniffing the trees and grass. His hand finds mine again, but this time he puts our entwined hands in his lap. "I know we have so much shit from the past to deal with, but I wish we could leave it back there and start fresh."

"In a perfect world we could," I say.

His gaze stays on Grover who walks as slowly as my grandma Rita.

"Do you think you'll ever forgive me?"

This man next to me isn't the Dean I knew. He's not the man I married years ago. That man would've assumed I'd forgive him with a flippant apology.

"I wouldn't be here if I didn't. I'm hesitant, Dean. I might've been the one who walked out, but I broke my own heart before you had a chance to finish the job."

His head turns in my direction, his eyes transparent and showing me how much my words cut him just now.

"I didn't say it to upset you."

His head is already shaking before I can finish. "I know."

"I'm terrified you'll break me, but you were right."

"I was right?" An uptick in his tone pulls a smile from me.

"Well, rare occurrences do happen every so often." I knock his shoulder with mine. "This pull to you is just as magnetic as it was when I was eighteen. I'm not naïve enough to believe in fate, but I can't deny this."

His hand leaves mine and he swivels his body to face me. Everything slows. I don't think about the fact we're in public or the lady on the park bench. It's just me and Dean as his hand lifts and cradles my face. The love overflowing from his eyes as his lips descend toward mine has me choking back emotion.

There's no rush to his affection. In fact, some might think it's our first kiss with the gentle way his lips land on mine. His tongue licks the seam of my lips and I part them for him. We kiss under the dark sky of Chicago with the quiet ripple of waves from the lake only steps away and chaotic nightlife of a big city in the other direction. Somehow, we find our happy medium and enjoy our kiss like a slow dance that could go on forever.

Grover's front paws land on my legs and I pull back. Dean takes his time pulling away, his large palm lingering on my face. "I'm going to have to have a conversation with him."

I smile down at a panting Grover who just wants some affection for himself, and then I lay my head on Dean's shoulder.

"I'm not sure we've ever done anything like this," I say, a quiet satisfaction in my voice.

His hand grips my knee. "I think we're getting old."

Grover lays down at our feet after I pet him briefly.

"I like it," I say.

"I like anytime you're near me."

A new rush of flutters ignites in my stomach. I love the magnetism between Dean and I when we can't get enough, but I love this, too.

"I'm not going to sleep with you tonight."

He chuckles. "Okay."

"It's not that I don't want to because my body is literally begging for me to strip you every time you enter a room." He chuckles again. "But I still want to spend the night with you."

"Okay."

I lift my head and wrap my arms around his neck. "You're so accommodating." My lips press to his cheek and right away, Grover's paws land on Dean's knees.

"I have no complaints. I've already gotten so much more than I've deserved from you. I could care less... well...I can't lie. I want inside of you as bad as I did that time you borrowed my teammate's catcher equipment and wore nothing else underneath, but what I'm trying to say is, I'm good with this, too."

I chuckle at our shared memory. I was so sexually unin-hibited with this man.

Dean leans forward and clicks the leash on Grover's collar then stands, holding his hand out for me. We make our way back to his condo. When we near his building, I'm still surprised that he lives somewhere so nice. Don't get me wrong, after we married, we talked a lot about the money he'd be getting paid if he went pro. The nice things we'd buy. That we'd be able to have nannies, so I could come to every game and travel with the team. Pipe dreams of poor kids. Now that I'm older and smarter, I don't think I'd be following my husband around from town to town.

Clark rises from the desk when we walk in the condo building's foyer.

"How was the walk Grover?" he asks, staring down at the dog whose tongue is hanging out of his mouth and seems in desperate need to lay down.

"It's a beautiful night," Dean remarks, pressing the elevator button.

"Having a beautiful woman at your side helps." Clark nods his head at me and I'm sure I must be blushing.

"You're right about that," Dean says, his hand seeking mine. "It's amazing how much things change when you have that."

Clark smiles and the elevator doors open. "Have a good night," he says.

"Good night, Clark." We each wave and the doors close.

"I still can't believe you have a doorman."

"Half the city has one."

I shake my head. He's crazy.

"I'd ask you to move in, but I'm not going to ruin the night."

"Do you ever stop pushing?" I ask.

"No."

"Fair enough." I shrug.

The elevator doors open, and we end up at his condo door moments later.

"I just want to give you everything I couldn't before," he mumbles as he shuts the door behind us, unhooking Grover.

"Was I not supposed to hear that?" I ask, not walking into the rest of the condo. As comfortable as I'm getting with Dean, his condo says he's a different man than I remember.

"Drink?" he asks, walking around me and into the kitchen that extends to the family room.

"Sure."

I sit on the breakfast stool, watching him move around his kitchen. The only sound is Grover's slurping from his water bowl. Dean bends down into his freezer and I enjoy the show of his ass prominently on display. If I only had a quarter to bounce off it.

"Milkshake?" He pulls out vanilla ice cream. Kicks the freezer door shut and then opens the fridge, pulling out chocolate sauce.

The man and his chocolate shakes.

"Perfect." I smile at him.

While he digs around for the blender and other supplies, I can't help but feel helpless. You don't come from a large family and not have it ingrained that you should never be sitting down when others are doing things.

"Are you going to tell me what you meant?" I ask.

His hands land on his granite countertop and his eyes peer into mine. "It's nothing really. When I blew out my shoulder, I ruined the chance to give you a life like this." He raises his hand in front of him. "Before you say anything, I know it's not what you would've gotten if I had been drafted. Maybe not right away, but eventually if I'd made it you wouldn't have wanted for anything."

I slide from the stool and round the corner of his counter, my gaze never leaving his. His body swivels in my direction when I approach, and I place my hands on his cheeks. "Do you think that's why I married you?"

"No, but I'm sure it helped." He tries to turn away, but I keep hold of his face to force his gaze to remain locked with mine.

"You want to know why I married you?"

He says nothing.

"I'm going to tell you." I slide a hand down his chest, slow and seductive, until I cup his package. *Bad idea. Such a bad idea.* "This. Your giant dick."

His eyes flare and it grows to full chub in my hand. I'm teasing him now, but I just wanted to lighten the mood. I'm so not used to us being this serious.

I step back and start scooping the ice cream into the blender. He comes up behind me, his hands gripping my hips, his chest pressed to my back, his dick pressed against my ass.

"You're playing with fire," he whispers.

"I like matches."

"I don't have any extinguishers." He picks up the chocolate sauce and squirts it into the blender.

"Good."

His forearm flexes as he adds the milk. I close my eyes and inhale a deep breath to try to rein in my sexual appetite. Dean always did have the best forearms. A pitcher's forearms. It seems at least that much hasn't changed.

I put the lid on the blender and press the 'ON' button.

We go on making our milkshake as though he never opened his vulnerable side to me. As much as I hate myself for not letting him go there, I just couldn't risk it. If he did, then I'd have to and I'm not ready for that. Not ready to discuss the totality of everything that tore us apart. There's something he still doesn't know.

More than all that, I'm not ready to fall completely back in love with him again…yet.

Chapter Seventeen

On Monday when I arrive at the office, Victoria and Hannah are both in the office before me.

I glance at the clock when I walk in.

"No, you're not late. Hannah's early." Victoria smiles and I see another picture is adorning her desk now.

"Who's in the new picture?" I ask.

She picks it up and it's her, Reed, Jade, and Henry on the SeaDog at Navy Pier.

"Cute."

I head down the hall, hearing two sets of heels following me.

"I have no funny dating story for you guys this morning," I say. I have a feeling our Monday morning divorcee dating stories are about to fizzle out unless Hannah hops on the dating bandwagon.

"We know," Hannah says.

They file in, Hannah taking a seat and Victoria standing at the door on the off chance she has to grab the phone. Our usual positions.

I stare at the tall crate on my desk. "What is this?"

"Delivery was waiting outside the door this morning." Victoria's face morphs into a sappy love look like she's watching someone experience their happily ever after once more.

"And you guys don't think I need privacy to open it?"

"Not really." Hannah glances over her shoulder at Victoria and then back my way, shaking her head. "Come on. We've been making bets."

I drop my bags on my chair and untie the ribbons around it. The wood creaks open and a plant, an alive plant lives inside.

"I'm going to kill it." I pull it out and place it on my desk.

Victoria steps into the room and I know that mom instinct of hers wants to know exactly what it is, so she can google it.

I pluck the card out.

It was nice going down memory lane with you this weekend. Thank you for the opportunity to make new ones.

Love Dean

As much as my heart pitter patters, I don't cling to the note and press it to my chest like some love-sick teenager. I place it neatly on my desk and lean down to sniff it.

"Jasmine," Victoria says, and I roll my eyes.

"Seriously, Vic."

She shrugs. "I could smell it when I brought it in."

I can tell she's lying.

"Poor Jade," Hannah and I both say in unison.

"When you two have a daughter, you can judge." She waggles her finger between the two of us. "A plant is not a diary."

"I don't remember the card saying your name on it," I say in jest.

"It wasn't hard to figure out, okay? I searched the company name and voila, there were only a few options that came in that crate."

Hannah and I laugh at our neurotic and impatient assistant who is always one step ahead of us. I guess we know why.

"So?" I cock one eyebrow at Vic.

She smiles but says nothing.

"Tell me," I force her to tell me what she found out.

"Jasmine is the flower of memories." She bites her lip and I shake my head.

"Yeah, I figured it from the note, but just wanted to make sure you were on the ball."

The phone rings and Victoria says, "You know you love that I have my PhD in Google." She leaves the room.

After she's gone, Hannah stays in her seat, her legs crossed, her hands clasped together with her elbows on either armrest. "Nice weekend?"

"Yeah." I place the crate next to the trashcan, sliding the plant to the corner of my desk, placing the instructions nearby to read once I get settled.

I pull out my laptop and planner and position everything the way I like it on my desk.

"That's it? That's all you're giving me?" Hannah asks. "Memories mean you talked about the past."

"Well, we cleared up a little, yes."

"Did you sleep with him?" No hesitation. Point blank. Again, let me be reincarnated into Hannah Crowley in my next life.

"No, but I really wanted to." I lean back in my chair, remembering his chest pressed to mine and how it made me weak in the knees.

"Why didn't you?"

Victoria's heels click at rapid pace down the hall. "I can't believe you're leaving me out of the loop." She heaves a breath. "It was just Jagger."

Hannah laughs.

Victoria rolls her eyes.

"I need to meet this guy at some point," I say, intrigued by her ex-boss in L.A.

"Trust me—" Victoria puts up her hand.

"You don't," Hannah finishes.

"What did I miss?" Vic asks.

Hannah slides over and Victoria sits in her chair. I guess RISE is taking a time out to hear about my date.

"She didn't sleep with him," Hannah says like one of those reporters on TMZ.

"Why?" Vic's all wide eyes. "If it's a body insecurity thing, you're insane. Talk to me after your stomach has been stretched out to here." She holds her hands a foot out in front of her.

Internally, I cringe but ignore her comment.

Truth is I was self-conscious for a little bit, but then I realized if he doesn't like me with my clothes off then that's his problem.

"No. I just…I wanted to. So badly, but we went on this walk with his dog and—"

"He has a dog?" Victoria's eyes grow soft again. "Jade's been begging me for one." She looks over at Hannah.

"You should take Lucy. We're not jiving at the moment."

Hannah's dog Lucy is a German Shepherd puppy who's yet to figure out house breaking or the fact that a La Perla bra is not a play thing. I'd give my right tit for a La Perla bra. Then again, I wouldn't have a tit to fit into it if I did that. *Okay, focus, Chels.*

"You will. She's a puppy. Give her some time," Victoria says.

"My bank account is about to cut her off."

We laugh because none of us is quite sure why Hannah got a dog, let alone a big guard dog.

"Back to you not having sex." Hannah's back straightens and they both sit at attention like two teacher's pets.

"I wanted to see what it was like to be around him without the sexual aspect of our relationship. We were either fucking like bunnies or not speaking at all when we were married. I was enjoying this in between we've found, and you know how sex can screw everything up."

Hannah nods.

"It didn't with Reed and I," Victoria says.

"I hate to break this to you, but Reed is a great guy. He wouldn't have let it. Dean runs hot. Sex has never been a problem with us. The daily living, the casual day to day encounters and communication is where we don't thrive."

"Are you suggesting that my sex life is boring?" She crosses her arms over her chest.

"Not at all. I'm sure Reed rocks your world, but you have to admit he's probably ready to cuddle before you are."

She uncrosses her arms and her silence says I'm right.

"There's nothing wrong with Reed. He's perfect." Hannah places her hand on Victoria's.

"Okay, because I drew blood the other night I'll have you know." Victoria nods her head about a million times per second as though neither of us believe her.

Reed's so fucking hot there's no way the guy doesn't know how to work a woman's body. The nice factor of him says he's probably perfected his moves and knows what Vic wants before she does.

"Dean's just a different species than Reed, that's all I'm saying."

"I think it's good," Hannah says. "Keep those legs closed until you're ready to give up the milk."

We all laugh because the whole analogy is such bullshit. If I give him a taste of my milk and he doesn't want to buy the cow than fuck him, I don't want the asshole farmer.

"I'm losing my will, but I was proud to hang on strong that night," I say.

They rise from their chairs. The workday needs to begin at some point.

"We'll let you go call and thank him," Victoria says, ever the romantic.

"I think I might run over to his office at lunch and thank him instead." I bite my lip wondering if I can walk into his office and not imagine that kiss we shared against his desk.

"Watch it or you'll end up having an afternoon delight," Hannah says on her way out.

We all laugh and then they're gone, leaving me alone with my thoughts.

I pick up my phone to text Dean, but I think a surprise is so much better.

YOU'D THINK there was a city grandfather clock that chimed at noon from the swarms of people rushing down the streets to get lunch. I'm spoiled from having The Sandwich Place on the main floor of my office building.

They know us so well now, half the time I don't have to give my order.

The sun glares off the million-dollar skyscrapers and onto the city streets, so I decide to walk instead of taking a taxi to Dean's office. I'm still crossing my fingers he's not in some sort of meeting or lunch date.

I round the corner after having been shouldered five times on the walk over and smile as his building comes into view.

I'm in so much trouble.

As slow as I want this relationship to go, my body is not relenting on getting what it wants—Dean.

I press the walk button, glancing at everyone around me with their earbuds on and missing the beautiful spring day. The city is so much more alive when the weather is nice.

My mood is light and buoyant as I cross the street. Even the cab's horn blaring at me when I'm not fully on the other side yet doesn't make me flip him off.

Turning left, there's a big group of men stepping out from his building's doors. After the group of men, Dean emerges out of the building. He pauses, running his hand through his dark strands. I admire the man who took my heart so long ago. The one who refused to give it back the last five years even if he didn't know it. Even with the stressed look on his face, I can't help but notice his tall body, lean muscle, and strong shoulders. I'm not close enough, but I can imagine his heart shaped lips, piercing dark eyes and straight nose all outlined with a chiseled jaw.

A woman walks by, her predatory gaze on him the entire time she passes.

Yeah, hands off. He's mine.

I step forward, just as he swivels on his dress shoes, heading in the opposite direction.

"Dean," I call out, but the loud sound of a delivery truck revving its engine drowns out my voice.

I increase my speed, figuring I'll catch him at the next light. Surely at lunch time in the city he won't get that far in front of me. I imagine covering his eyes and him wrapping his arms around my middle lifting me with the surprise.

The light turns just as I'm midway through the block.

Shit.

"Dean!" I yell again, but he doesn't hear me.

A few people glance over at me and I ignore their inquisitive looks.

Damn. I didn't wear the best heels to try and chase someone down. Seduction? Yes. The hundred meter dash? Not so much.

I make the crosswalk in time, but I'm panting when I reach the other side. Continuing my pursuit, I see him sneak into a McDonald's under the Brooks Building. My footsteps slow when the red hand flashes at me. He'll be there for a while at this time of day, so I have some time.

Casually, I wait at the corner for the crosswalk to light up, scouring the windows for a glimpse of where he is, but it's overfilled with people coming in and out and I can't find him.

"Oogum Boogum Song" by Brenton Wood streams out of the window of a cab sitting at the light and my head and shoulders start moving. The best part of spring and summer is the different kinds of music coming out of the cars. The city gives you its own soundtrack during the warmer months.

I cross the next street and finally those golden arches are prominent on the awnings in front of me. I finally reached him.

Swinging the doors open, I step into the foul smell of perfume mixed with cologne mixed with fast food and it clogs my nostrils. My eyes search one way and then back the other way.

No Dean.

I wait by the front door to see if maybe he went to the bathroom, but after seeing five men go in and out, I doubt that's where he is. Walking over to the bathrooms, I wait outside and when a man comes out I stop him.

"Anyone else in there?"

"Well, lady I'm an eyes-front kinda guy." He steps away and then turns back around. "But I think I was alone."

My shoulders sag and I refresh what I saw in my mind. He ducked under the awnings and I saw him walk through a door.

Leaving McDonald's and looking like a lost girl from Kansas, I search for any other door he might have gone into. I pull out my phone, when I see nothing—no other signs that indicate there's another food joint in the building —figuring I'll forget the element of surprise, and just text him.

Me: *Hey, where are you eating for lunch?*

I wait for the three dots as people rush by me talking about their bosses, their schedules, their kids, their marriages. It's Monday, which means there isn't much optimism to be found even with the nice weather.

A nicely dressed woman opens up a door down from me and I quickly follow. Maybe that's where he went.

She walks up a set of stairs, turning when she hears me and smiles. I return her smile.

Is this creepy? A little. Desperate? So much so I don't want to admit it to myself.

She turns right into a room and I follow. My feet freeze when I enter the room.

"Are you new?" A man approaches me from behind. How did I not hear him?

"Um…"

"No need to be shy. Come on in." He ushers me into the room.

"I think I'm in the wrong place," I say, trying to move back the way I came.

I freeze when I spot the woman in the short skirt and revealing blouse talking to Dean at a table with coffee and sandwiches placed in the middle. His lips are straight as she carries on about something.

I glance around the room. "You've got to be kidding me," I mumble.

The circle of chairs.

A man at the front says hello to a few people and heads lift in his direction because he's the man in charge.

No. This cannot be happening.

I back step quietly as everyone moves to their seats. I'm thankful Dean hasn't seen me yet.

"Please, come in. You don't have to speak," the counselor waves me in and all eyes, including Dean's, land on me.

He tilts his head, one eyebrow raised.

"I, um…"

Speak Chelsea. Speak!

"I was you once, I understand. Come and sit by me." The woman who was talking with Dean stands and loops her arm through mine, guiding me to a chair right across from Dean.

Our eyes meet and the smirk on his lips says he's never going to let me live this down.

Chapter Eighteen

"If she doesn't want to join, I don't think we should force her," Dean says. The entire room stares at him like he's an asshole.

"Don't be silly." The woman seated beside me shoots him a mean look and then directs her attention back to me. "I'm Pam and just stay and listen."

"I can't." I rush to my feet. "I'm very sorry. It was by accident that I ended up here and I shouldn't hear the things that are talked about here."

Pam's head rears back.

"What do you think this is?" Dean asks, the smile unable to stop playing on his lips. "We could be a swinging group looking for new members."

I narrow my eyes at him and then look at the instructor.

"This is Alcohol Anonymous?" He nods.

"I'm not an alcoholic."

The instructor stands. "Can I ask why you're here then?"

My eyes flick to Dean, the instructor follows my gaze.

"You know Dean?"

"She's my ex-wife." For some reason, hearing Dean call me his ex out loud hurts. We've come so far from that word, but how can I be mad? It's the truth.

All their shoulders fall and their eyes swim with apology.

No. Nope. Not doing this.

How much has he told them about me? About us?

"I'm very sorry for intruding," I say and rush out before anyone can put their arm around me or try to comfort me.

Dean follows me, which I expected I suppose.

"Chels," he calls out to the empty hall.

"I'm so sorry, I went to your building to surprise you for lunch and then I was trying to catch up to you and followed you here."

"Why did you follow me? Because you didn't trust me?" He pushes his hands into his pockets.

"I yelled to get your attention but there was so much noise on the street and then I texted you and you never answered."

He pulls out his phone and nods. "I silence it when I come here."

"Oh."

There's an awkward silence between us for a few seconds before he speaks. "I've been sober three years now."

"That's great." I hope he can hear the sincerity, and if I'm honest—relief, in my voice.

He nods slowly, his head moving up and down, his eyes on me the entire time. "Do you want to stay?" The cocky twinkle that's always in his eye is replaced with a timidness I've rarely seen.

"No, I shouldn't hear their stories and private thoughts."

"They don't care and plus, I'm talking today, and I want you to hear it. I think it will help us move forward."

"I can't, Dean." Panic wells up inside my chest until I feel like I can't breathe.

He's already shaking his head. "Don't worry, I promise it will be fine."

Both his hands slide down my arms and he links our fingers, pulling me away from the wall. "I want you to see this part of me."

He leads me down the hall, both of our dress shoes clicking on the linoleum floor. When we enter, the instructor eyes the two empty chairs.

We sit in them and I feel all the eyes on me. I'm not one of them...in fact, I left one of them while he was in the deep throws of addiction. They can't see me as a good person.

"This is Chelsea," Dean says.

Everyone says hello.

"It's been almost three years sober for me."

Everyone claps, including me.

"It took me forever to seek the help I needed. Chelsea and I divorced five years ago and as much as I hate to admit it, our marriage was probably my idea when I was half blasted. We were in Vegas on a trip with some teammates of mine and we tied the knot on impulse. Chelsea was only eighteen and I was twenty-one."

I knot my fingers together in my lap. It all sounds so stupid when you tell other people. At the time I'd thought it was romantic. No wonder my family looks at me like I'm a complete moron.

"I used to play baseball...slated for the big leagues. But I was also drinking too much, and I had a temper. After some guy hit on my wife, I got into a bar fight and messed up my shoulder." He glances my way. This was the start of our demise. "If I hadn't been drinking that night the fight might not have even happened. Who knows. After baseball was ripped away from me, the drinking only grew worse. I'd be out half the night, roll in long after Chelsea was in bed. I never called to let her know where I was or who I was with. At first, Chelsea tried to keep up, but when she wouldn't join me, I'd tell her she wasn't any fun to be around. I'd say she was wasting all her good years."

I'm staring at my hands in my lap and I don't have the heart to look up, to see all the faces looking at me with what's probably pity. I'm sure our story isn't foreign to them but rehashing our sordid love affair reminds me how stupid I was.

"I stopped communicating with her. If she ever called me out on my bullshit I'd resort to fighting with her as a way to keep from discussing what was really the problem— me. I treated her badly over and over again. In the end it probably felt like she was married to a stranger." He heaves out a deep sigh. "Just so we're not here all night, I'll condense it."

Thank God. There's only so much I can handle.

"She did the right thing and stopped enabling me, eventually leaving me one night." I look up to find him looking at me. "Morning probably."

I nod more to myself than him.

"It took me two years of just barely getting by to seek help and three years clean before I could actually face her." His hand seeks mine out, entwining our fingers, gripping tight. "We're trying to move forward, start something new, something better."

Tears prick the corners of my eyes and I attempt to slow my beating heart. There he is, my Dean Bennett, the side of him no one else saw in college. The side of him I denied existed after we parted—as if the kind, honest side of him was a mirage and had never really been there.

"That's great, Dean. Congratulations on three years sober and remember, it's just one day at a time," the leader says. "Chelsea, you're welcome anytime you'd like to join us, but maybe you'd like Al-Anon, it's a program for families of addicts. It might help you to forgive and move on—with or without Dean."

The word forgive lodges in my throat like a thick piece of steak I forgot to chew.

We stay for the rest of the meeting and people don't seem to mind me listening to their stories. All of them different than Dean's but similar at the same time. They've all hurt loved ones, and some don't know how to mend those relationships. Dean offers advice to one, telling him that all he can do is try. They discuss the twelve steps and how you can't make anyone forgive you. They're allowed to have their feelings.

As I sit in a plastic chair with the smell of stale coffee around me, it's as though someone finally gave me the pen to connect all the dots. For the first time, my heart does believe he's changed.

By the end of the meeting, I only want to be alone with Dean, my arms wrapped tightly around him, not letting him get away from me again. This man...his strength knows no bounds.

After everyone says the Serenity Prayer and Dean and I say our goodbyes, he leads me out the door and down the stairs to the streets of Chicago which are quieter now since the lunch hour is over.

"Do you need to go back to work?" he asks.

"I think I'm going to play hooky." Hannah will understand and there's nothing on my to-do list that can't wait.

His hand tightens around mine. "Lunch?"

I turn to face him, my eyes burning into his. "At your condo?"

He unhooks his hand from mine, clasping my shoulders. "Are you sure? We should talk."

"Dean, I'm done talking. I just want to be with you." I don't want to discuss anything else that might ruin this moment for us. So, I wrap my arms around his stomach, my lips finding his jaw. It's smooth today with the scruff he seems to grow out only on the weekends shaven away.

"Everything I said in there is the truth, but I didn't say it, so you'd sleep with me."

"Are you cockblocking yourself?" I ask, my lips continuing to dot kisses along his jaw and neck.

"I just want to make sure you're positive." His voice is gruffer now.

"Where's that man from weeks ago who brazenly kissed me in his office?" I reach down and grab his ass.

"Right now, he's rising to the occasion."

His hard erection presses into my stomach.

"Then take me home and give us both what we've wanted for a while."

He raises his hand for a cab and he grabs my free hand, pulling me toward the taxi that's pulled up at the curb.

Sliding in, I want to make-out—grab his clothes and force my lips on his, but we're in Chicago and that might be something for late night, not during the day when we're in so much stop and go traffic. It wouldn't be just the driver getting the show.

Dean's fingers weave a pattern across my palm and I count down the blocks until we reach his condo. What seems like a lifetime later, I climb out of the taxi, my panties already wet. Not wasting any time, he pays the driver and then grabs my hand once more, pulling me through the doors.

"Hey, Clark," he says, not waiting for him to attend to us, but pressing the button for the elevator to come.

"Good afternoon. Miss Walsh, nice to see you again."

The doors ding open and I stumble forward from him yanking my arm, but he catches me and it's all good.

"Bye, Clark." I wave as the doors slowly close between us.

"I don't care about cliché." Dean pushes me against the wall, his hands planted firmly on either side of my head, his body way too far away. He bends down, his lips capturing mine as the elevator rises.

I half expect him to press his body to mine, let me feel how aroused he is now that we're finally alone. Instead, he keeps his distance, only making sweet promises and kinky expectations with his lips and tongue.

The ding alerts us that we've hit his floor, and the doors slowly slide open, but Dean doesn't move.

"I'm going to ask you again. Are you sure?" His dark eyes are now filled with lust.

"Take me to your condo and fuck me every which way. Is that clear enough for you?"

A smile teases his lips. "Crystal."

His hands slide down my sides, cupping my ass and lifting me up. Our lips touch and the ease of his movements send shivers up the back of my legs now that my dress is up around my waist.

He stops, my back pressed to his door, and expertly holds me up as he fiddles in his pocket for his key and inserts it into the lock.

We tumble in, but Dean never loses his grip on me. His shoulder comes to mind, but I'm not blowing this mood with talk about the past.

He kicks off his shoes and props me up on the kitchen breakfast bar, sliding my ass so it's hanging off the ledge. Painfully slow, his hands run along my torso, bypassing my breasts until they cradle my face.

"I can't wait to be inside of you."

He brings my lips to his once more, the firm and frantic nature of our kiss already making them swell. Not that I'm complaining. I always loved when Dean was unrestrained and wild. That's when I knew how much he wanted me.

My legs tighten around his waist, but he's busy shaking his leg behind him, so I break our kiss and look down, seeing Grover humping him.

"He has to go out," I say, looking over Dean's shoulder.

"He can wait."

Grover stares up at me with pitiful eyes like he's already crossing his legs so he doesn't pee in his master's house.

"Dean," I sigh unable to enjoy the way his lips and tongue are devouring my neck.

"Chelsea, he's fine." His tone is impatient, and I smile knowing he'd rather his dog crap all over the house than take his hands off me.

"I'm not going anywhere," I assure him.

"Last time we walked him you decided against sex. Forgive me for not taking my chances."

I laugh pulling back and his head falls into my lap.

"Let the dog out and then we can get to know each other again. I should probably call my boss anyway."

Dean groans, pulling open my legs and presses his lips to the outside of my panties.

My hands fall back on the granite counter top, my eyes drifting shut.

Grover who?

Arf.

That Grover.

As though reading my body language, Dean's hands slip up my dress and grab each side of my panties sliding them off my body. "I'm taking these then." He shoves them in his suit jacket pocket, stepping away with his eyes zeroed in on my pussy.

After retrieving my purse from the floor, he props it up next to me. "You are not to move." He points at me, a stern expression on his face. "I want you spread-eagle when I return because I'm not even close to being finished tasting you."

Without tearing his eyes from me, he grabs the leash and clasps it on Grover's collar whose tail is happily wagging now.

"I can't believe I have to take out the fucking dog," he mumbles. "You better be fast."

Before he slides out the door, he gives me one more fleeting look like he has to burn the image into his head. The door shuts and then reopens. "Oh, and no taking off any clothes. That's my job."

The heavy door slams shut, and I fall back to the counter blindly searching for my cell phone to tell Hannah and Victoria that I won't be back in the office. I refrain from the details that I will, in fact, be enjoying an afternoon delight. And if I'm lucky more than one.

Chapter Nineteen

I do as Dean dictates, staying on his counter hammering out a quick text to the girls.

Me: *I won't be in for the rest of the day. Something urgent came up.*

I put them on a group message. Really need to rethink that next time.

Hannah: *oh lala…*
Victoria: *Was it the jasmine that did it?*

I shake my head, but the door opens, and Dean walks in without Grover. Not saying a word, he lets the door shut, stripping from his suit jacket, letting it fall to the floor and I can't even question what the hell is going on before his mouth is on mine.

Our lips devour one another, his tongue searching for mine, his hands planted on my cheeks. And as though no time has passed we're back in that frantic dance we perfected years ago.

His mouth starts kissing across my cheek and he angles my head with one hand, sprinkling open mouth kisses to my heated flesh.

Again, he pulls me into him so I'm flush with his body. His hard-on hasn't diminished.

"Dean," I sigh, loving the feel of him all over me.

"Down the hall. The teenage girl is going to dog sit for me." Then he's kissing me again, his fingers finding their way to my back and unzipping my dress. "Don't mention Grover again," he mumbles against my skin.

He kisses all over my body like he's in a game show and has to touch every inch of me within a certain time frame. His large hands pull down my dress from my shoulders and his lips skitter along one collarbone to the next.

I slide my hand out from my dress, left in only my red bra. He pulls back for a moment, his gaze glued to my chest. Taking the opportunity, I grab his tie and pull, unknotting it as he stares down at me.

"So beautiful," he murmurs, his knuckles gliding along the swell of my breast. "I almost don't want to unwrap you."

It's then that I witness Dean taking me in like a piece of precious art he's waited decades to view. His tongue slides out and he licks his bottom lip.

While he admires me, I pull his shirt from his body, letting it join his jacket on the floor. I look at a man five years older, more muscled, more defined. We've grown. His flat stomach now has more dark hair trickling down past his waistband, his nipples more prominent on stronger pecs. He's turned from boy to man and I missed the transformation.

He lets me look him over the same way he does me. Finally, his hands cup my breasts right before his fingers find the clasp in between my mounds, releasing it. The fabric pulls apart, revealing me completely.

Worry flashes through my head. Have they lost the fight with gravity?

His palms cover me again, his thumbs running over my taut peaks. "Just as I remembered."

I close my eyes as he caresses me, my core heating up more and more.

"Dean?" I break up the mood. Not that I'm not enjoying what he's doing, but Dean doesn't do gentle caressing.

"Uh-huh," he murmurs, his lips touching my skin and finding their way down to my breasts.

"Don't treat me like I'm damaged goods." He lifts his head and stares at me like I'm a crossword clue he can't figure out.

"What?"

"You don't need to be gentle with me just to prove you've changed."

The one side of his lips lift. He knows exactly what I'm referring to. Our sex life was never tame—it was break the table, shatter the lamp kind of sex.

"Are you asking me to fuck you, Chelsea Walsh?" A full smile creases his lips, his forefingers and thumbs now pinching my nipples harder. A moan falls from my lips.

"I'm asking you to show me exactly how much you want me."

"Well, I do always aim to please you." The pressure on my nipple intensifies, sending a current racing through my body. A glorious pain I've missed more than I've admitted.

"Dean," I sigh, my head falling back to his granite countertop.

One hand covers my right breast and he squeezes and then massages it. The fine art of hard and soothing—no one knows it better than him. He bends down taking my nipple into his mouth as his arm slides under my back along the counter. In one motion, he pulls me up to him. My legs wrap around his torso so that he doesn't have to stop tormenting me with small bites to my pebbled nipples while he carries me to the living room.

The cool air-conditioned room quickly warms with the heat our bodies are throwing off.

My breast pops out of his mouth and he loosens his grip enough so that I slide down his body. The cool metal of his belt pressing on the bottom of my ass. He lets me unhook from him, allowing my feet to fall to his hardwood floors, but instead of letting me unbutton his pants, he swiftly turns me around.

"Place your hands on the couch, gorgeous." His voice transforms to that authoritative mix of stern and sultry that I love.

I do as he says, my ass out for his viewing pleasure. One hand smacks my ass and then slides down, gripping and squeezing.

Then my body ignites with the sound of his belt being unbuckled and the thud as it falls to the floor, along with his pants.

"I'm torn on having you strip me down the rest of the way, or me bending you over and hammering into you." I close my eyes as shivers rush across my skin.

I wait for instructions or him to put my body where he wants.

"Tell me, baby." His hand runs up and across my stomach, gripping the other side and swiveling me around to face him.

His mouth claims mine and he steps into me, his boxers soft on my skin. I stare at his lust-filled eyes that already promise me what I want. His one hand slides up to the base of my neck and his fingers tighten on the strands of my blonde hair. "You want me?" he asks like I'm not resembling Grover—salivating for his next instruction.

"I want you."

He twists my neck and his lips fall down on me like a vampire, nibbling on my skin all the way down.

"Apologize for making me wait," he demands, his tone firm and ready to dominate me.

"No."

His fingers tighten, and the strands of my hair pull on my scalp. My fists pound his chest.

"No?" I feel his lips widen and he's struggling to hide his smile at our play.

"You apologize for ruining our marriage." My fists open and I run my nails down the front of him, purposely using enough force to leave a mark.

His teeth scrape down my chest and he bends me over the back of the couch. Licking his fingers, he rubs my clit in circles, his one finger teasing my entrance.

"I already apologized. You weren't all innocent." The five o'clock shadow of his chin pricks my skin as he continues to bite me on his way down my belly, to my center.

"You were a drunk and you gave up on us," I pant.

His palms grip on the inside of my thighs, pulling my legs apart for his viewing pleasure. "I never gave up on us. You were the one for me. Always have been and always will be." He takes my clit between his teeth, gentle enough not to hurt but firm enough to send an electric current through my body.

"Why did you wait so long?" My eyes close, the clenching of a soft throw pillow not nearly enough to grab on to.

He stops the torment of his tongue, his fingers pushing

in and out of me, one and then two, stretching me slowly, making sure he won't hurt me, but the promise of his roughness still there.

"You know the answer. You're a smart girl."

He flattens his tongue, licking the entire length of my folds, twirling it around my nub.

My body needs the release but knows it should hold out until the very end. Let him take me to that edge over and over again until he lightly taps me, and I free fall into him. Dean was a magnificent baseball player, but the man is a fucking king in bed.

Sitting up enough to see him, I grab a fist full of his hair and pull him up. "Tell me."

He fights the smile again and it's hard to get into character when we're talking about our demise and the residual feelings.

"I had to be the man I promised you."

Tears want to fill my eyes, but I pull him up by his hair and smash my lips to his. Our tongues diving in, our hands pulling and tugging. I'm able to get a hold of his boxers and I push them down his legs. He steps out of them and kicks them off.

His dick is poised and ready at my opening. "Protection?" he asks.

For the first time since I committed to this, I pause, unsure.

"Never mind." He picks me up and I wrap my arms around his neck.

I assume he'll take me to the bedroom, but he heads back into the kitchen, laying me on the table.

"You stay here." He backs up and it's the first time I can admire him fully.

He's just as big as I remember, just as hot and since my

body is already a five-alarm fire, it just went to inferno status.

I hear his feet slap along the floor, a drawer open and he returns with a bottle of lube and a condom.

"What do I get for staying in place?" I ask coyly, and his lips tick up.

"One huge cock."

I slide off the table and onto my knees, wrapping my hand around the base of his erection and taking him into my mouth.

A growl escapes him, and his hand moves to the back of my head, directing me like I don't already know exactly how he likes it. Hell, he was the man who taught me how to do this.

"I need you up." He removes his hand after only a couple of minutes. "Time for that later, right now I need your pussy."

I stand, wiping my mouth with the back of my hand and move to the table. I hop up, but he pulls out a chair and sits down.

"Our first time together and you think you don't get what you want?" He pats his bare thighs. "Ride me, baby."

I take the condom off the table and straddle him. He twitches when my fingers touch his dick as I slide the condom over the head. While I'm making sure we're protected, he squirts lube on his fingers and my back falls to the table as he massages it into my pussy.

His mouth sucks my tit as his hands encourage me up and over him. I place my hand on the base of his cock, and then slide down, letting him fill me.

Glorious, oh so fucking glorious.

How I've missed him and in this moment by him, I mean his perfect cock.

"Tell me how much you missed me." He holds my

head in his hands. "How many times did you masturbate to memories of me?"

"Never."

"Chelsea." His tone is more teasing than mean.

I ride him, my thighs flexing as I push up and down. He helps me, lifting his pelvis.

"I'm not admitting shit." I can barely get the words out.

His hands tighten around my head and he brings me closer so our eyes lock.

"I refuse to fuck you until you tell me." He ceases all movement.

Our heavy breathing has our chests rising up and down.

"What do you want?" I challenge him the way he likes.

He thrusts up and a squeak rises up my throat. I want him so bad I can't even remember what he asked me.

"I want you to tell me I'm the best fuck, that every time you were with another guy, you thought of me, of us together. That you missed me just as much as I fucking missed you. That what's between us isn't going away and that you'll open up your heart for me again."

Tears burn in my eyes. I knew he wanted me back, but usually our sex was 'tell me you're mine.' Even his words and promises have grown up. Finally a teardrop falls to his chest.

"I can't promise," I whisper.

He thrusts again, and my body begs to be lazy and fall into his arms.

"You won't," he grinds out.

I press my palms on his chest, trying to distance myself, but he won't have it.

"This isn't some movie where you can win me back in two hours."

He shakes his head. "Tell me and I'll give you the release you want."

His pelvis rocks up and down, slowly and although that might get some girls off, it does nothing but cause sexual frustration for me. "Fine."

He gives me a satisfied smile. "There's my girl."

His hands loosen on my head, but he still keeps me in place as the truth escapes my eyes. "I never stopped loving you. Yes, every man was compared to you. My heart has already opened, so you better not fucking break it again." I slap his pecs.

A slow smile crosses his lips and he thrusts up into me faster.

"I promise, it's safe this time."

He grinds into me and I claw at his shoulders. His hands fall to my ass, slapping, squeezing and gripping. By the time I'm ready to let go, he only has to bite my earlobe and whisper, "Come."

I do. Not on his command, he can just read my body so well that even after five years he knows when I'm at the edge. I told you the man is a fucking king.

His fingers dig into my hips and his hands push me so my back rests on the table edge. He watches himself moving in and out of me, with a hand on my belly.

My body floods with a spike of new arousal watching him watch us, and the look of utter rapture on his face.

I'm ready to face the truth, that I might have hated him, but our love is one that doesn't die because of distance or inattention. It's not a classic princess fairy tale, but it's an epic love story nonetheless.

Chapter Twenty

*D*ean's large hands run along my sweaty back, urging me forward. I fall onto his chest willingly. He rises from the chair, my legs barely able to stay wrapped around him.

"I should get back to work," I say, and he stops abruptly in the middle of the hallway. I can't look at him, so I focus on the blank white walls.

"Don't even try it." He starts moving again and we pass by a bedroom door before we walk through the door at the end of the hall.

A king-size bed sits in the middle of the room with a plain headboard. Everything inside is either gray, black or steel. Typical bachelor pad. He deposits me on my feet and heads toward what I assume is the bathroom.

My gaze sweeps over the surroundings, taking in more details. Another dull room with no life to it. Not even a clock next to the bed. Other than the view of the sun playing peek-a-boo between the surrounding high-rises, it feels cold and the complete opposite of how I usually feel when I'm with Dean.

The toilet flushes and a chill wraps around my body.

"Nap time." He goes to what I assume is his side of the bed. We weren't together long enough to each have a side of our own. It went from the two of us in the middle, to one of us on the couch.

"It's like four o'clock," I joke, starting to feel slightly exposed and more than a little vulnerable.

"Do you have somewhere to be?" he asks, laying the comforter and sheets out farther.

"No."

"Then let's take a nap and then we can order in food."

"Dean, I have a life."

He stares at me a moment, as though for the first time he's at a loss for words. Then he breaks the distance, his hand already prepped in position to cup my cheek when he steps into me. My stomach flutters and my tough girl act crumbles.

"Tonight, let me be your life." He presses his lips to my forehead, his hand gliding down my arm until my hand lands in his.

He doesn't pull or yank me toward the bed, he takes one step at a time, leaving enough slack between us in case I don't follow. Which means he knows we're still not close to where we've been.

"Half an hour," I say begrudgingly.

He eyes me, nods, though the smirk on his face says he doesn't believe me. I wouldn't believe me either.

Waiting at the edge of the bed, I crawl in first, suddenly exhausted from the hottest sex I've had in half a decade.

"Half hour and then I'll replenish you." He pulls me into him, his arms secure around me, his lips sprinkling kisses on my forehead and temple. Our legs are in a tangled mess, and my cheek is pressed against his muscled chest.

"Did you mean what you said?" His voice is soft and insecure, sounding nothing like the man who just withheld my orgasm until I told him what he wanted to hear.

I prop my chin on his chest, my own hand running along the small patch of hair on his chest.

"Well, you were holding my orgasm back with your delicate thrusting."

I smile, he doesn't.

Shit, where is the Dean Bennett I know? The one who would challenge me.

"And I'll do it again." His lips curve a bit, but he's still holding back.

"Dean." I direct his eyes back on me, sliding up a little so he has no choice but to focus on me. "Orgasms don't make me lie. I'm in this. I can't deny that I'm terrified, but you've done more than enough to prove to me that you've changed so far."

"Do you ever think we still need to clear the air? Let it all out…talk about *everything* that happened?"

I slide back down, my head finding relief in the crook of his neck. The manly smell that's his alone is like a security blanket to me. "Not today, okay?" I murmur.

"Okay, I'll give you a pass." He kisses the top of my head and before I can think about when and if we'll have to have that conversation my eyes drift shut and I'm fast asleep.

IT'S nighttime before I wake from the deepest slumber I've had in a while—at least when alcohol wasn't involved. Although Dean's blinds are open, the sky is ominous with tall dark buildings blocking the view of the moon. People are home from work and the windows are lit up like a game of connect the dots.

I scoot down and out of Dean's arms, sliding off the bed setting my feet on the ground. Heading down the hall, I tiptoe as quietly as possible. Whatever happened to carpet? Why does no one have carpeting anymore? It makes it much easier to sneak around.

The sound of my phone vibrating is like a screeching alarm in the quiet place. My footsteps increase in speed and I dig into my purse, retrieving the vibrating device.

My hand freezes and the phone drops to the counter.

It bounces around like my unicorn cock vibrator after I come when I drop it between my legs.

The word Mom flashes from the phone as it shakes along the table.

She's probably using that sixth sense to know I'm here with Dean. The man I'm certain she's hired a hitman to kill.

I grab Dean's shirt from the floor, buttoning it up.

"Don't go getting dressed." His groggy voice sends an electric current down my body, like it's saying I'm ready for more.

Down girl.

I turn to see him in a pair of basketball shorts—bare-chested, hair askew and droopy eyelids. This is my Dean.

"Don't go thinking you can boss me around." Sliding my phone off the counter, I drop it back into my purse.

His fingers begin unbuttoning his shirt. "I love you in my clothes, but not tonight."

Once he's done, he lets the fabric fall open and his hands run across my stomach, his fingers dangerously close to the area between my legs. "I'm not sure you ever like me dressed."

My phone vibrates again, and I circle around in his arms.

"Tell me that's not a guy."

I wrap my arms around his neck, pressing my breasts into his strong chest. "Worse."

"Nothing is worse than having to compete with someone, especially when I feel like the deck is stacked against me." I press my lips to his chest and his hands slide down my back and cup my ass.

"I'm here. Why would you be worried?"

"I had you here once and I lost you."

"Well then try harder this time." I smile to break the mood. We do better with funny than emotional.

"I gotta run down and get Grover, but first I'll feed you." He smacks my ass, much lighter this time around and then turns to head to the other side of the breakfast bar.

"You'd leave me naked?" I button up his shirt.

"I'd eat my meal off you." He opens the fridge and grabs two white Chinese boxes. "Lo-Mein and Mongolian beef?" He sets them on the counter and then pulls out two more. "Fried rice and egg rolls."

"Did you suspect I'd be here?" I round the counter, jumping up on the surface. Chinese food is my favorite.

"You forget, I introduced you to Mongolian beef."

He has a point. Up until him, I only ate fried rice and egg rolls.

"No one likes a know-it-all." I crack open a container, and my stomach rumbles. Funny thing is, I like cold Chinese food more than warm.

"Come on, we'll Netflix and chill with it." He bundles the containers in his hands, digging out two forks from a sliding drawer.

I grab two waters and follow him to the couch. "I think we already did that."

He sits down and places the containers on the glass table. "And we'll be doing it again. Are you sure you don't want to let me eat off your body?" He winks, and his gaze rolls over me like I'm a six-layer chocolate cake and he's PMSing.

Just like that, he kick-starts my lady parts into wanting another ride on the Dean Bennett rollercoaster.

"I know it's none of my business, but who was on the phone?" he asks.

I cozy up and put a blanket over my lap, grabbing the Mongolian beef. It's been a five-year stretch without it. Too many memories.

"My mom." My face morphs into the annoyed expression I always wear whenever we're around each other.

"How is Babs?" He opens a container, grabs the remote.

How my mom doesn't put the fear in him as it does me baffles me. She went to our apartment after I left and from what I heard from our old neighbors, ripped him a new one. It was the one and only time my mom and I were on the same side.

"She's the same. Still pissed I didn't allow her to throw me some elaborate wedding."

He turns to me, his lips down. "I did apologize to her for that."

"What did she say?"

"She said that your next one will be huge when you marry the *right* man."

I nuzzle into his arm and lay my cheek on his shoulder. "She's just protective."

"Uh huh. She was right you did marry the wrong man the first time. But the second time I'll guarantee you marry the right one." He clicks on the television and it illuminates the dim room.

It takes me a moment to process his words. "I don't plan on ever getting married again."

He doesn't even look my way. Just clicks through the channels.

"You heard me, right?" I ask.

"I heard you." He brings a forkful of Lo-Mein noodles to his lips.

"But?"

"But nothing."

"Fine. Don't tell me." I stab a piece of meat in the carton.

He chuckles. "I'm not going to waste my breath. You're not there yet."

"Not where?"

His eyes are still focused in on the television, never veering to me once. "Ready to see us."

"Speak English, Dean."

He swivels in his seat and places his container down on the table. "You've let me in and I'm not going to scare you, but Chelsea, I won't give up until that ring is back on your finger."

"Dean," I sigh trying to ignore the flipping and flopping of my heart like it's screaming he wants us, he wants us.

"See." He points to me. "This is why I wasn't going to say anything. You're not ready for that declaration."

I laugh. "Are you sure we didn't warp back to the seventeen hundreds? Maybe you want to go ask Barb and Ted for my hand. Do you have a dowry? Or is it me who is supposed to have the dowry?"

His lips tick up. "Relax, Chelsea." He winks again.

"I'm not going to push you into something you don't want."

He's so smug. He thinks because he landed me in bed that he's going to convince me I want to get re-married? Who is he kidding?

"I have to go to the bathroom." I stand, leaving my fork in the Mongolian beef. He had to go and ruin that for me by talking about the future. I'm still processing that I'm even here right now. That I just slept with him.

Deciding on his en suite bathroom instead of the one in the hallway, I step in and turn on the lights.

Again with the dreary black, gray and white. Who decorated this place?

I shut the door and head to the toilet, but a flash of color on the monochrome canvas of his bathroom walls draws my attention. In slow motion, my feet move forward and my need to use the bathroom suddenly vanishes.

It slides off the towel rack when I clutch it in my hands. The Moroccan style towel my grandma sent us after she heard the wedding news. I thought I took them all. They weren't the most beautiful things in the world. More colors than a kaleidoscope, but it was the only domestic wedding gift we got.

Bringing it up to my nose, I inhale and smell Dean. Memories float through my brain of the happy times I'd pushed as far back as they could go. Placing it back down, I open the bathroom door, ready to tell Dean he's right, I'm not there yet, but yet doesn't mean never.

He's sitting on the edge of the bed watching me with a schoolboy look to him. As though, I'm the principal and he's been sent to the office.

"I shouldn't—"

"No. Don't say anything," I say, stepping into the opening of his legs.

His hands run up and down my thighs, sneaking under the back tail of his button-down.

"Let's just let this play out, okay? I know it's hard, but date me all over again," I say. I place one leg on either side of his waist and straddle him with my hands around his neck. "I'm not saying no."

His lips touch my collarbone, his hands growing more firm on my ass.

"Deal." His tongue slides up my neck. "To think it was only weeks ago you said I'd never lay a hand on your body again." A light chuckle comes out of him.

"Watch it, Bennett." I do nothing to refute him. He's not lying. I move my head down and he doesn't miss a beat, smashing his lips to mine.

My mind says I'm playing with fire, but my body overrules it. I always liked the danger that came with Dean Bennett.

Chapter Twenty-One

The following Saturday, I'm watching a little girl dancing to some YouTube-gone-viral movie in my living room.

"You must be thirsty, Jade." I put the root beer on the table.

She falls into my couch, catching her breath. "Thanks, Aunt Chelsea," she sips it.

My heart warms at her use of the word aunt, because I'm not. But I look at it as a term of endearment.

"That's an interesting dance." I look at the kid on the television swinging her hips and her arms. I don't really understand it, but whatever.

"It took me a long time to figure out. My friend Henry still can't get his hips right." Jade sits on the edge of the couch sipping her drink and watching the television.

"Your mom lets you watch this?"

Babysitting Jade for the night was a win-win for me. First, it does Victoria and Reed a favor so they can have a guilt-free night, not leaving her with Vic's mom again. Second, I get to see how Dean will fit into my life. I'm not a partying college kid anymore. I'm not exactly domesti-cated, but Jade and my niece and nephew are a part of my life now.

"Yeah, Reed can do the floss. Mom." She cringes.

I stand up, pressing the button to start another video. "If Reed can do it, I can do it."

The video starts and some ten-year-old boy is swinging his hips so hard I swear he's going to tear a muscle.

I move my hips and my hands, but they're not going where they're supposed to.

"No, Aunt Chelsea." Jade giggles, falling onto the couch.

Being the perfectionist I am, I continue trying, but the only thing I accomplish is Jade spitting out her root beer all over my coffee table. Like mother like daughter.

A knock lands on the door as I'm scrambling back from the kitchen with a roll of paper towels.

"Here." I hand Jade the roll of towels and then head to the door, checking the peephole to see Dean.

I open the door and he holds up a brown paper bag. "Sundae supplies. I got extra cherries." He winks, and I open the door wider.

"Great, Jade loves cherries."

Dean's jaw drops slightly, but he recovers fast replacing his disappointment with a smile.

"You're Victoria's daughter?" he asks, stepping into the apartment, positioning the bag in one hand and holding out the other.

"And Pete's. Reed's?" She stops and thinks. "I guess I'm kind of like Reed's daughter too. I'm moving in with him."

"Dean met Reed and your mom at Hannah's party."

She smiles. "I love her dog Lucy." She gets a lovesick look in her eyes. "Do you have a dog?"

"Yeah, his name is Grover," Dean says.

"Do you have pictures? Why didn't you bring him?" She perks up, moving to sit at the edge of the couch.

"I would have had I known." He heads to the kitchen. "I'll put these away and then I'll show you some pictures."

Jade shrugs, turning on the video again after Dean and I disappear into the kitchen.

"Care to fill me in?" Dean unloads the groceries. Whipped cream, cherries, sprinkles, chocolate sauce, butterscotch sauce.

I put everything away and then hold open the freezer, waiting for him to hand me the ice cream.

"I told Vic I'd watch her tonight. They had some big fancy dinner thing for Reed."

Dean folds up the paper bag. "Cool."

"Did you forget the ice cream?" I ask, my eyes bugging out of my head. If I don't send Jade back high on sugar what kind of faux aunt am I?

"I didn't buy any."

I shut the freezer door. "Were they out?"

He places the paper bag on the counter, his hands landing on my hips, and he thrusts me into his arms. His nose glides over my jaw and neck. "I thought you were going to be the sundae."

I giggle in his arms.

"I had plans of licking whipped cream and chocolate off your delectable body. Why do you think I bought extra cherries?" His teeth latch on to my earlobe, giving a firm tug.

"Well, maybe you should have a sleepover tomorrow night."

He squeezes my ass. "Is that a sly way of telling me no sleepover tonight?"

"Since Jade sleeps with me, I'd have to say no."

"I have a question for you." He draws back, leaning on

the counter and I'm suddenly rethinking my plan. An entire night of not being able to touch him feels like torture at the moment.

"What?" I ask.

"Am I here as a test?"

I wrinkle my brow.

He raises his.

I tilt my head.

He tilts his in the opposite direction.

"What?" I feign ignorance.

"You heard me."

"I don't want to say."

He captures me before I can escape back into the living room and his fingers torment me with tickles. "Admit it."

"No." I laugh.

He laughs. "I'm not going to stop."

I wiggle and slide around but he's got me cornered and let's be honest, I'm not trying very hard to get away. If I really wanted to, I'd knee him in the balls.

"Fine. Maybe."

He stops for a second. "Maybe as in yes."

"Maybe."

He tickles me, but his hands skitter up my chest. "God, I want to strip you right now. These damn clothes are a fucking tease. I can see the outline of your body, but there's still a barrier."

"Aunt Chelsea," Jade calls out. "Someone just knocked on the door."

"Don't answer." I look at Dean. "Not a true test, I just wanted to see how you'd fit into my life now. How you'd handle it when it's not just all about us."

A cocky smile plays on his lips. "Like everything else, with perfection." He presses his lips to my cheek. "I'll grab the door."

My hands grip the counter, preparing myself for a night of temptation.

By the time I get to the living room, Dean's shutting the door and he's got the pizza in his hand.

"The money was on the table."

He shakes his head.

"I bet you're a cheese girl, right Jade?" he asks.

"How did you know?" She follows him to the small kitchen table.

"Is that the floss?" Dean asks, placing the pizza on the table and opening the box.

"Yeah." Jade's hips start moving and her arms swinging from side to side.

Dean steps back from the table, watching her and then he juts out his hip. "Move your arms back when you swing your hips sideways."

Jade looks like the kid from the video and Dean looks like if you put the video in slow motion.

I lean against the doorframe of the kitchen watching the two interact.

Jade's easy, I know that. She's not going to act like a brat or give him a hard time. She'll say her pleases and her thank yous. Still, it's nice to see the two of them joking around.

"Have you ever done the Cupid Shuffle?" Dean stops attempting the floss and starts singing the cupid shuffle song and doing the dance.

Jade watches his feet, mimicking him.

"Wait, wait. We need the music." Dean grabs the remote from the table and searches Cupid Shuffle on YouTube. A minute later after an ad, the song begins and Dean pushes the coffee table against the couch.

He motions for Jade to come to the dance floor. She looks at me and I nod, then she runs to join him. Dean takes her hands and the two follow the directions of moving to the right and then to the left. They go through the entire dance together, her following Dean's steps and movements. Even the flexing of the bicep.

"Can we do it again?" Jade asks with a big smile and sparkling eyes.

"If Chelsea joins us." Dean looks in my direction, clearly issuing me a challenge.

Jade runs over to me, grabbing my hand and tugging me toward them.

"The pizza will get cold," I protest.

"Excuses, excuses," Dean says, tsking me.

"Watch us," Jade says, eyeing Dean to press play.

"Sweet Jade, I'm the master." I puff my chest out.

"What happened to the pizza-will-get-cold girl?" Dean teases, stepping to the side to give me some space.

"I just didn't want to show you up." I wink at him.

Dean laughs, and presses play. "Then show me up, beautiful."

Jade's all in and has most of the moves down. Oh, to be a kid again. She's strutting along the floor, her hips in sequence to the rhythm and she's even singing the lyrics. "You're really good, Aunt Chelsea." She shoots a fleeting look in my direction.

Dean dances over to the pizza, grabbing a slice and eating it while he watches us.

"A plate wouldn't kill you," I say over my shoulder.

His deep chuckle grows closer and he leans over my shoulder, biting a piece of the pizza.

"You want to see Aunt Chelsea flip out?" Dean asks Jade.

She turns and continues her dance as she watches us.

"You're buying me a new rug if you drop it." Although it's making me slightly worried, I'm going to let this go.

"Deal." His arm wraps around my waist and he holds it up in front of my face. "Live on the edge and take a bite."

"Nuh-uh." I shake my head.

"Come on Aunt Chelsea." Jade jumps up and down next to us.

I look down at the girl and then to Dean, opening my mouth. I figure a small nibble will do, but Dean puts the entire piece in my mouth and walks away.

I chew and they both laugh at me and my chipmunk cheeks as I try to chew it enough to swallow.

"HOLY…" Dean screams as Beyoncé's "Put a Ring on It" starts. "Now this is Aunt Chelsea's song. She sang it to me one night five years ago."

My cheeks instantly heat. I search for the remote, finding it in Dean's hands, wiggling it back and forth in the air.

"She can show you how to dance to this."

"You danced to this?" Jade sits down on the floor and watching the woman on the screen who's barely clothed dance around.

"Inappropriate," I mumble over the last bit of pizza.

"It's Beyoncé." Dean makes a face like whatever.

"Please Aunt Chelsea," Jade begs from the floor, her hands clasped together.

"Let's eat first."

"I don't think you should dance on a full belly." Dean sits down in a kitchen chair, helping himself to another slice of pizza. "Not to mention this song is all about female empowerment. It sure put me in my place." Dean smiles that smug look that somehow makes him even more attractive.

I narrow my eyes.

"Please Aunt Chelsea." Jade pulls on my arm.

The video continues playing and Jade starts following Beyoncé's dance moves in the video.

"One time and then we eat." I put my finger up and Jade glances over her shoulder to Dean like we did it.

Dean doesn't look surprised. He knew I couldn't say no to Jade.

"Should I start from the beginning?" he asks like he's not going to.

He starts the video over again and I start moving and shaking it like I'm in college again and half corked. I'm surprised I never forgot the choreography.

I keep my eyes on Dean the entire time, remembering him at that bar that night—him with his buddies, his ridiculous idea that we really should get hitched after I finished dancing.

Shit, I'm the reason we married. It was meant to be a joke, me and two of the other player's girlfriends were playing around. They didn't go to a chapel and marry their girlfriends. Only Dean.

The song ends and I almost collapse, leaning forward to catch my breath.

"You're so good, Aunt Chelsea. Can we do it again?"

I pat her dark chestnut hair. "After we eat, okay?"

"Okay." She skips over to the table eating the pizza Dean already has out for her. "Don't you love Lou's?" she says as cheese hangs from her mouth.

"I'm actually a Gino's man." Dean laughs, knowing he's asking for a fight.

"My mommy loves Gino's."

I go to the kitchen to grab some water before I pass out.

"What about Reed?" Dean asks.

Jade starts talking about Reed liking whatever Mommy likes and how her dad loves Lou's, but only the deep dish.

Who knew a conversation about pizza could keep a girl so busy?

Dean comes up behind me while I'm shuffling things around in the fridge. He slides his arm past me into the fridge, his body pressed against my back. "Do the dance for me in private sometime?" he whispers.

"Depends how much it's worth to you."

He backs up after grabbing three waters with one hand.

Magic fingers, I'm telling you.

"If that little girl wasn't here, you'd already be spread-eagle on the table with my head between your legs."

I push him away. "She's right there," I whisper.

She's on to Henry and her grandma's pizza preferences now. Only in Chicago.

"That dance confirmed for me that I wanted to marry you," he says in a serious voice.

"Let's try to push that memory back." I start to walk away, but he grabs my wrist.

"I never want to forget our first marriage. I don't want to erase our past no matter how dark it was."

He gives me that look again. The one that says we still have things to discuss.

"Not tonight."

"I know not tonight, but this week okay?"

I nod. "Okay."

"What about you, Aunt Chelsea?" I walk back to the table and take a seat.

"I'm a Lou's girl."

"You guys are split then?" she asks with astonishment.

"Not on only pizza. She's a Sox fan." Dean thumbs in my direction.

"Aunt Chelsea," she whines. "I liked you the most." She shakes her head in disappointment.

"I bet she'll teach you that dance now," Dean says.

I kick Dean under the table.

"Yay!" Jade's face lights up.

"Yay!" Dean's fists rise, and he shakes them in the air like he's a cheerleader.

With a chuckle, I say, "Payback will be swift."

His foot slides up my leg, inching my thighs apart. "You wanna make a bet?"

I shut my thighs. "Absolutely not."

Smiling, I think of all the ways I can extend his torture —mostly with my mouth.

Chapter Twenty-Two

*T*he following Tuesday, I'm deep in ad launches for the fundraiser, making sure every logo of each company that's donated is accounted for when my phone dings with a text message.

Minute Man: *Lunch at my place?*

Shit, I never did change his name. I quickly edit his name.

Me: *Why do I think I'll be your lunch?*

Heat rushes between my legs.

Dean: *You always were a smart girl.*
Me: *Mr. Bennett, are you asking for an afternoon delight?*
Dean: *Call it whatever you want. As long as it entails me underneath you.*
Me: *You do know I don't have to ride you every time, right?*
Dean: *I like having your tits in my hands. We're both winners.*

Me: *Are you going to feed me?*
Dean: *Unless you want a very vulgar response, I suggest you use that smart brain of yours and figure it out.*

I laugh.

"What's so funny?" Victoria hollers from her desk. She'll be in here any minute with her stealthy mom P.I. skills.

"Nothing."

Me: *I'll be there at noon. Don't make me wait.*
Dean: *I think that's my line. Clark has a key for you.*
Me: *A key?*
Dean: *Too soon?*

I drop the phone on my desk. Is it too soon? I don't really know.

Me: *Don't expect one from me.*
Dean: *I expect nothing from you.*
Dean: *Strike that. Just a wet pussy.*

My cheeks heat just as Victoria stops at my door, coffee cup in her hand like she's just stopping on the way to the break room. That move might work on Jade, but not me.

"Who are you texting?"

I glance up at her and then quickly type out another message.

Me: *Then we're on the same page. You better be hard by the time I get there.*
Dean: *I'm already hard thinking about you bent over my couch.*

A shiver runs through my body and I squirm in my seat.

Me: *Okay, I need to work. To be continued…*
Dean: *I was just unzipping my slacks :(*
Me: *Use your imagination.*
Dean: *Just send me a pic?*

"Chelsea!" Victoria's loud voice pulls me from my internal debate over whether I'd actually send him a pic.

Me: *In your dreams Rico Suave. Noon.*

I shut off my screen, placing my phone face down on my desk. Knowing Dean, he'll send me a picture of himself.

"Sorry, what?" I say, realizing Hannah's there now, too. She and Hannah walk in and sit down.

"So, things are good?" Hannah asks, crossing her legs.

"They're progressing, yes."

"Are you taking him to Vegas with you?" Victoria asks, sipping out of her coffee mug. See, she's a con artist.

"God, no. I don't want to end up married again," I joke.

"You think you would?" Hannah asks.

"No." Then I frown while I think about that for a second.

"Jade adores him," Victoria says. "Said he's the best dancer. She brags about him so much, Reed was trying to choreograph his own dance last night."

"Reed's got no competition, but I have to admit he was good with her. He started breakdancing for her at one point."

"She showed us." Victoria smiles, silently giving me her

blessing should I want to jump back in the Dean pool again.

"You've fallen for him again, haven't you?" Hannah asks.

I shrug.

If I told them the truth, I'd be admitting it out loud. And that makes it more real. I've been dodging my family for the past few weeks because I know they'll see it on my face.

"We aren't going to judge you," Hannah says, dipping her head to catch my eye.

I look up through my eyelashes and nod.

Hannah smiles.

"Am I the stupidest woman in the world?" My forehead hits my desk.

"No." Victoria sets her coffee cup on my desk and comes around to my side. She puts her arm around my shoulders, propping herself up on the arm of my chair. "Not at all."

"But Hannah said people don't change."

Hannah laughs. "What do I know? I barely know the guy except for the fact he's a good tax lawyer."

"What if he destroys me?" I voice my biggest fear.

"What if he doesn't?" Victoria says, her lips pressing against the top of my head. "I know it's scary, but if you're already scared of being hurt, it's too late. Now you have to jump in with both feet."

"I'd rather put my toe in."

Hannah laughs. "You already did. You're going to feel the hit if it doesn't work out anyway. Don't stand in the way of working out yourself. Understand?"

"Kind of." I shrug.

"If Dean called you right now and said he met someone else, how would you feel?" Hannah asks.

Her words send an adrenaline rush through my body and my chest constricts. "I'd be crushed."

Hannah raises her shoulders, her lips pursed in a 'see, you're invested' mannerism. I know she's right. I felt it Saturday night. The pit of my stomach said I crossed the line. That he won and weaseled his way into my heart again.

"So both feet huh?"

Victoria squeezes my shoulder. "Yep, but don't worry, Jade's a really good judge of character."

"She loves Pete." I look up at her and roll my eyes.

Victoria laughs at me bringing up her ex-husband. "Every girl has the hero complex for her father."

She's right. "Has Dean really changed?" I ask the same question that kept me up last night.

Victoria's hand lands on my chest, covering where my heart is. "Only this can tell you."

Hannah rises from the chair and walks toward the door. "You know, Chelsea, when I hired you, it was between you and another woman. Do you know why I hired you?"

She stops in the doorway.

"Why?"

"You're a fighter. I knew you'd go all in and get the job done. The same goes for a relationship. Let's remember why we're all divorced."

Victoria and I say nothing.

"We're divorced because the men we married *weren't* all in. A successful relationship takes two people who will give one hundred percent. I know Dean disappointed you before, but he seems all in by everything you've told us. The question is, are you?" She leaves the room with a soft smile.

I look up to Victoria, whose lips are pressed together.

"She's right. I never really did think of it like that, but she's got a point." She pulls me in for a hug and then stands.

"Yes, she does," I mumble after everyone's left.

I open my desk drawer, pulling out my jump drive. My stomach rumbles with nausea as I wait for it to load on my computer until the small thumbnail images pop up.

I click on the first picture. A selfie of Dean and I. Were we really that young once upon a time? His arm is slung around me, my lips pressed to his cheek, a million-dollar smile on his face.

I scroll forward to photos of us at his games, us at parties, out with our friends and the only constant is Dean is by my side. Even when I'm with my friends, he's photobombing in the background. A smile comes to my lips remembering how much fun we had during those short months.

Checking the time, I see it's eleven thirty. I grab my purse and phone off my desk.

"I'll be back after lunch," I say, not waiting for a response.

"Well then," Victoria says but the door shuts and I press the elevator button before I hear more.

It's always been Dean. I need to finally give him all of me.

I USE my new key to open Dean's apartment and I'm greeted immediately by Grover, his tail wagging and drool hanging from his mouth.

"Hey Grover," I say, looking around for his leash. "Do you want to go outside?" I bend down and pet him, spotting his leash on the table by the front door. "Okay, let's go."

I drop my stuff, attach the leash and move toward the door. It opens before I can grab the knob.

Dean strolls in, his tie already loosened from his neck. A smile warms his entire face and I'm reminded of the pictures I looked at moments ago when I walked down the aisle toward Elvis at that small chapel in Vegas. I really wish I'd been more coherent, so I could remember marrying him better.

"I like this scene way too much." Dean places his computer bag on a chair and bee-lines it right over to me.

"Grover needs to go out."

"I pay a dog walker. He was here a half hour ago. He's fine." His head burrows into my neck and he lifts me into his arms, inhaling deep. "I need you more."

"You spent all day Sunday with me." I laugh, my head falling back, and his teeth nip along my neck.

"I need you every minute of every day." He kicks off his shoes.

Grover's leash slips out of my hands.

I cup his face between my hands, staring down at the man I'd convinced myself I loathed for the past five years.

My head drops, and I capture his heart-shaped lips, my tongue searching for entry. He opens as though he's been waiting for this moment all day. Our tongues glide and explore one another's mouth. He tastes like the mint he must have had on the way here.

He gradually releases me until my feet touch the floor. His forehead lands on mine and he searches my face, for what I don't know.

"Something's changed," he says, his fingers feeling for the zipper on the back of my dress.

The zipper sliding down is the only sound in the condo while our gazes remain locked.

"Nothing's changed."

"The imaginary wall that was between us isn't there anymore," he says with a touch of wonder in his voice, like he can't believe it.

His hands glide up my back, slowly lowering the dress off my shoulders.

"I'm just happy." I close my eyes and inhale as my dress falls from my shoulders.

He helps it find its way to the floor and I stand there wearing only a black bra, panties and heels—not a self-conscious bone in my body.

He wants me, and I want him. End of story.

"I'm happy, too." He smiles and cups my breasts, teasing my already erect nipples.

I arch my back into his hands and he tugs the cups of my bra down, brazenly admiring my breasts. Sliding my hands to my back, I unhook my bra and let it fall between us.

"I should spank you, it's my job to strip you." He steps into me, my naked chest rubbing against his suit jacket and vest.

"Let's get you undressed before you start getting kinky on me."

He takes off his jacket and tosses it on the couch. My fingers go to work on his vest as he stands there watching me undress him.

"I could get used to this," he says with a smirk.

The vest joins my dress on the floor. Since his tie is already loosened, my manicured nails make quick work of finishing the job. I lay the striped tie across the back of my neck, letting it hang over my breasts.

He inhales a deep breath. "Now you go and cover up? You're playing a game you aren't going to win."

I smile seductively, working all the buttons on his shirt. Soon it slides off his strong shoulders and pools on the floor.

"Just a few more items, Mr. Bennett." My lips press to the warm skin of his chest. Cedarwood and melon overwhelm my senses. Since when did this man start wearing cologne?

As though he's testing himself, he doesn't let himself touch me. My skin aches for his rough handling.

I unbuckle his belt, unbutton and unzip his pants all while my mouth sprinkles kisses along his chest. Still, he hasn't placed a hand on me. Is he trying to tease me until I'm dripping wet?

I slide my hands to his backside, pushing his slacks until they drop to the floor along with his belt, landing with a thud.

His rigid length bulges out of his black boxer briefs and my mouth waters. I'd never tell him, but he was right. I do love his cock. But what he doesn't know is that I love his reaction when I go down on him more than the actual act.

Slowly, I slide down his body until my knees land on his hardwood floor. Teasingly, I run my finger along the waistband, staring up at him through my eyelashes.

His eyes are locked on me, heat radiating from the dark depths of his irises. Rubbing him through the thin fabric with my palm, I watch his chest rising and falling with fast breaths. His mouth hangs slightly ajar, but his hands have yet to guide me.

Dipping down the front of his boxers, his dick springs out as though saying 'play with me, lick me, suck me.' Finally, a groan erupts out of him and his hands move, but he doesn't allow himself to touch me and the ache between my legs grows more intense.

I use my tongue to lick up his length, my hand wrapped around his base so I can cover his tip with my mouth.

"Fuck," he murmurs, fisting his hands at his sides.

I love the way he's about to lose his self-control.

It's easy with Dean, I know what to do to get him off, but today I want to do other things, so after sucking up and down a few times, I let his cock pop out of my mouth and slide my tongue down his long length. Twisting my head, I suck his balls into my mouth as my hand continues to stroke him up and down.

He leans forward, his hands landing on the edge of the couch, which only spurs my thirst to drive him wild. I use my thumb to rub the pre-cum around his tip.

"Please Chelsea," he begs.

As though I was waiting for those words, I move my mouth up and fill it with his length once more, bobbing, sucking. He flexes his hips and the tip hits the back of my throat.

Still the same Dean.

Releasing my hand, I allow him to fuck my mouth as my hand cups his balls. With a loud groan, he erupts in my mouth and finally his hands touch my skin, one hand on my shoulder the other on the back of my head.

An electric current travels through my entire body. My eyes locked with his, I swallow and let him fall from my mouth. He's still hard.

Dean holds his hand out to help me up and when I do he pulls me into an embrace. "I told you. You love my cock more than me."

I smile and let him think that. Although I really can't complain, he does have a wonderful dick.

"Come to my bed." He grabs my hand and leads me down the hall.

"I should get back to work."

He stops, stares at me for a few seconds. "It's not an afternoon delight if you don't get off. Let big daddy please you."

"Yeah, that doesn't do anything for me."

He chuckles, not letting go of my hand. Not that I'm pulling away anyway.

Chapter Twenty-Three

The sun is spilling into his bedroom when we enter. Dean doesn't pull me to him but guides me to the bed and nods his head for me to sit.

I'm waiting for him to be the dominant he usually is and dictate exactly how he wants me—tell me what he's going to do to me, ask me questions about how much I loved sucking him off.

That's us. We fuck. We fuck rough and we both get off on it.

That doesn't happen.

As baffled as I was in his family room that he never touched me until he came, I'm even more so now.

Gradually he lowers to his knees, his eyes on me, his hands resting on my knees. Without ever tearing his gaze off of me, his palms run along the length of my inner thigh, and he inches forward into the space between my legs.

He hooks each side of my black panties and drags them down my legs. A tingling starts at my ankles and runs up my legs. When the tips of his fingers move closer to my center, he runs them along the outside of my pussy, building an ache in me that I'm not sure can ever be quenched.

"So beautiful," he says, and all expectations fade from my mind.

His tongue dips between my legs, up through my folds until he sucks my nub into his hot mouth, twirling it with his tongue.

I spiral into a state of passion. Wanting his body over mine. Needing his hands on every inch of me. As though he's channeled my thoughts, he slides his tongue up my stomach past my breasts and kisses me. Slow and deep, and the pit of my stomach quivers.

Without a word he encourages me to climb up on his bed, his lips not leaving mine. I fall into the softness of his mattress with his weight on top of me, his thigh pressed to my core, my hands gripping him, not wanting him to leave me.

We kiss, we caress and for a brief moment, it's just us, in our happy bubble like we used to be. There are no bills to pay, no job to go back to, no pressure of our past mistakes. It's Dean and I in our purest and most honest state and a tear drips from my eye when his knuckles run along the side of my ribs.

All I want is him. For him to never stop touching me, never stop kissing me, never stop being the man I need.

From tight grips to softer touches, we explore the bodies we've grown into over the past five years, finding new places that illicit sounds of pleasure instead of falling into the routine we mastered years before.

His hands are warm and gentle as he flips my body over and hovers over top of me, his lips not letting one part of my flesh go untouched. All the insecurities about us disappear and a newfound love for the man he's become buds inside of me.

He brushes my hair to the side, his kiss on the back of my neck spurring a line of goose bumps along my spine. Flipping me to my back, he hovers over me, ready between my legs. Our eyes lock and he shifts, his arm stretching out toward his dresser.

I grip his wrist and he freezes in place, questions filling his eyes. I shake my head once and he comes back to me, laying his forearms on either side of my head.

"I love you," he whispers, his lips sealing the promise he made on my skin.

Inch by inch he sinks into me. I've never felt fuller in my entire life. My heart and my body are filled with Dean from my head down to my toes. He leads us to the brink with lingering kisses and unrushed touches that add fuel to my building orgasm.

He pulls back, his eyes locked with mine and suddenly we're lost to one another. It's only us. He grinds into me and I meet every thrust as my feet slide along the sheets, his thighs pushing my legs farther apart. Deeper and deeper he plunges until a wave ripples on the surface and I tighten my core to stop myself from coming. I never want this moment to end.

My fingers cling to his rounded shoulders and my back arches, pushing my breasts to his chest.

He leads me farther into the abyss until the ripples turn into small waves that cap at the ocean's edge. My toes curl and he thrusts deeper to the point you'd think it'd hurt, but it only sends my pleasure soaring higher until I'm in a raging sea near the middle of a hurricane. Wave after wave pounds at my willpower, begging for release. I clench around him and a strangled groan erupts out of him.

My fingernails scrape his skin until there's too much

pressure to hold back. I can't control my impending release any longer.

His lips crash into mine, his tongue taking what he wants, and I lose all control, the water breaching my levies and flowing over. I descend into my climax and it's like being caught up in a whirlpool as bliss thunders through and around me, dragging me down until this feeling is all I know. He stills inside of me finding his own release.

All my muscles feel like Jell-O and I lay on the bed amazed at what we just experienced.

He lays on top of me and then slides to the side of my body. His hand turns my head and he kisses me softly on the lips and then kisses my nose. "I'll be right back."

When he disappears into the bathroom, I don't move.

Returning only seconds later, he has a towel and cleans me up.

"I'm assuming you're covered?" he asks, folding the towel over and wiping my thighs.

"I am." I languidly sit up and swing my legs over the bed. "I have an IUD."

"Figured."

I stifle a smile. I bet if I asked him he has no idea what an IUD is, but it doesn't matter. I kiss his lips. "Thank you."

"I should be doing the thank yous." He pulls me into his chest, kissing the top of my head. "Thank God I came before that otherwise, I would've lasted about two seconds."

I giggle into his chest.

"I have to go back to work," I say, even though it's the last thing I want to do right now.

"Me, too." He backs up from the bed, offering me a hand. "Sleepover tonight?"

I giggle as I head to the living room where my clothes are. "What are we, ten?"

Before I can even slip on my panties, his arms are around my waist, his head in the crook of my neck. "I liked rediscovering you today."

My head falls back to his firm chest and my hands cover his forearms. "So did I."

His lips press to my temple and my eyes fall closed. Pure heaven.

"Come on, I'll take you back to the office." He lightly taps my ass before backing away.

Can I stay here forever?

"I HAVE a drawer at my place for you," Dean says with his classic smirk on his face as we exit the elevator and head to the RISE offices.

"How very kind of you."

"Are you going to accept it?" he asks, holding out his arm for me to exit first.

"I don't know. It's awfully quick." My voice is light because let's face it, he just gave me the best sex of my life. Am I really going to deny being able to keep a few fresh pairs of panties and a toothbrush in a drawer? No.

"I'm not offering a whole dresser." He opens the door to RISE.

"Thanks for the clarification."

"Unless you want one. I'm trying to keep things at that granny speed you prefer. You know I'd buy you your own dresser if you'd let me."

I walk through the door laughing. "It's not granny. It's like mom minivan speed."

"When's the last time you ventured out of the city?" he

asks. "Suburban minivan moms drive the fastest."

I stop and look at him. "Really?"

He nods.

"Okay then." I stop and look up at the ceiling, thinking. "How about a kid who just got his license? The one who gets the good student discount for insurance. The one who listens to their parents. You know the type. Not the adrenaline junkie jock like you were."

I laugh and look at Dean wondering why he hasn't responded. His eyes are set on the chairs in our waiting area, unblinking.

"Or the way you still are." My mom's voice rings out and I whip my head around to see her standing from a chair. She straightens her blouse by the tails and slides her purse up her arm. "Chelsea, may I speak with you?"

"I've got phone calls to answer, but here you go," Victoria says, putting a cup of coffee on the table in front of my mom.

"Sorry, I—I didn't know you were coming."

What do I say?

"Chelsea." My mom's tone becomes more impatient. "Office. Now."

Dean doesn't reach for my hand. If anything, he distances himself.

"You remember Dean?" I ask her. No sense ignoring the pink elephant in the room, or ex-husband as it were.

Her gaze flicks to his. "Nice to see you coherent." Then her eyes are back on me with a look that demands privacy now.

Dean steps forward, putting his arm out. "Mrs. Walsh, it's nice to see you again."

My mom stares at his outstretched hand and for a moment I think she'll never shake it. Eventually, she does, and Dean puts his hand back in his pocket.

"Dean's a lawyer now. He's doing pro bono work for the foundation."

"Interesting." She fake smiles.

"I better get back to the office." Dean steps forward and I rear back. Then I bend forward and his head tilts back. After an awkward dance, his lips make contact with my cheek. "Dresser offer still stands," he whispers, and a smile graces my lips.

"Mrs. Walsh." He nods like some trained elitist. "Please give Mr. Walsh my best."

"Dean," she says the four letter word like it *is* the four letter word.

He steps out, catching my eye before he leaves. Can we please go back to a half hour ago?

"Your office. Now." Mom heads down the hall without waiting for me.

"Hey, Vic, hold all my calls."

Victoria gives me a 'I'm sorry' smile. It's not her fault. I'm sure when I check my phone there'll be messages from her.

By the time I enter my office, my mom is on my side of the desk.

"Shut the door," she demands like we're in her office, not mine.

Nonetheless, I follow her instructions.

She hasn't even heard the click of the door before she's laying into me. "How could you? He's the worst person for you. What are you, going to marry him again?"

"Just relax. He's changed."

"He's changed." She throws her hands up in the air. "A tiger doesn't change his stripes, Chelsea. He's still that selfish bastard who let you down five years ago. A man who can't take care of himself, let alone a wife."

"I'm twenty-five. Do I have to remind you of that?" I clench my fists by my side in an effort to control my anger.

"Funny. You said that same line to me when you were eighteen and newly married." She sits in my chair, taking a calming breath and then sets her focus on me. "Chelsea, just because he's some lawyer now and dresses in nicer clothes than baseball shorts and t-shirts doesn't mean the inside of that package has changed. You're a smart woman, he's just always had this power over you."

"Because I love him," I mumble, crossing my arms over my chest.

"You do not. Don't let him convince you to feel things you don't." Her hand slaps down on the desk and I jolt.

"He's not, Mom. I do. I love him. I love who he was five years ago, and I love him for the person he's become. I knew you wouldn't accept this."

"There's nothing to accept."

"There is. We're in a relationship." I bring my hands back down to my sides and puff my chest out. "He just offered me a drawer at his place."

"How sweet of the man." She rolls her eyes. "Come back down to Earth, Chelsea. You're sleeping with him, so he's offering you a drawer so you can sleep with him some more." She stands and leans toward me with her hands pressed down on my desk.

"Did you ever think that maybe I was as important to him as he is to me and that's why he offered a drawer?"

I can't believe I'm having an argument with her over a drawer.

"I think that men like Dean get what they want no matter how many lies they have to tell people to get it. I think as soon as he's done, he'll leave you again."

"I left him," I grind out.

She scoffs and shakes her head at me in pity. "Don't

fool yourself, he left you way before you walked out that door."

I plop down in a chair that's supposed to be for guests in my office, almost defeated. She always plays to win no matter how deep she has to plunge in the dagger.

"Stay out of it," I say, staring at my knotted hands.

"You're my daughter."

I know I'm not wrong this time. I know it.

Standing back up, I decide I'm not going to let her dictate my life. She doesn't bring much joy to it anyway.

"I'm going to continue dating him, Mom. I'd like you and Dad to give him a chance and see how he's changed, but if you can't do that, fine. But know that I'm not changing my mind. I've decided to give him a second chance." I cross my arms for effect and she stares me down, calculated and waiting for me to crumble under her narrowed eyes.

After a prolonged silence, I speak. "Now this is where I work, and I have to get back to it. If you want to talk about this further, call me." I walk over and open my office door.

"Chelsea, I'll leave because I'm not going to make a scene, and everyone knows you need the money, but you can engrave this into stone. That boy is going to ruin you —again."

"That's where you're wrong, Mom, he's a man now, not a boy."

She shakes her head and leaves, stopping just after she's cleared my doorway. "You can tell your father. I don't want to upset him."

"Will do."

She walks down the hall and I lightly swing my door shut, even though I want to slam it for all it's worth.

Am I the only one who can feel the tsunami brewing?

Chapter Twenty-Four

"Whoa, what a mama bear." Victoria cringes while she peeks into my door.

"A grizzly to be precise. She's not being protective."

"Oh, I think she is. She's worried." She helps herself to a seat and of course Hannah is right behind her.

"I'm going to take the chairs out of my office," I grumble.

Hannah smiles sweetly, one that says, 'no you're not, all is well.'

"Hey, it doesn't matter what your mom thinks, it matters what you think." Hannah's hand reaches over and grabs mine.

"Exactly," Victoria says.

"Speaks the woman whose mom loves her man."

"Not always." Victoria shrugs. "My mom hated Pete."

I stare blankly at her.

"Yeah, okay I see your point." She brings her fingers to her lips and zips. Even pretending to throw away the key. Is this what happens to people after they have kids?

"Truly I don't care, it's just going to make it uncomfortable at my cousin's wedding." I slide my hand out from Hannah's and type my password into my computer.

"What are you going to do after that?" Hannah asks.

"I'm going to disown my mom."

Hannah and Victoria glance at one another.

"Seems viable," Hannah says. "Or you could try to let them see the good in Dean."

"They've never seen the good in Dean. Actually" —I hold my hand up—"they weren't that upset when they thought he was going to be a number one draft pick. After he hurt his shoulder and they figured out the money train vanished, that's when they decided they really hated him."

"They were okay with you marrying him at eighteen?" The judgment in Victoria's tone is clear and she's probably put herself in my mom's position in her head. Jade marrying someone right after she leaves for college. I get it, shortly after we were married I made myself a promise that if we ever had a daughter, she'd know all the mistakes I made so she didn't repeat them. Not like I really have to worry about that anyway.

"No. Not at first. They warmed up once they found out about his bank account prospects. Then they were down on him again." I click on some emails not really in the mood to rehash all this family drama.

My phone dings in my purse.

"Probably Dean." Hannah side glances Victoria.

I pull it out of my purse and sure enough, she's right.

Dean: *Glad to see the wicked witch of the Midwest is still kicking.*
Me: *Please I've tried to drown her in a bucket of water. Nothing.*
Dean: *LOL…need me to come over?*
Me: *Nah, the girls are already in my office.*

I glance up at the two sets of eyes focused on me.

"I think we should go to Torrio's tonight." Hannah nods like it's already a done deal.

Me: *They're talking about going out tonight.*
Dean: *I thought we were having a slumber party. :(*

"I can call Reed. He can pick up Jade from my mom's."

Me: *I can come over all sloppy drunk and you can take advantage of me.*
Dean: *I prefer you coherent, but thanks for the offer.*
Me: *Sorry, I shouldn't have said that. Sometimes I forget that I shouldn't bring up drinking with you.*
Dean: *Don't apologize. Part of sobriety is having to deal with the fact that everyone else in the world is not an alcoholic.*
Me: *You sure?*
Dean: *Definitely. Now what about tonight?*
Me: *I'll have to get back to you.*

"Why don't you invite Reed and Chelsea can invite Dean?"

"What about you?" Victoria asks.

Me: *Hold up. You might be getting an invite.*
Dean: *I'm not crashing girl's night.*

"I'll be fine. If we're at Torrio's, I know plenty of people."

Now Victoria's gaze flickers to mine because I guarantee you we're on the same page here—the silver fox.

"Cool. I'll go text Reed." Victoria slides out the chair and leaves my office.

"What do you say? Ready to let Dean come out and play?"

I drop the phone on my desk. "What does that mean?"

Hannah tilts her head in her classic, 'you're not a moron, you understand exactly what I mean.' "You've been hiding him from everyone like he's your mistress."

"Technically, he'd be my... what would he be called?"

Hannah chews on the inside of her cheek, thinking.

"Misteress?" I offer.

"That's lame."

"Bushdog?"

She laughs.

"Fuck boy?"

She points her finger at me. "I'm not sure I care what that word is, but I like that one. God knows they have enough derogatory names for a woman who enjoys sex."

"Masteress?"

"That sounds more like a dom. Not to mention I would never give a man the satisfaction as having master part of his name."

"Oh, forget it. Dean's not one of those anyway."

Hannah snaps her fingers. "Manstress."

I nod because she's probably got it right. I lean back in my chair my thoughts heading in another direction. "Do you find it funny that there are all these names for women who sleep with married men, but none for the actual married man and none for a man who sleeps with a married woman?"

"Yet another example of why I started RISE. When I was getting divorced, Roarke Baldwin tried to find out if I was cheating. He had me followed, pictures of every man I had come into contact with since my separation came up, twisting the truth to try to get me to admit to something that wasn't true. But Todd? Nope. My lawyer had hotel receipts for a room every Thursday. My lawyer had pictures of him groping her in public, them having sex in a lingerie changing room."

"Ew."

She nods. "But Illinois and their no-fault bullshit. Somehow Mr. Baldwin took me for more than that son of a bitch should've ever gotten."

"I'm sorry, Hannah. I know I joke about you liking him. But I realize now why you must loathe him."

She chews on the inside of her cheek again, her eyes darting around until they land on me briefly. "I do," she says simply.

My phone vibrates on my desk.

She shakes her head as though the vibrating has stopped her train of thought. "Anyway, check with Dean. I'm going to call ahead and see if I can get us the curtained-off room."

I'm giddy with excitement. It's like Hannah's got connections to the latest boy band and I'm thirteen again.

"Thanks, Hannah."

She walks out, and I pick up my phone.

Me: *You're coming out with me tonight. It's a speakeasy though. That okay?*

My shoulders sway back in forth. My mood ten times better than after my mom threw her little tantrum.

Dean: *I'd rather be coming inside you on my bed. And yeah, that's fine.*
Me: *I never said that couldn't be arranged.*
Dean: *Tell me more…*

Instead of telling him anything, I place the phone

between my legs under my desk and snap a picture. It's teasing, clearly showing the opening of my legs with a triangle patch of my black satin panties visible.

I click send.

Dean: *It's so unfair, you can send me a pic with your clothes on and my dick goes as hard as granite. Am I supposed to send you an outline of my dick? Somehow, I don't think it'll have the same effect.*
Me: *That's what you think.*

A minute later my phone dings and sure enough, it's the shape of his hard dick outlined in his boxers.

My mouth waters.

Decisions, decisions.

Torrio's or Dean's…

Can't a girl have both?

DEAN and I stand at the end of the alley where you enter Torrio's. Trying to look inconspicuous waiting for Hannah, Victoria, and Reed. His back is to the brick building, his hands on my hips, our lips attached.

Ever since this afternoon, I can't seem to get enough of him.

"I wanted to clear something up," he says, his hands sliding up and down my hips.

I rest my chin on his chest. "What?"

"This afternoon, I said I love you."

"Oh." My heart speeds up in my chest.

He shakes his head before I can say anything. "I just want you to know I meant it." One hand tucks a strand of hair behind my ear. "It wasn't some declaration after an orgasm that I didn't mean. I've never stopped loving you. I know we're taking this slow and I don't want to rush, but I didn't want you thinking I said it just because my mind was in overdrive."

I lay my cheek on his chest. The V-neck t-shirt he chose to wear is soft and edgy just like him. Most men will still be in suits, but I know he doesn't care. His confidence never left him.

His arms tighten around my waist and I still don't say anything.

Staring up at him again, I kiss his jaw.

"I love you, too. I thought that love died, but it never really did. It was laying dormant. Waiting."

"Did you just compare your love for me to the state of a volcano?"

I slap his stomach lightly. "No. It just means inactivity."

"That's comforting. Can I tell our love story like that?" he pauses. "Chelsea said during our five years apart the love she had for me was inactive until I popped back into her life."

I giggle like the school girl he turns me into. "It doesn't sound that bad."

"Let me give you my rendition." Again, he pauses for dramatic effect. "I loved Chelsea from the first moment I saw her on a bar stool laughing with her friends. I had to eat the hottest wing they had and not drink anything for five minutes, but I'd do it all over again. The first time I told her I loved her, I didn't know that I'd never be able to live without her. After my shaking hand signed the divorce papers delivered to me the morning after a binge, one would've thought it was over. But the seed of love was planted when we were barely adults. We starved that tree after only a short few months. Still, someone was watering that tree because it grew a little every year. It wasn't until five years later when I held her in my arms again that the branches grew, and leaves budded. People would say it's beautiful now, but I think it was just as beautiful when it was only a seed planted into life's soil."

Tears fill my eyes. His thumb swipes one away before it slips off my cheek to his t-shirt.

"But you're right, that whole love was inactive line is the better of the two." He smiles, and I swat him again in the stomach.

I rise to my tiptoes, planting my lips to his and when I pull away, I stare into his eyes. "I love you, Dean Bennett."

His palms mold to my hips. "Enough for a dresser or a drawer?"

I smile at his humor and fall back down to my heels, wrapping my arms around his stomach, holding on for dear life. Pretty soon fate is going to want us to water that tree again.

"Aren't you guys the cutest." Hannah steps out of a taxi. She pays the driver and I see she's upped her game tonight.

"Hannah," Dean says, sliding his hand down my arm until it's locked in his. "Nice to see you off the clock."

"Technically you don't punch a clock for me since you're helping pro bono." She smiles, leans forward and kisses my cheek. "Glad you could make it."

"Nice outfit," I comment, and she rolls her eyes. "It's nothing."

"Uh-huh," I say low enough that no one really pays me attention.

She's in a short black skirt and see-through blouse with a gold bra under. She's asking for it tonight. And if I had my guess, I'd say she's hoping a silver fox will hunt her down.

A black SUV pulls up and stops beside the curb. Victoria and Reed file out. Uber express, I'm sure.

"Great, we're all here. Let's go have some drinks and make some memories." Hannah leads the pack down the alley as everyone says their hellos.

Reed and Dean shake hands and discuss some new judge or some legal thing I'm not interested in.

I'm wondering if I should've gone with my gut and taken Dean up on his offer to head straight to bed. Suddenly I really don't want to share Dean.

Chapter Twenty-Five

*E*ver notice how time flies when you're happy? It's been three weeks since Dean and I declared our love to each other and I'm not sure I've stayed at my own apartment since.

The saying ignorance is bliss comes to mind, too.

I haven't spoken to my mom more than I've had to with Skylar's wedding nearing. I'm still surprised she's kept Dean and my relationship a secret from my entire family. I know this because cell phone towers would crash if they knew. I'd be getting calls from Skylar, Zoe, Mikey and whoever thinks it's their business that I'm back with Dean.

Tonight it all changes. Tonight is Dean's coming out party. Actually it's a birthday party for my Aunt Liz but I have a feeling Dean will be the center of attention rather than my aunt.

"I really wish you'd told them." Dean steps out of his bedroom in a pair of charcoal slacks and a t-shirt with a long coat that only enhances his broad shoulders. He clasps his silver watch around his wrist.

"Surprises are better."

He raises his eyebrows. "Says you. I'm the one people are going to give the cold shoulder to. Sky and Zoe will have you hidden in the bathroom."

My heels click on the floor as I break the distance between us. "Good thing you're a lawyer."

"Why is that?"

"Because you know how to set everyone at ease." I lift my heels and kiss the hollow of his neck.

The smell of his cologne awakens my lady parts.

"I think you're getting lawyer confused with mediator." He squeezes my hip and pats my ass to get moving.

I walk in front of him to grab my purse.

"Sorry, Grover." I bend and pet his head. "They don't even know about the big guy yet. Next time." I reach over on the end table, grab a Kleenex, and run it along the flaps of his mouth.

"I think Grover is pretty smitten with you. Maybe you should just move in." Dean winks then busies himself putting his wallet into his pocket and his cell phone into the front of his jacket.

"Moving a little fast there, cowboy," I remark.

"Oh, I forgot, we're still going five under the speed limit."

I laugh, throwing away the Kleenex and grab my clutch.

"You're catching on."

Neither of us taking it very seriously, he opens the door, I file out and we enter the elevator.

"Remember the days when you wanted to make-out?" I joke because this might be my first elevator ride with Dean where his hand isn't on skin. Skin that he shouldn't be touching in public.

"The night is young." He winks and straightens forward.

Just when I think we've already moved into comfortable territory, his hand reaches for mine, grabs my wrist and tugs me next to him.

"Sorry, I'm just a little nervous." He kisses my temple.

"Look at me." He glances down as I tilt my neck to look up. "Don't be. I don't care what they think."

His smile is tight and I'm not sure he believes me, but he will.

The elevator dings open and I walk out, nodding at the night doorman.

"Evening Mr. Bennett. Ms. …"

I tilt my head and wait for him to figure out my name. The poor young kid's face reddens.

"I'm sorry." He looks to Dean like he's going to be mad.

"Tell me, Sean, do you not know my name because Mr. Bennett has so many women come through here?"

His eyes widen. "No. You're the only one I've seen."

Dean's chest hits my back, his hand molding to my hip. "Let's leave the new guy alone, shall we Ms. Walsh?" He chuckles.

"Sean, you seem like a good guy. You'd tell me the truth, right?"

I'm totally joking, and this kid looks like he might have a panic attack if I keep it going.

"Yes. Honesty is the best policy. For sure, Ms. Walsh." He smiles over my shoulder to Dean.

He can't be more than eighteen. Where did they find this guy? A gnat could intimidate him.

"Don't worry, Sean, she'll be Mrs. Bennett soon enough," Dean says.

I shake my head at his assumptions. "Can you believe the arrogance of this guy." I thumb behind me.

"How many times have I told you, it's confidence, not

arrogance." Dean pulls me by my hand away from the doorman's desk.

"Have a great night, Sean." I wave.

"You too, Ms. Walsh. Mr. Bennett." He nods.

"Please tell me you aren't that insecure about where you stand in my life," Dean says as he flags a cab for us.

My hands slide under his jacket and I nuzzle into his body. "No. I was just playing with the guy. But you better watch it. You're on the Autobahn with the moving in and now marriage comments."

"One day." He winks, not saying anything else as he opens the cab door for me.

I slide in and he joins me telling the cab driver the name of the restaurant.

I settle into the leather seat since we'll be leaving downtown and heading to the outskirts. I'm crossing fingers my entire family can behave themselves tonight, even if it's not in their nature.

CROSSING my fingers didn't work.

We drop our coats at the coat check, walk into the private room that's already disturbing the restaurant with their laughter and loud talking. Half the group is probably already drunk.

The doors open, and I thought we could slide in unnoticed, but Dean can't slide in anywhere.

You'd think we just came in with ski masks and guns, sounding a warning shot. My Aunt Liz's jaw is on the floor. Skylar's eyes are already slits focused on Dean. Zoe's wrangled Caiden away from the cake with a small smile on her lips. My mom, well, her chest is heaving from how pissed she is that I brought him, and my dad sits there stunned.

"Don't you people have any manners?" I ask, tightening my grip on Dean's hand. It's cold and limp.

Aunt Liz approaches first. "Chelsea." She kisses me on each cheek, her eyes on Dean the entire time. "Dean." She holds out her hand. "I'm sorry, I didn't know." Her eyes focus back on me.

Guess I should have told them.

"Chelsea thought it would make a good surprise," Dean rats me out.

Aunt Liz's displeased eyes land on me, piercing me with guilt.

"I don't see what the big deal is," I continue to fight my decision.

"Don't play that innocent game with me." Her eyes dip to our clasped hands. "So, you two are together?" She waves her finger between us. "Again?"

"We are," Dean answers and for some reason, my stomach flips from his declaration. Maybe my family won't make him run away from me.

"This isn't about a bet or money or some twisted joke?" she asks.

"No," I answer.

"You're not pregnant?"

My stomach lurches. "Please give me some credit."

She nods.

"A few more things." She turns her attention to Dean. "What do you do with yourself now?"

"I'm an attorney."

She cringes and glances at me from the corner of her eyes.

"Tax attorney," Dean clarifies so she doesn't think he's an ambulance chaser and she smiles.

"Drinking?"

"Three years sober."

"I'm to assume that means no drugs as well?"

"Yes, ma'am."

"And you're ready to give this one hundred percent?" She crosses her arms over her chest.

"Okay, Aunt Liz," I plead for her to stop.

Dean's squeezes my hand, he knows he's getting somewhere with her.

"Definitely. I'm in it to win it."

They share a laugh.

"Well then." She extends her arms out. "Welcome back to the family." She hugs him to her body and my eyes swell with tears. Why couldn't my mom have a little bit of Aunt Liz's DNA?

Once they part, she sets her eyes on me. "I'm still not happy about you surprising everyone by bringing him here. It puts everyone—including Dean—in an awkward situation." She shoots me those judging eyes only a mother can accomplish, and the feeling of disappointment falls over me.

"I'm sorry," I whisper.

She nods and then hugs me into her body. "Congratulations. You look very happy."

"I am."

Pulling away, she turns to face the room. "Okay everyone, I know this was a huge surprise, but I've cleared the air. Dean is back in the picture. He's an attorney now."

Grumbles ring out in the room.

"A tax attorney," she clarifies.

They all sigh like that's okay then.

"He's been sober for three years. No drugs and he promises he won't hurt our girl."

A few people smile, a few whatevers ring out. I'm not sure why it has to be some big announcement.

She pats my hand. "Good luck." She walks away,

picking up her grandson from Zoe's arms and telling him how he needs to behave and how that's Great-Grammie's cake.

Now that Zoe has her hands free she makes her way over to us. "I should beat the shit out of you out back," she says to Dean.

"If it makes you feel better, let's go. Three free hits."

She shakes her head, a smile already playing on her lips. "I'm not as easily sold as my mom. I'll be watching you." She points her fingers to her eyes and then to Dean.

"Understood." He nods.

A few other people come up to shake our hands, but Skylar keeps her distance. It isn't until we're at the bar that her fiancé, Beckett, approaches us.

"Chelsea," he says, taking a swig of his beer. "Always making an entrance."

I give him a sour look like I'm seven and boys have cooties.

"Beckett, great to see you again," I say, dripping with sarcasm.

"How come I don't think you mean that?" He takes another swig of his beer, his eyes landing on Dean. "Hey, I'm Beckett, Skylar's fiancé."

Dean shakes his hand. "I saw you two on the news."

Beckett shrugs. "Not sure why it's news, but I guess when two Winter Classics medalists get engaged, people find it interesting."

Dean steps closer to me. "See Chels, at least we dodged that. Imagine if our short marriage was splashed on magazines and news channels."

I roll my eyes. The pity of the entire U of I campus was enough for me to hightail it out there and head to concrete skyscrapers.

"So, you two?" Beckett leaves the question in the air.

"Yes," I answer, and he takes another swig of his beer. "I'm glad. You seem happy."

"If only your fiancée would actually talk to me tonight." I really should leave this topic alone. Let Skylar act like I'm invisible and Dean isn't here. Let her act like a childish brat when it has nothing to do with her.

"You know her. She's a ball buster."

"To everyone but you." My tone turns bitter and Dean's hand squeezes my hip, telling me to quiet down. He knows better. That move never worked on me.

"What can I say? It's my charm I guess." He holds his hands out to his side like 'check me out.'

"I think it's your dick."

"Chels," Dean says my name with warning and I have to say I like the way he's trying to keep me in check.

"Listen to your boyfriend," Beckett says with a chuckle.

"Are you suggesting your dick isn't impressive enough for her to go easy on you?"

"And that's our cue." Dean's hand slides across my lower back, capturing my hand, ready to pull me away. "We're going to take a breather."

Dean ignores my uncle Jim who tries to say hello to us on the way through the room and pushes open the back door into the alley.

I struggle to free my hand from his grip, but he doesn't let it go until he cages me in with his body against the wall.

"I like your thinking." My hand slides down the front of his shirt bumping along his abs until my finger slides under the waist of his slacks.

He takes his hand and stops me, spurring my gaze to shift to his.

"You're cockblocking yourself?"

"What's with you?" he asks, his eyes appearing darker than normal.

"Beckett and I have a mutual dislike of one another."

He doesn't say a word, just stands there brooding and silent. His hand eventually leaves mine and he places it back on the brick that's currently scratching my back.

"Talk to me," he says, all serious.

"How about I taste you?" I fiddle with his belt and again his hand clasps down on mine.

"Chelsea?" There's that warning tone again.

"Dean," I return the same one. "Since when do you not want to fuck me?" My hand wiggles out of his grip and I dip under his arm.

"What's up with this whole night? You not telling your family I was coming? Not going up to Sky? Being a bitch to Beckett? I know you well enough to know you're not dealing with something and that's why you're acting like this."

I pace up and down the filthy alley that reeks of old spaghetti and spoiled veal.

"Skylar can do whatever the fuck she wants. She wants to be a brat, fine. I don't care."

He leans his shoulder against the brick, his arms crossed and lets out a long sigh.

Yeah, we both know I'm talking bullshit.

"This isn't about Sky."

I stop pacing, meeting his gaze. "It will never be like it is for them." I choke back tears.

"Like what?" His arms drop, and he pushes off the wall.

"Beckett and Sky, everyone is so happy for them. No animosity, no anger. They just accepted him into the family."

A tight smile forms on his lips and he slowly walks toward me.

"So maybe it does bother you more than you think that your parents don't accept me?"

I shrug.

"It's okay, you can tell me I'm right later."

I huff out a small laugh. He reaches up and cups my cheek. "Baby, one day they will. What we have is complicated and none of them understands. All they see is some has-been baseball player who lost his shit in a bottle of Jack. A guy who left his new bride alone and abandoned. But that Dean is gone and maybe they haven't realized it yet, but you have. For me, that's all that matters. But if those people in there matter this much to you, then I'll make damn sure they know what we already do, that you're number one in my life."

I shake my head. "You shouldn't have to do that. It should be enough that I know, and I tell them so."

His large palms slide down my bare arms, taking each hand in his. "Your family is important to you. I've always known that."

I step into his strong arms and he holds me tight to his body.

"But the bitchy girl who's throwing a tantrum because she didn't get what she wants has got to go."

I jab him in the stomach, but he never moves an inch.

"You love my bitchy side."

He chuckles into the night air. "I love every side. But I think everyone in there would prefer to see a different side of you."

"How fitting I find you both in the alley?"

Dean steps us to the side so we can see who it is, but I'd know that voice anywhere and I prepare myself for round two.

Chapter Twenty-Six

"Thank goodness you have clothes on this time." Skylar's arms are crossed, her eyes throwing daggers at me.

I slide out of Dean's embrace, stepping in front of him as though I'm protecting him.

"Let's remember one thing before we get this started, I never gave you shit about Beckett. If anything, I pushed you toward another man, so he'd realize he loved you."

"Okay girls."

"Stay out of this, Dean," we both say in unison.

Dean steps out from behind me. "Fine. Go at each other's throats."

Skylar and I are practically like sisters. We grew up together, playing tag around holiday dinner tables, secretly telling one another our crushes. Jeez, with the same last name, people thought we were a set of adopted twins all through school. This isn't the first time we've thrown it down, and I know it won't be the last.

"I'll be inside." Dean opens the door, passing Skylar with a shake of his head.

"Were you never going to tell me?" Skylar asks, her gaze narrowed on me.

Anyone passing by would probably think we're minutes away from pulling each other's hair out. That's not us though, we punch and kick. We just haven't done it since we were sixteen.

"Obviously from your reaction tonight, I chose correctly. I don't need your doubts."

Her exaggerated huff echoes in the dark. "You're the one who calls him your biggest mistake."

"Maybe I was wrong." I shrug.

Her shoulders lose the fight and sag.

"Maybe he's changed. People can change," I say.

Her hands leave her hips. "I never said they couldn't, but Chels—"

I raise my hand in the air. The dim yellow light above the door our only way of seeing one another.

"I don't want your negativity. I love him, okay? I know very well I'm lighting the match on the explosive and my entire life could blow up. But maybe it won't. I don't need you and my mother and Zoe and anyone else who wants to weigh in telling me he's no good."

She steps closer and there's a glimmer of a smile on her lips. "You're so intense right now."

"I was there for you."

"I know," she says softly.

"I never told you how horrible of a guy Beckett was even when he was being the biggest douchebag."

She stops in front of me, her smile on full display now. A glimmer of hope sparks inside me.

"I don't need another mother, Sky. You're supposed to be on my side."

Her hands touch my shoulders. "Okay."

I roll my eyes. "Okay? It's that easy?" I cock a hip out to the side, not fully believing her.

"Let's remember who got in that awful pink dress for that dinner reception your mother forced you to have after you and Dean ran off and got married. I stood by your side then and I'll stand by it again, Chels, but this time if he hurts you, you better have money for bail."

She pulls me into an embrace.

"Is that a deal?" she asks. "If he hurts you, I take a meat cleaver to his nuts."

"That's fine because his dick will already be a hood ornament if he does."

She laughs, and I wrap my arms around my cousin's body.

"So, are you going to keep stuff from me from now on?" she asks. "Because I'm going crazy with this wedding. Everyone is all over me in there. I have to thank you for taking the pressure off Beck and I for a while."

"No one can take the shine off the golden couple," I say like the sullen child I'm acting like.

She breaks away from me and tilts her head. "When you and Dean get married again, you'll be a golden couple, too."

What is it with everyone shifting gears so fast?

"Marriage is way down the line," I say. "If ever."

"I don't know, you and Dean always do things fast."

"Sky—"

She holds her hands up, walking backward toward the door. "I'm not judging. I'm just saying."

I nod. She's right. We move fast in everything we've ever done. Whether it was five years ago or present. Taking my time around Dean always seems like a waste.

Skylar and I return inside through the back door of the restaurant, my eyes immediately finding Dean at a table with Vin, Mikey, and Beckett. He's telling a story that has all of them laughing.

"Looks like he's already in with the guys again," Skylar says.

"My husband was practically giddy when you walked in." Zoe comes up next to us with a sleepy Caiden in her arms.

I run my hand over his dark hair. "So peaceful and sweet."

"When he's sleeping." Zoe stares down at her son with love bursting from her eyes.

My gaze scatters across the room, and then double take to my mom's who's currently glaring at Dean and my dad who has refused to look at me all evening. It's his usual M.O. Let my mom handle all the dirty work.

I elbow Skylar. "That'll never be fixed."

Sky and Zoe follow my line of vision. Sky's arm sliding through mine. "She'll come around eventually. Between my mom and everyone else, she'll get there."

My mom won't make a scene here and maybe that's why I slid Dean into this family gathering. That way he's here and she won't attack him. What would people say if she took me by the arm and escorted me out of the room, or worse was seen yelling at Dean outside the restroom? I'm not sure if her disdain comes from being protective or spiteful.

"Come on, let's go join them." Zoe walks toward the table, just as her daughter Molly meets us on the dance floor. She's doing the floss.

"Way to go girl." I hold my hand up in the air. She smacks it and then her arms start moving as fast as Jade's did at my house.

Aunt Liz and a few of my other aunts are watching her

and laughing. She's bragging about her only grand-daughter and how smart she is.

Two arms wrap around me, and a chin rests on my shoulder. "What are you thinking about?" Dean asks.

My hands cover his. "Nothing really."

"I'm assuming since Sky just punched my shoulder but smiled at the same time that we're good?"

I giggle. "Yeah, another Team Dean inductee, well…"

"Your mom will come around, Chels. Just give her time," he whispers, kissing my cheek. "Come and have fun with your cousins."

He leads me back to the table and I slide into the seat next to him.

Mikey's smile is bigger than when he's about to get laid. Maybe he knew something I never did.

My mom's eyes flicker to us every now and then, but she never says a word and neither does my dad.

"MOTHER FUCKER!" I walk down the hall, thankful that there's no clients or potential donors in the office. "I fucking hate Mondays."

"First off, language. Second of all, I have a soft spot for Mondays." Victoria types away on her computer.

I roll my eyes. "Still in that love bubble I see."

She points a newly manicured nail my way. "You are too, unless something just went horribly wrong this weekend." She stops typing, spinning her chair my way. "Did it?"

"Well, I can't find the fucking string to my IUD, so now I gotta make a doctor's appointment. I don't even know if it came out or it's floating around somewhere in my body right now." I cringe.

Victoria's face pales.

I point to her, circling my finger around her face. "You take those thoughts and spin them back your way. I'm not pregnant."

"Oh good." She lets out a breath and brings her hand to her chest. "You guys use condoms?"

"First off, I had an IUD, they're like ninety-nine percent effective."

I ignore the boulder in my stomach reminding me that it's not the getting pregnant part that's my problem.

"Not if it falls out," she adds helpfully.

I stand, wishing I would've said nothing to her.

"I should call the doctor and see when they can get me in." I head to my office, my heels clicking on the floor.

"I'd be happy to go with you." She calls out from her desk.

"Thanks, but I'll be fine. Plus, you don't want to be there when my hoo-hah is all open for investigation." I shut the door to my office, sit in my chair and the entire memory flashes in my head like a car crash. Slow motion and just as hurtful and painful. I cannot go through this again when Dean and I are just now getting to a good place.

I pull out my cell phone, seeing a text from Dean, but ignore it since the doctor is more important at this point.

The receptionist puts me on hold forever, but after I explain what happened, she gives me an appointment for the next day at three. Not ideal, but I'll take what I can.

I pull the text from Dean up.

Dean: *What do you want for dinner?*

Such a simple question. One he's sent me before, but this time I see the path we're going down. My apartment sits deserted most of the time since Dean's is closer to downtown and about ten times as nice.

Me: *I'm thinking about chilling at home tonight. Is that cool?*

The three dots appear and then disappear until another text pops up.

Dean: *You want alone time?*

I stare at my computer for a second, staring at the selfie I took of me and Dean by the lakefront two weeks ago.

Me: *Well…*

I type and then I delete.

Dean: *It's cool if you do. My hand doesn't do nearly the job your mouth does, but I'm sure you can make up for it next time. LOL*
Me: *Assumptions, assumptions.*
Dean: *In all seriousness, I'm good with you wanting a night alone. I can take care of myself.*

A small part of me is saying tell him, tell him, tell him that if you come over, there is no sex because you have no idea where the little thingy that's not supposed to come out went. The other part says, but if we tell him, he's going to think we could be pregnant and then goodbye easy times and hello dredging up the past.

Me: *I just have to hammer down some things here and I might go and crash. I'll definitely be up for some phone sex though.*
Dean: *Well then, I'll practice my deep gruff voice and sharpen up my dirty talk.*

Me: *Your dirty talk is just fine.*
Dean: *Not when I can't use my hands and mouth at the same time.*

I laugh, my thumbs poised on the screen.

Me: *Then it's a date. Ten o'clock. You call me.*
Dean: *Have Rambo ready to go. ;) See you at ten.*

I wait for more, but there's nothing. Maybe Dean really has changed because years ago he would've protested any time apart.

TWO HOURS LATER, Victoria walks into my office with a black box with a pink ribbon wrapped around it. "Another special delivery." She places it on the corner of my desk.

I snatch the note off and it only reads:

For your eyes only.

"Thanks, Vic." I sit back down at my desk and return to the email I was sending.

She clears her throat.

"Sorry, it's private." I glance over to her.

Her smile falters. "Oh, I see how it is. Let me guess that's not going in the trash." She smiles and then grabs the knob of the door. "I'll shut this for your *privacy*."

I circle in my chair and the smile won't wipe off my face. "Thanks."

She nods and playfully rolls her eyes before closing the door.

My chair almost crashes into the wall behind me from how fast I spring up to my feet. I untie the ribbon and tear off the matching pink tissue paper and then collapse back into my chair.

"Oh. My. God."

My feet tap on the floor and I can barely hold in the scream I'm dying to let out. This man knows me better than I know myself.

I pick up the piece of paper labeled Instructions.

- *Use the bath salts to take a long and warm bath at nine o'clock.*
- *Soak until the water runs luke warm.*
- *Dry yourself with the towel.*
- *Lotion your body up with my favorite smell on you.*
- *Slip into the nightie.*
- *Have the vibrator next to you in your bed.*
- *Plug earbuds into your phone and answer my call at ten pm sharp or be prepared for a spanking.*

My smile doesn't tease my lips, it lights up my entire face as I inspect each item. The silk of the lingerie, the softness of the towel.

I don't send him a thank you text because I'm sure he knows I got it and my thank you will be later tonight when his cum shoots out him like a rocket.

Chapter Twenty-Seven

*a*t ten o'clock sharp my phone rings.

"Tell me you followed the directions?" He's lowered his voice to a deep timbre and my limbs dissolve into my mattress.

"I have."

"Good girl," he says softly. "First of all, you can't touch yourself until I tell you that you can."

"Okay," I whisper.

"So compliant tonight."

"Well—"

"Run your hand down your chest, through the valley between your tits and slide the nightie up, exposing yourself."

My fingers graze the silk fabric and I pull up the edge of my nightie. The coolness of the ceiling fan makes my center come alive.

"Slide your finger along your pussy and tell me how wet you are."

I do just that finding myself already soaked. Not that I'm surprised.

"I'm wet."

"How wet? Wet enough I could slide right in?"

"Yes." I let out a breath imagining how he'd be touching me if he was here right now.

"Good start, but I like you dripping."

Me too, I want to scream. Bring it on.

"Put your finger in your mouth and tell me how you taste, but run that finger up the front of yourself, letting the nightie slide up another inch."

I do as directed, my finger hovering over my erect nipples that beg for attention.

"Do not touch your tits," he orders in his domineering voice.

How does he know?

"Just once?" I practically beg.

"Chelsea." My name wraps around me like the softest of silk.

"Fine," I groan.

"Lick your finger, slowly teasing yourself with only the tip at first."

I twirl my tongue around the top of my finger, and it gets me thinking, I have no idea if he's undressed. This whole taking a back seat thing is hard.

"I'm swirling my finger like I do the tip of your cock."

His groan leaks out over the line.

"Why I'm busy tasting how sweet I am, why don't you fist your hard, thick cock for me."

A low chuckle falls out of him. "You just can't let me take control, can you?"

"We do this together."

Another chuckle, but he doesn't fight it and the rustling of sheets says he's doing as I asked.

"My hand is on my dick."

I let my finger pop out of my mouth. "You slipped

out." Making another exaggerated slurping noise, I get more aroused from tasting myself.

"Leave your finger in and then cup your tit with your other hand, pinching your nipple."

"Thank God." I lower my free hand and put pressure on my breast like Dean does, using my forefinger and thumb to pinch my nipple.

"Harder," he demands, and my fingers tighten. "How does that feel?"

"Not nearly as good as when you do it."

He laughs, and I hear a bottle open on the other end.

"Lubing yourself?"

"Well, you're not here to coat my dick."

I close my eyes, imagining the liquid flowing over his tip and his strong hand wrapping around his big cock as he spreads it all around.

"Are you imagining that it's me who's made you so wet, Dean?"

"Is that finger out of your mouth?" he asks since I'm speaking freely.

I quickly put it back in and keep up with the exaggerated noises.

"Remember only I can tell you to touch yourself."

I playfully roll my eyes. He can't see me.

"Don't roll those beautiful blue eyes."

I let a low chuckle loose. "I didn't."

"You did and we're getting off track."

"Sorry master."

"My dick just twitched."

A low heat runs through my body, my blood set to simmer.

"Cup your pussy, diving your finger between your folds, into your wetness and tell me how good it feels."

I do as he says, leaving one hand on my tit, the slippery

silk becomes damp as the ceiling fan does nothing to cool me down anymore.

"I'm dripping." My voice is low and sultry and matches exactly how my body is feeling.

"Grab the vibrator and turn it to the lowest setting."

Reluctantly, I take my hand off my tit and grab the pink vibrator and it buzzes in my hand.

"Lightly place it on your clit."

It tingles, and I clench, loving the arousal coursing through my blood.

"Close your eyes baby and finger yourself. Imagine those are my fingers."

My back arches and I buck into the vibrator needing more. "I need you," I pant, and he chuckles.

"No, you don't. Up the intensity."

The vibrating along my clit has me on the brink and I squirm around the sheets trying to find a release that's still too far away.

"Better?" he asks in a low voice.

"No, I need your dick. Come over now."

"I appreciate the compliment and I wish it was your pussy wrapped around my cock instead of my hand, but your groans and moans are going to be what makes me come tonight."

We're both quiet for a moment, each enjoying our own pleasure and the sounds the other is making.

"Go ahead and slide that hand under your nightie and grab your tits again, play with your nipples."

When my hand cups my breast and my finger runs over my nipple, I actually believe it could be his hand.

"Better?" he asks.

I release a strangled groan. I'm about two seconds away from coming. My hips rise off the mattress as if he's really here on top of me.

"God, yes," I moan.

"I appreciate the reference. Now drop the vibrator."

"No!" I screech, just one more level up and I'm there.

"Chelsea, drop it," he orders.

"Why?" I whine.

He chuckles. "Because I'm about to be inside of you."

The vibrator drops between my legs and I sit up. "Are you here?"

Sweet Jesus tell me he's surprised me like that night months ago. I don't need the donuts and Mickey D's. Just his dick and his hands and his mouth. Okay, and his arms to hold me close afterward.

"No."

My body flops back down to the mattress. "You got me all excited."

"Sorry." He chuckles. "Put two fingers inside that soaked pussy and play with yourself exactly how you do when you're thinking of me."

I roll my eyes but does as he says and my body sinks into the mattress once more, content that I'm about to fall off the ledge at any moment.

"Do it like you normally do, Chelsea. You can get yourself off, and I want to hear exactly how it sounds when you do."

I do as instructed, playing with my clit and then putting my fingers back in. Moans fall from my lips and my breathing rushes and then slows.

"I'm so fucking hard," Dean grates out and I can tell he's trying to hold back.

"I'm so fucking wet."

"I wish I could grab you and plow into you right now."

"I wish your fingers could dig into my hips and you ram in and out of me."

Our breathing labors over the line and if it wasn't for the headphones, I would've dropped the phone.

"Next time, I promise baby."

"Oh, Dean, it's coming."

"Don't fight it."

My mind blanks and sails over the finish line with a cry out of his name as my body pulses with pleasure. Afterward, my hand falls from between my legs as I lay limp on the mattress, tired and sated.

"Fuck baby, that noise you make."

And then I hear nothing except some panting and grunting as he finishes himself off. I don't look at a clock, but it isn't until we're both breathing even again that one of us cuts the silence.

"Don't take this the wrong way. I love having sex with you any way I can get it, but I really wish you were next to me right now," he says.

A smile comes to my lips. "To snuggle?"

"To lick up my cum, but I guess to snuggle, too."

"If you were in front of me, I'd punch you in the gut."

He laughs. Not the steamy rougher chuckle from before. This time it's his honest and true laugh.

"I gotta clean myself up."

"I don't want to hang up," I say.

"Me either, but you need your sleep. Sweet dreams, Chelsea."

"Good night."

"Love you," he whispers.

"Love you."

The line dies, and I pull the earplugs out of my ears and roll to my side, wishing the other side of my bed wasn't empty.

Chapter Twenty-Eight

*T*he next day at three o'clock on the dot, I sit in a waiting room filling out papers with pregnant women all around me.

Some are glowing, and some look like they could murder someone. Others are trying to control their young kids and some are rubbing their stomachs smiling at nothing.

Shaking my head, I concentrate on my family history. Why do I have to fill this out every year? I answer the yes and no questions to every disease imaginable, sign the privacy form and put my insurance card on the clipboard.

The receptionist handles everything and gives me back my insurance card, leaving me again in a waiting room.

"Did you just find out?" The woman with a swollen belly glances at my flat stomach.

I stare down at it to make sure it's actually not showing a bump. I had a big lunch but other than that I'd bet the largest casino's vault I'm not pregnant.

"Oh, no, I'm not pregnant."

She smiles and waves me off. "I always forget that

women don't only come to an OB because they're pregnant. Are you trying? I hope I didn't offend or upset you."

I smile although it's not genuine because if I were trying, I wouldn't discuss it with a stranger. A stranger who is pregnant. "I'm not trying either."

"Oh." Her eyes fall over me, taking in my dress and heels.

Digging my phone out of my purse, I decide to lose myself in anything but conversation with this lady. I'm not sure if she thinks I'm some woman who never wants to have kids or what, but frankly, it's none of her business. I don't even talk about this stuff with the people I'm closest to.

Women come and go and I look at the clock on my phone. A half hour since my scheduled appointment.

Finally, my name is called by a nice nurse with red hair pinned into a bun. We do the whole dreaded weighing and blood pressure routine. Once I'm in the exam room, I explain my problem. She smiles nicely and leaves the room.

Twenty minutes later, my panties are hidden under my dress folded up on a chair with my shoes neatly tucked underneath. The paper gown scratches my skin as I double check I'm not flashing my ass. Not that it should matter, I'm going to spread-eagle any minute.

Would it kill them to turn down the air conditioning in here? I have goose bumps all over my body now.

A knock sounds on the door.

"Come in."

"Miss Walsh, I wasn't expecting to see you again so soon." My doctor, a woman in her forties or so walks in wearing scrubs. "I apologize for the wait, but I just got back from delivery."

"No problem." My stomach twists in nervous anticipation. I just want to get this over and done with.

She sits down on the stool, her laptop poised in her lap.

"You think your IUD came out?" she asks. "When did we put that in again?" Her fingers scroll on the mouse, never looking up at me.

"A few months ago. My old one had expired. I never had a problem with the old one."

She sets the laptop down. "It says February we gave you the new one. I bet the strings are just shorter this time and you just can't get as good of a feel." She slides forward putting up the stir-ups. "I'll check and we'll make sure you're okay. It's rare that it comes out or dislodges, but I can't say it doesn't ever happen."

Gently she moves my feet into the stir-ups. "Scoot down to the edge of the table for me. Just like that. Good."

I lay down on my back, staring at the ceiling tiles that so many women before me have seen as well. They should put motivational messages up there or something. My hands grip the edge of the bed in preparation for the medieval torture device to open me up.

"So, how have you been?" She begins the awkward small talk like I'll forget she's looking into my honey pot. Meanwhile, I'm praying she sees two strings coming out of my uterus.

"Okay. Busy with work."

Not that my busy work is equal to hers. I mean she probably gets woken up to deliver babies on the daily.

"I hear that. Any one special guy in your life these days?"

Why is she asking me that? Because there are no damn strings, I bet. My breathing becomes labored and I mentally will myself to calm down, doing some deep breathing exercises.

The instrument closes and I finally can breathe.

"Um, too early to tell."

Yeah, yeah, I lied. So what?

She takes off her gloves and puts them on the table and I wait for her to hold her hand out to help me up, but she doesn't. And she doesn't try to get me out of the stir-ups.

Shit, shit, Shit! Dean and his giant cock.

Her hand finally outstretches, and she helps me up. "Stay undressed below the belt for right now. I can't locate the strings to the IUD. There are so many variables that I don't want to tell you anything until I can get you in for an ultrasound."

My face must pale because she doesn't wait for me to respond.

"Don't assume anything. If you're worried about pregnancy, I guess we don't really know how long it's been missing. Have you been sexually active?"

I swallow.

"Yes, but—"

She stands up, rolling the chair back to the desk area. "Let's just wait and see where we are before we start talking crazy. Let's handle the ultrasound first. I'll be right back."

I'm silent as she walks out the door. Once alone the despair wraps around me like a straight jacket.

This cannot be happening. Not now. We aren't ready to face something like that. It will ruin us. Again.

Lucky for me she knocks a minute or so later but leaves the door open.

"I know this isn't the best, but I was able to secure an ultrasound between two patients to have a look really quick. Would you like another sheet?"

I hop down. Let's get this over with. "Nah, I'm good."

"Okay, it shouldn't take but a few minutes. If it's okay,

I'll grab your clothes so you can change in there. I'm sure it just got dislodged and maybe came out. Nothing too serious."

I follow her two doors down into a dark room with the only light inside emanating from the machine.

"Have a seat."

I weave my body through the stir-ups and lay down, looking at the wand. Memories flood back to me as she puts the latex over the top and squirts lube on the tip.

"Okay, you ready?" she asks, holding the dildo looking device in her hand.

My hands grip the side of the table. "Yep." I blow out a shaky breath.

The pressure between my folds eases when she's in and her eyes focus on the screen. Her free hand clicking buttons. She rotates it around and I try to see something, anything, but she has the screen turned away from me.

"Okay, Chelsea, the IUD must have fallen out because I don't see it. My guess is when we put it in that it wasn't placed properly. Sometimes they slip out during a bowel movement or maybe during your period and go unnoticed."

I'm silent for a moment, taking in her words. "Then we can just pop in a new one?"

I hear a noise and then she pulls the wand out of me, slipping off the condom and throwing it away while sanitizing the instrument. Her hand reaches out to help me up, but I don't want to.

As soon as I'm sitting up, I see her face and I know she's about to tell me the one thing that will destroy Dean and me.

She tears off something down below the ultrasound machine and holds it in her hand. "We can't do another IUD yet." Her expression is pensive.

"Oh, do I have to wait a certain amount of time or something?" I ask, grasping at straws. "Weird since they literally took out my first one after five years and popped in another, but whatever."

"Under normal circumstances, we could but, Chelsea—"

"Nope. Don't say it." I shake my head.

"Chelsea, please, I know your history, but there are things—" She passes me the paper and I don't even bother to look down at it.

"How far along am I?" I whisper.

She smiles. "You're six weeks."

I squeeze my eyes shut. "That's impossible." I jump down from the chair, pulling my phone out to check. "I had my period." I find it on my app. "A-ha, I had it three weeks ago."

The doctor's lips fall. "You can have your period when you're pregnant, especially in the beginning. Was it a lighter period?"

"My periods are always light."

She releases a breath. "I understand being scared." She steps forward as I'm already fumbling and putting my underwear on. Fucking lube.

"Wait here for one second, okay?" she asks.

I don't agree or disagree. I just need to get out of this office.

I step into my dress, finding the zipper and pulling it up as I slip into my heels. When I open the door, a nurse stops and stares at me.

"I think the doctor is coming right back."

I walk by her without a word.

"Miss Walsh?" she asks, but I head through the maze of their office to find an escape. I feel like a rat caught in a maze as I go down one row only to end up at an emergency exit.

"Chelsea."

I turn around to find my doctor there with a bag in her hands. "I just need to absorb the news."

"Please, come into my office." She opens up the door next to her.

Of course, I end up cornered by her office.

I walk in, taking the seat in front of her desk, inhaling a deep breath.

I am strong. I can do this.

She rounds the desk and places the bag down. "First of all, I know you're worried, and we're going to be super cautious with you."

"I can't. I just can't." One tear slips down my cheek.

"I wasn't your doctor before, so I can't speak to that, but with your medical history we can try to stay on top of this." She stands, rounds her desk and takes the seat next to me, her hands grabbing hold of mine. "I can't promise everything will go smoothly, but I can't promise any of my pregnant patients that. The pills I have in the bag are your prenatal vitamins and the extra folate you need to take."

It feels like a vise is constricting my chest and I can't speak for a moment past the lump in my throat. After what feels like forever, I voice the secret I've kept to myself for the past five years.

"I thought there was no way I could carry a baby?" I practically whisper.

Her hands squeeze mine. "We're going to stay on top of it. Give you the extra folate your body needs."

I want to believe her. I really do. Could the thing that destroyed us, solidify us five years later? I'm just not sure.

Chapter Twenty-Nine

Dean: *Okay, I need the live version of my girl tonight. I'll order Chinese.*

I flip the phone over so it's upside down on my couch and I can ignore it a little longer. The ultrasound picture lay next to it. The little bean. My hand falls to my stomach. The only plus is I don't have to tell him that we have to use protection. That ship has sailed. A while later my phone pings with another text and I reluctantly reach for it.

Dean: *I'm coming over.*

Shit, I knew he wouldn't keep his distance.

Me: *Sorry, I'm with Skylar. A week before the wedding is a hectic time for a bride.*
Dean: *That's why we made the right decision to do it in Vegas.*

I shake my head and smile.

Me: *Well, we were drunk. I'll call you when I'm done with her.*
Dean: *No need to call. Just come over. No matter the time.*

My gut tells me to trust him with the news. No way it will turn out like it did before. He *has* changed. But still, that small amount of doubt inside is spreading like a bad rash.

"Not yet." I touch my stomach. "We'll tell him when it's safer. Stay strong little one."

I rise from the couch, grabbing my computer and search up statistics of successful pregnancies with the MTHFR Mutation. For the rest of the night, I read as much information as I can. I read about women who suffered numerous miscarriages before finally successfully carrying a baby. I read about women who never even knew they had a problem until their second pregnancy. I'm obsessed with getting as much information as I can about my situation. At the end of the tearful, hopeful, and devastating stories it looks like I've got a fifty-fifty shot of being able to carry this child to term.

A knock lands on my door and I slam my laptop lid down like the person can see through my door and I've been caught watching porn. Standing up, I head to the door and glance at the time on my entertainment center, finding it after ten already.

Through the peephole I see Dean, his hand already positioned to knock again.

"Dean?"

I look around my apartment seeing the ultrasound picture on the couch. Running over, I shove it into the first thing I find, my purse.

"Chelsea," he says, knocking once more.

"I'm coming." I take the bag of pills from my doctor and drop them behind my couch.

When I open the door, Dean walks in without an invitation—like usual—his gaze taking in every inch of the room.

"Are you okay?" he asks, staring at the pile of Kleenex on my end table.

Shit, I forgot about that.

"Yeah, just reading a sad article online."

Not a complete lie.

He nears closer to me, his hands running down my arms. "What's going on with you? I feel like you're dodging me."

I shake my head.

Tell him. Just tell him.

"I think I know what this is about." He smiles like he's the most brilliant detective there is.

"You do?"

No way he does.

"I know you want your family to like me and with it being Skylar's wedding it makes you remember us and how horrible it was after we announced our marriage." He pulls me into his arms, his hands holding my head to his chest. "Don't worry baby, eventually it will all turn out okay. They'll accept me. It might be fifty years from now, but it will happen."

I say nothing, letting him think the assumption he's made is correct. My mom's approval can stay shoved up her ass.

My arms tighten around his middle, needing the comfort of his arms. I pray things turn out differently this time around.

"Come on, you look exhausted." He shelters my hand in his, locks my front door and guides me down the hall. "I'll even keep my hands to myself tonight."

We enter my bedroom.

"What about Grover?" I ask.

"He can stay by himself and I'll run back home before work." He strips down to his sweatpants, leaving him stark naked.

"Are you going to be able to keep that thing away from me tonight, too?"

He slides under the covers. "I'll try, but you know he's got a mind of his own." He winks, and the news sits at the tip of my tongue.

"Come." He pats the bed next to him, his hand propped under his chin and holding his head up.

"You didn't have to come," I say.

I take off my clothes and pull back the covers. When I slide in, his arm drapes over my stomach, pulling me flush to his chest. "I'm not going to let you hide from me. We face this together."

My body loses the fight and I sink into his hold, his one hand flat on my belly.

He should know. I should tell him.

Somehow, I just can't get the words out.

His other hand grabs hold of my breast and I flinch.

"What's the matter?" he asks. He massages it with his hand and I resist the urge to pull away. "Were you too hard on yourself last night?"

"What?" I ask.

"When I told you to pinch yourself? Are you super sore today?" His voice is low like he doesn't want to disturb someone else in the apartment.

"A little." Another lie slips out and more guilt piles on top of me.

His hand falls down and releases my breast. "Sleep baby," he whispers, his thumb running a small circle around my stomach as though he knows our little bean is in there and he's soothing it to sleep, too.

Oh Jesus, when did I get so emotional?

Oh yeah, when my hormones went into overdrive to grow a baby inside me.

At least I hope that's what it's doing.

THE NEXT MORNING, I'm at my desk. Early because I made up the excuse to Dean that I had an important meeting and I just didn't have time to have breakfast.

I hear Victoria enter, her footsteps clicking down the hall.

"When I call you, I'd like an answer." She sits down in the chair across from me.

"Sorry," I respond, pretending to write down something important.

"What did the doctor say?"

Fuck me. Why didn't I prepare an answer for her? No way it's fair if I tell anyone before Dean.

"She scheduled me for an ultrasound."

I say a silent prayer to be forgiven for all the lies I'm telling. But they're necessary to protect the people I care about.

"So, it is out?"

I nod slowly.

"How? That's scary."

"She said when they inserted the new one a few months back, that maybe it wasn't placed properly." I shrug acting like it's no big deal.

"So could you be…"

Of course, Victoria would ask me straight out. But if I tell her about the pregnancy and the fact I didn't tell Dean, she's going to tell me how wrong that is.

Yeah, yeah, I know she was right the first time she

told me to talk to him when he first started pursuing me again. If I hadn't, I wouldn't have him in my life right now. A man who knows me so well, he shows up at my apartment late at night because he knows something's wrong.

"We didn't talk about it."

Her eyes narrow. "The doctor didn't ask you if you could be pregnant?" The sarcasm drips off her words like ice cream off a cone on a scorching hot summer day.

"She just said she'd have to schedule an ultrasound to make sure it's not lodged inside me somewhere."

Another lie. How many am I up to now?

"Chelsea," she says, and I meet her eyes for the first time. "You're lying."

"No, I'm not." I shake my head, swallowing down the guilt of all my lies in the past twenty-four hours.

"First off, you're way too calm for the fact that a foreign object could be floating around inside your body somewhere. Usually you'd have entertained me with some crazy story about your gyno appointment. Second of all, you're antsy." She looks side to side and then leans forward. "Are you pregnant?" she whispers.

Hearing the question point blank makes it so much harder to deny. A tear falls down my cheek and drops on the paper I've been writing a to-do list on as a distraction from her.

"Oh, sweetie." She stands from her chair and comes over to me, wrapping her arms around me.

I don't stand though or reciprocate the affection.

"Why are you upset?" she asks.

My gaze meets hers. She's such a great mom. Loving and caring and has that 'tell me anything and I'll still love you' look in her eyes when she talks to Jade. Like she's strong enough to take any weight on her shoulders.

"It's not my first time being pregnant with Dean's baby," I say.

She tries to cool her reaction, but I see the shock on her face.

Hannah barrels in, surprising us both. "What's the matter?" Her eyes widen and she stands on the other side of my desk.

Victoria stares at me and I nod.

She turns her attention to Hannah. "Chelsea's pregnant."

Those two words are now out in the world to people other than the little bean's father. Guilt rips at my chest, but there's a small amount of relief that at least I'm not lying to everyone I know anymore.

"And it's a bad thing?" Hannah asks, honestly curious.

"I think their shared past might make it a bad thing." Victoria chimes in and studies me, waiting for me to give them more information.

For the next hour, we talk about what happened five years ago and why I loathed Dean as much as I did. As hard as it was to talk about, it felt good to get it out. Even if it brought my feelings closer to the past with Dean than my future with him.

Chapter Thirty

Skylar and Beckett stand up at the altar, pretending the priest is telling them what to do. I stand two back with Zoe in front of me and Sky's friends Mia and Demi behind me. Across the way is Beckett's two buddies, Grady and Dax along with Mikey and Vin.

Caiden and Molly sit on the steps. Molly's sulking from not being able to practice with real flower petals today while Caiden's busy sliding his butt down the stairs.

I glance out to the pews which hold a few of our relatives as Dean steps into the church.

He came right from work and although I've been dodging him with excuses of feeling sick all week, he still glows with a smile that says there's nowhere else he'd rather be. I slept at my own place for three nights, but last night I met him for dinner and slept at his place.

His gray suit is buttoned, the heels of his dress shoes clicking before he sits a few pews back from my parents. My mom must notice my face because she never turns around to see who came in and her blinking increases exponentially.

"I now pronounce…" the priest lets the words trail off and Skylar and Beckett smile. "Now you'll walk down first."

Skylar slides her arm through Beckett's and they dodge Molly and Caiden as they walk back down the aisle. Molly and Caiden follow. Zoe and Grady, me and Dax, Mia and Mikey and Vin and Demi bring up the rear.

Dean winks at me as I pass him by. Once we get to the end, Aunt Liz rushes over with her phone.

"Picture time!" she screams.

"I'll have enough pictures tomorrow," Skylar says.

"Come on, one of you guys up on the stairs." She steps aside and Skylar huffs but starts to head down the marble walk way.

"I need lipstick then." Skylar turns back around. "I left my purse in the bride's room."

"Who cares, we need to get this over with. Caiden and Molly are about a minute away from losing it. The out of town guests are probably at the restaurant already. You don't need lipstick. It's a picture for Mom." Zoe lightly pushes Sky on the back.

"Says you. They're my wedding pictures."

I think the wedding stress is getting to everyone, not to mention everyone here probably has a hunger bitch going on.

"You can use mine," Zoe says, grabbing her purse next to mine, digging in.

"I can't pull off that red. I need more of a coral." Sky looks around at the girls. "What are you wearing, Chels?"

Beckett rolls his eyes, heading down to the front with his buddies. They're both razzing him about how great the pipe is in New Zealand and how behind he is because of all this wedding stuff.

"You can use mine." I turn, but Zoe's already wrestling with my purse, digging through every nook and cranny.

"I'm organized," I say. "Grab the makeup bag."

Zoe walks toward me, her focus on the bag, her hands probably messing everything up. "I don't see a makeup bag."

Caiden jumps off a pew landing on Zoe's back. "Horsey!" he screams.

Zoe looks behind her, scowling at Caiden, and my purse tips in her hands. She falls down to her knees, Caiden laughing thinking his mom is actually going to be a horse right here in St. Matthews. All of the contents in my purse spill out before the purse plops down like a dead fish in the middle of the aisle.

"Caiden!" she screams.

Vin grabs hold of him. "No, Mommy was going to be a horse," Caiden tells his dad, struggling to get back on her.

"Not today," Vin says.

"That's what you said last night. Why is she a horse for you but not for me?" Caiden crosses his arms, a scowl across his face as all of our eyes widen in surprise.

"Shut up. All of you." Zoe points as everyone in the circle giggles like someone just said vagina and we're six years old.

"Maybe you should lock your doors." I laugh.

Zoe narrows her eyes at me. "The kid can pick a lock. Hence the fact" —she looks at a still very pissed off Caiden — "he saw me and Vin playing horsey and cowboy last night."

All of our combined laughter echoes off the stained glass and beamed ceilings.

"Okay now. Everyone stop," Aunt Liz tries to get everyone in order.

"Grow up," Zoe mutters.

Vin comes over and puts his arm around his wife, an arrogant smirk on his face.

"Chelsea," Dean says, and I look over my shoulder.

My heart shudders and almost stops, the breath leaving my body.

He's holding out the ultrasound picture with half the contents of my purse packed back in, the rest still scattered on the ground.

"What's that?" Aunt Liz asks and then her eyes widen. She finds my mom a few people back. She points, and my mom steps up, grabbing it from Dean's hand.

"Chelsea!" she scolds me. "Is this…is this yours?" She holds it up and everyone gasps around me, their eyes pinging between the ultrasound and me. They want answers.

I stare into Dean's eyes. "Yes."

His head falls back between his shoulder blades and his hands fly up to cover his face. There's no happiness in his body language.

It's silent for a moment and after a minute he holds his hand out. "Can I see that Barb?"

To my surprise, my mom hands it to him.

He looks it over. "We need to talk." His tone is clipped and his face holds no emotion.

My mom holds out her arm at him as he approaches me. "Not with that sour look on your face. You will not do to her what you did to her five years ago."

Dean's feet stop, his eyes turning darker than I've ever seen. His gaze flicks to my mother. "Good thing this isn't five years ago then." He takes her arm and moves it to the side of her.

"I…"

"Not here," he says to me.

"Dean." Zoe grabs his arm.

He pulls his arm free.

"You've known this entire week." He towers over me and I meet his stormy eyes.

"I have," I say in a quiet voice.

"Oh, Chels," Sky sighs and I catch her and Zoe sharing a look.

Dean stands there, tucks the ultrasound in the pocket of his suit jacket. "We're going to talk now."

I walk up the aisle and through the doors, standing in the lobby area. Dean makes sure to shut the doors behind us.

"When are you ever going to forgive me?" He sits down at the pew on the wall, his head in his hands.

"I did forgive you."

"You clearly didn't. You refuse to talk about what happened. I've tried so many times to get you to talk about it. And now this…"

I throw my hands up in the air. "Why would we talk about it? So we can feel the pain again or should I say so *I'll* feel the pain. You'll probably just deal with it on your own like last time."

He leans back like I slapped him. "I was fucked up then. I was an alcoholic. I wanted to talk to you about the miscarriage because I wanted everything from our past out in the open. A clean slate for a fresh start. Now you're pregnant again and hide it from me? Just like the first time."

My eyes close, losing the fight against my tears. "I didn't know I was pregnant the first time."

"You expect me to believe that now?"

"You expect me to feel bad for hiding it from you? I sat in that hospital when they told me that I'd been pregnant and I didn't even know it. I was the one who bled alone in a sterile room. No one to hold my hand, no one but a fucking nurse to tell me I'd be okay. And then for the doctor to tell me…" I stop because saying it out loud means this baby inside of me is in jeopardy of my body rejecting it and I can't deal with *that* and *this* right now.

"What? What possible reason could there be for you not telling me about this baby?" He stands and stalks toward me. "You have to let me in Chelsea. This will never work otherwise."

I cross my arms over my body and shake my head. "While you were drinking with your buddies or passed out on the couch, a nurse I didn't even know wrapped her arms around my shoulders as a doctor told me that I might never have children. I have a mutated gene and my body can't turn folic acid into folate. I was eighteen and I didn't know what the hell he was talking about. Just that I might never be a mother and you weren't there. You weren't there!"

He steps into me, but I push him away. He fights, his arms around me and I sob into his shoulders.

After a minute, I collect myself and finish telling him what he needs to know. "The chances of this baby making it is only fifty percent. That's why I didn't tell you. Because more than likely I'll end up in the hospital bed again."

Dean steps back, his arms falling off me. "Alone?" he asks.

I shrug.

"You still think I'd do that—ignore your texts and calls. You still see me as a monster."

I shake my head, but I can tell he doesn't believe me.

"You can deny it all you want, but your actions and your lies this entire week say different." He slowly backs away from me.

"A tiger doesn't change its stripes," I whisper.

A condescending huff erupts out of him. "How original." He keeps stepping backward away from me.

"Do you think you'll ever truly forgive me?" he asks, now a good distance from me.

"I do forgive you."

"Keep putting that on repeat and maybe you'll believe it one day."

I swipe the tears from my cheeks. "What do you want from me?" I almost yell, my mixed up emotions getting the best of me.

"I don't know anymore." He looks as heartbroken as I feel right now.

My anger comes fast and furious. "How fitting. Just go then." I point to the doors of the church.

Dean stares at the door. "I'm not sure what more I can do to prove it to you."

"Maybe you can't."

"You're giving up on us?"

I shrug. "Maybe you're right. Maybe this thing between us was a disaster from the beginning."

"You believe that?" he asks.

I shrug again.

"Say it, Chelsea. You say the word and I'm out. But you can bet your ass I'll be a part of that kid's life." He points to my stomach. "But I'll leave yours if you think you'd be happier that way."

I swallow and cast my gaze to the floor. "Do what you want, Dean."

"Which means what exactly?"

"Maybe we need some space. This whole thing is crazy. I mean in a couple month's time, we're supposed to erase the past and get back together and have a baby? This isn't a Lifetime movie. Things don't end up in a perfectly wrapped box."

He stands there, his eyes not leaving mine for an uncomfortable moment. "Tell Skylar and Beckett congratulations." He walks toward the doors.

I say nothing, falling into the pew as the click of the doors bounce off the walls, sealing our fate.

My hand runs along my stomach.

The doors of the church open and I expect to see Zoe and Skylar, but my mom comes over and sits down next to me.

Her two hands take mine and rest on my lap.

"I'm so sorry, Chelsea. I had no idea."

How could she? I told no one afterward. They knew about the miscarriage because my health insurance was under them, but I never told them what the doctor said. Now I guess everyone knows.

I lay my head on my mom's shoulder. "Guess you were right about him."

Her hands tighten with mine. "Somehow I don't think that's the last we'll see of Dean Bennett."

Chapter Thirty-One

The next morning Skylar stands in front of the mirror, her white dress puffing out into a million layers, her bodice beaded down to her waist. She looks stunning.

I'm trying to forget the whole mess with Dean and the fact that I didn't hear from him after he left the church last night. Today is my cousin's big day and I can't let my situation overshadow that.

"I still say you should've planned it like most people do. This whole whirlwind wedding stuff is a lot." I sit down on the couch in the bride's room, checking out my shiny blue bridesmaid dress in the mirror across from me. "And I know you say I'll wear this dress again, but I'm calling bullshit, I won't. And you'll never wear the one I made you wear."

"Noted, but I have to say, mine is ten times more beautiful than the pink number you put me in."

"Your groom is ten times better, too," I grumble, unable to completely put the man I love from my mind.

"I won't fight you on that. He's slow out of the gate, but he sure knows how to make up ground."

"That's where I went wrong. Mine was fast out of the gate and then didn't know which lane he should stay in."

Her eyes meet mine in the mirror and I ignore the look she's giving me. It's the same one she's given me all last night and all day at the hairdresser. Go after him. Get him.

"Why did we rush again?" she asks. Maybe I had it wrong and she was thinking of herself...not that she shouldn't, this is her day.

"It wasn't a rush. It was four years too late." Demi walks in with her veil in her hands.

Four years.

I slide out from the bride's room, needing some space to think. This is Skylar's day and I'm not going to ruin it. I find some space down the hall on a bench, enough to see some guests, but far enough that no one will come up to me.

I'm leaning with my head against the wall, eyes closed, trying to draw in some strength and fortitude to get through this day when somebody sits next to me. Before I can see who it is, something falls into my lap. "Here."

I look up to find Mikey, his eyes wide.

When I glance down I see my phone and I shake my head, tears threatening once more. "No."

"Stop being bullheaded and stubborn. What you went through, Chelsea, it's horrible and I was all for you punishing Dean, but now you're just punishing yourself, too."

"No, I'm not."

He stops, pausing for dramatic effect and urges the phone back at me. "You are. You're miserable. Just apologize to him. Tell him that you still love him. Be honest with him. Open your heart to him. Let him in."

"You make it sound easy."

"There's a reason I'm single...the way you look at him and the way he looks at you...I haven't found that yet. And I'll make you a promise. If I ever do find it, I'm not going to lose it. I'll protect it. Whatever the cost."

I reach over and squeeze my little cousin's hand. "Look at you, talking so grown up."

"You can deny it all you want, but you never stopped loving him. I know it's scary, but if you're going to make this work, you have to be vulnerable. You have to risk getting hurt." He pauses for a moment to let me take in his words. "When I ran into him a few years ago, I punched him because I was still protecting you. I wanted to make sure he knew what an asshole he'd been. But right now, he's looking like an angel and you're looking like the one who should be punched."

I scoff, and he knocks his shoulder against mine, smiling.

"You're supposed to have my back," I complain.

"I do, which is why I'm keeping it real with you. And now Dean's going to be the father of my newest cousin."

He taps the phone in my lap, stands and walks away. "Make it snappy. We're on in ten."

I stare at the phone. How Mikey got my phone, I have no idea, but the guy's sneaky. I remember when we were little, and he tried selling mine and his sister's bras and underwear to his friends. What a perv.

I click to see there's no new text messages or calls. I laid awake last night, guilt and shame gnawing at me knowing that as much as I've let him in, I also kept him arm's length away. He's nothing like the guy who broke me.

Without debating any further, I pick up the phone and dial his number.

It rings and rings, but he doesn't answer.

"This is Dean Bennett, please leave your name and phone number and I'll get back to you." It's his professional voice. It beeps and my own voice catches in my throat.

I clear it. "Dean. It's Chelsea. I'm sorry…you're right. I've been keeping a wall between you and my heart. That doesn't mean that I lied when I said I love you. I do. So fiercely that it scares me because I know how much it hurt last time things didn't work. And now I love you more…I don't know if I'd survive it if it didn't work again. I don't want to compare you to five years ago and I don't want to rehash what happened to us. I don't want to recount our horrible past. Because we had good in that past, too. And I don't want to forget our first kiss. Our first date. I don't want to forget how your eyes watered when you first bit into that chicken wing as I sat across from you. I want to remember our wedding night and how I never felt more wanted and more loved, and how you still make me feel that way. I'm sorry for not telling you about the baby. Being scared isn't an excuse. I know that. You know where I am today, and I'd love for you to come and join me. If not, I understand. Maybe we can sit down for coffee and talk about the baby. I guess I'll be having herbal tea… anyway…I won't have my phone with me, but I'll check it periodically. Please just call me back. Just know that I love you, Dean and that includes the past, present and hopefully the future."

I click end call. Zoe peeks her head out of the bride's door. "You just about ready?" she asks with a smile.

I get up and move toward her.

"Everything okay?"

I nod. "Yeah. You know Mikey's a lot smarter than we give him credit for."

She laughs as I step through the door. Putting her wrist on my forehead. "Are you sure you're feeling okay?"

We laugh, she might not realize how great her brother is, but I do. He's going to make some woman very happy someday.

Chapter Thirty-Two

Skylar and Beckett kiss after their vows and the entire church claps. I smile at my cousin for getting her happily ever after. Beckett and I may bicker like step-siblings, but there's no doubt that he's the one for her.

They walk down the stairs, Beckett unable to stop staring at her. As practiced we all follow as the guests smile on at us.

Once we're through the doors, everyone takes turns hugging Skylar and Beckett.

"We have the receiving line now," Skylar reminds Beckett and we all take our places.

All of my relatives walk through the line, kissing both my cheeks and telling me how beautiful I am. How I've grown. No one says congratulations which means my close family has been able to keep the news to themselves. Just like my first marriage, the perceived bad news has a way of staying on the DL.

Once it's over, we take pictures. I smile on as best I can. I'm happy for my cousin, but my head still turns with every person who enters through the doors and I wonder if Dean's called.

Finally, with sore cheeks, I make it back to the bride's room and I pull out my phone.

No text messages.

No phone calls.

I climb into the limo, my smile fading steadily the more time that goes by.

We get to Buckingham Fountain and the bridal party takes more pictures. The night that Dean took me here after the game comes to mind. My heart tugs because that was the first night I thought maybe there's more to him than the Dean of five years ago. Maybe Dean had changed. Hope bloomed inside me that night, but right now I feel as if my hope is fading.

I smile some more, growing irritated that I can't drink out of the flasks Mikey and the groomsmen have tucked in their tuxes. No champagne or wine with the girls. Zoe thought she was funny when she handed me one of her kid's apple juice boxes in the limo.

Throughout the day, I smile and make small talk with the other bridesmaids. Not that I have much in common with two women who ski professionally, but they seem like fun girls. Demi and Dax practically have sex on a park bench. No fear of PDA there. Mia and Grady don't stop kissing and going off on their own. Sky and Beck are lost in themselves as they should be on their big day. And Zoe and Vin are constantly wrangling their kids. Caiden almost fell into the fountain head first and it caused a small tiff over who was supposed to be watching him. Vin lost that one.

Mikey's been on his phone practically the entire time, texting numerous women no doubt.

Me, I get to sit and reflect in between shots. It's as though karma is shining down on me once again and saying I told you not to fuck with me.

"Party time!" Dax wiggles his ass like he's a Chippendale dancer on his way back to the limo.

I try not to roll my eyes. Polite and nice is always the best.

I really hope Dean is just holding out on me to make sure I realize he's the catch he is.

I climb into the limo unladylike and plop down next to a window. The sun is shining down on the lake and families are enjoying the early summer day.

"Whatcha thinking about?" Mikey knocks his shoulder with mine, staring out the window with me.

"How much I love Chicago."

"Bullshit. Don't doubt him, Chels. I see you checking your phone. Have some faith."

I face him, my eyebrows furrowed. "Where the hell did Mike Walsh disappear to? Has someone taken over his body?"

He pulls out the flask, unscrews it and downs a hefty-sized gulp. "I'm a closet romantic you know."

His whiskey breath hits me. "What are you drinking?" I can't keep the envy from my voice.

"Rock Hard Whiskey. My friend said it's the best. I picked up a few bottles at Miska's. Wish you could try some but since you're knocked up." He smiles to say he's joking.

"Haha." My face contorts into a disgusted expression.

"You probably would've had half the bottle already if you weren't." He glances over in my mother's direction.

"Whatever." I cross my hands over my chest.

Mikey's perma-smile dips and he leans in, his alcohol breath making me nauseous. "You know she'll come around. Especially after the baby is born. Babies bring families together, not tear them apart."

"That's it." I push him with my hand and he falls into Vin's shoulder. "A romantic life coach has taken over Mikey's body."

Zoe laughs, staring at her little brother as she tries to open a string cheese for Caiden. Is that what my life will become? I can only hope.

"Get the f...get off me," Vin catches himself.

"Close Daddy," Molly says.

I laugh at the girl who knows way too much for her age. I'd be lucky to have a kid like either of them. I can only hope I make it that far.

For the zillionth time, my hand touches my stomach as though the small bean can sense me thinking about him or her.

"No dollar for you." Vin points to his daughter. She smiles like he's her hero. I love that look.

We arrive at the reception venue twenty minutes later and I have to pee so bad I thought I was going to have to go in a champagne glass when we got stuck in traffic.

"I'll see you guys in there." I open the door, head in, weaving through the drones of extra guests Aunt Liz invited.

Lucky for me, all wedding receptions are held at the same place in our family, so I make it to the bathroom in record time, knowing the lay of the land.

I close my eyes as I pull my dress up and my underwear down. Narrowly peeking out of one eye, I check my panties to see if there's any blood. Once I see it's clear my shoulders relax and I exhale in relief.

I do my business, thankful for another moment. Although if it's like last time, the cramping will be what brings me to the hospital.

After I wash my hands and reapply some lipstick, I check my phone.

Still nothing.

It's not like Dean not to get back to me.

Well, it's not like the new and improved Dean.

How badly did I piss him off?

I open the bathroom door and step out to see most people are still enjoying cocktail hour and the doors to the actual dining hall haven't opened yet.

Sliding by a bunch of mingling groups, I say brief hellos and let a few older relatives hug me, pinch me and tell me how old they feel seeing me grown up.

Caiden and Molly are scanning the place cards on the table.

"Aunt Chelsea, do you see us?"

I help them, finding each of them their placecards. "You're table nine."

"Nine?" Caiden asks.

"Yep."

Molly looks over the cards again. "All the kids are at table nine. I don't want to be at a kid's table."

"Sweetie you are a kid."

"Hey!" she exclaims picking up a card. "What's Dean's last name?" Molly asks, staring at a card.

"Bennett."

Molly's eyes widen and she shows the card to Caiden whose eyes bulge out. "What did he do to be put at the kid's table?"

Molly shrugs.

I grab the card, clearly seeing that a seven has been made into a nine. I'm pretty sure Zoe or Sky had something to do with this.

"Do you think he'll dance with me?" Molly asks.

I start to fix one of her curls that's gone array from the wind by the fountain, taking out a bobby pin and repositioning her hair. "I don't think he's coming."

"Wrong," Caiden says.

"I know it's disappointing, but you'll still have fun without Dean."

"You're wrong, he's here," Caiden says with a tone that suggests I'm an idiot.

My hands freeze, the bobby pin falling from my mouth and it's all I can do to keep Molly's hair between my fingers until I can secure it again.

Dean stands at the entrance doors, his eyes searching through the crowd. Lucky for him, his height is an advantage. He meets my eyes and a small, shy smile crosses his lips.

Someone bends down next to me, and then hip checks me. "Go." Zoe nudges, taking her daughter's hair from my hands.

I walk toward him, and he walks to me. Our eyes don't waver from each other.

"I know you might not want me here," he says. "But I couldn't leave you alone here tonight."

"What?"

"I get that you want your space and I know we have a ton to talk about…"

"Did you not get my message?" I ask.

A confused look crosses his face and he digs out his phone. Scanning through his missed calls, his eyes light up. "I have no idea how I missed it."

"It doesn't matter. You're here." I step forward and he doesn't hesitate to wrap his arms around me. "I'm sorry. That's all the message says. I'm sorry for everything. You're right I was still holding you at arm's length."

"I can't expect you to shift gears so fast. It's me." He steps out of our embrace, his palm sliding down my arm until he has my hand in his. Guiding us outside, the stifling Chicago summer heat feels like walking into an oven.

"We really need to think about moving." He doesn't stop us until we're on the side of the building where no one can see us.

He cages me in with my back against the brick wall. "I can't spend another night without you beside me. Please don't make me." He gently places a chaste kiss on my forehead.

"Okay. I questioned how much you'd fight for us and I was wrong to do that when I wasn't even willing to fight myself. So, Dean." I hold his face in my hands. "I'm in this. One hundred percent whether it ends in I do, or I want a divorce."

"We already did the I do part." He smirks.

"We did the divorce part, too."

He laughs, stepping in so we're chest to chest. "So, we're all good again?"

"Yup."

"Man, we're so mature now. Not even a dish broken." I laugh remembering the crazy fights we used to have when we were younger. I guess that's the good part of sharing a past. They see you change for the better.

"We should go in, cocktail hour is going to end soon."

"We need to talk about the baby, but for now I'll take a kiss." He leans in, capturing my lips, his tongue moving at a slow and easy pace.

"You call that a kiss?" I question when he closes it.

"Oh, my little freak is back in full effect I see." He grabs the back of my neck, tilting it to the side and slams his lips to mine, displaying how bad he wants me from the way our tongues fall in line, fighting for dominance.

When he pulls away, he reaches for my hand and starts to lead me inside.

"I can't wait to see what pregnancy is going to do to your hormones," he says.

Rather than smack him on the chest, I laugh because I can't wait to see either.

Chapter Thirty-Three

"*Y*ou're actually supposed to be at table seven."

Dean glances away from the kid's table and over to the table full of Beckett and Skylar's friends from skiing. People we've seen on commercials and who have impressive careers in the limelight.

"I'm surprised I get to sit with the cool kids." He kisses my cheek. "Although I wish I was next to you."

"Dean! Dean!" Molly runs over, grabbing onto his suit jacket sleeve.

"What's up, Molly?" Dean asks, holding his hand up for a high five.

She goes to hit it and he moves it away. "I hope you can do better than that?" she asks.

"Whoa, did I just get dissed by a little kid?" he looks back at me baffled.

"I'm not little." Molly puts on the attitude that matches her mother's.

"Sorry, big kid." Dean puts his hands up in front of him.

"Come on." She pulls on his jacket.

"Where am I going?" he asks as he pretends to fight back.

"Your card says table nine," Molly says.

Dean pretends to put an arm out to me as though he needs saving.

"What do I tell the cool kids?" I ask with a laugh.

"Tell them I found cooler kids to hang out with." He winks. "Save me a dance."

Then he turns around and goes with Molly, pulling out the chair for her and then takes the other. A minute later, I can see that Molly introducing him and he's leaned over the table asking for high fives from all the kids.

"I'm still not sure, but I suppose he does seem different." My mom comes to stand alongside me.

"Don't be too apologetic there, Mother."

An older image of myself stands beside me looking elegant and sophisticated. Everything she wants people to think she is. So worried about outside appearances rather than the inside. If our relationship had been different, I would've told her about what the doctor said after my first miscarriage. Maybe she would've done more research than I did at the time and we would've found out some people have successful pregnancies. Maybe she would've taught me what it was like to be a mother, rather than showing me the type of mother I don't want to be.

"Well." She straightens the shoulder of my dress. "It is nice to tell my friends my daughter's boyfriend is a lawyer."

"Even though she's pregnant out of wedlock?"

Her face morphs into stone. "I assumed there'd be a wedding. I mean the two of you went off and got married in a rush when there was no baby. Surely my grandchild won't be born with me not knowing which name to ask for at the hospital, his or her mother's or father's."

"I don't know, Mom, I like to keep you on your toes." I

pat her on the shoulder. "There's no ring on this finger yet." I hold up my left hand.

"Chelsea," she warns.

My eyes go wide, stepping farther and farther away from her. She'll never raise her voice.

"Have a great night, Mom." I find my seat at the head table.

"I see I was right." Mikey pretends to straighten his collar like he's the shit.

"He's here, yes."

"All kissed and made up?"

I elbow him in the ribcage. "Yes."

"Good to know." His phone buzzes to life in his pocket.

"For heaven's sake, Mikey, what the hell is going on? Who do you have to talk to so much?"

"What can I say, I'm popular." He shrugs.

I roll my eyes. "Uh-huh."

For the entire meal and through all the speeches, my eyes find Dean from across the room. We share a smile every time we catch one of us looking at the other. He's the highlight of the evening at table nine based on the fact that the kids are all laughing hysterically and have the other tables giving them dirty looks.

"Seems like it's not only you he can win over," Mikey whispers, rising from his chair. "I'm going to the bar."

"Wish I could join you."

"See you in nine months." He laughs stepping off the stage, disappearing to the bar that's located outside the dining area.

Dean stands and places his napkin on his chair and nods for me to join him outside.

Since all my responsibilities as bridesmaid are over, I follow Mikey out the doors. More people funnel out toward the restroom or the bar, chatting with one another.

By the time I make it to where Dean should be, he's talking with Mikey and some of his childhood buddies. The guys are all drinking hard alcohol and what I guess is a tonic water is in Dean's hand.

"Trust me. The single life is not as great as they make it out to sound," I hear Dean say before I poke my head in their little circle. "I was just telling them, they have no idea what they're missing out on." He snakes his arm around my back, pulling me to his side. "I guess you're on my train for a while? Tonic?" he asks, holding his drink out to me.

"I think I'll just have water."

Dean waits for his turn at the bar to grab me a water. A second later I have a glass in my hand.

"Maybe I should put a lemon in it, so people don't ask," I whisper so only he can hear.

He sneaks his hand over the table and grabs a lemon, dropping it into my glass.

"What would I do without you?" I say, laying my head on his chest.

After last night I ache to have him hold me.

"Oh, you're no princess. You'd save yourself before you'd ever need anyone."

I kiss his strong jaw. "You know me so well."

He smirks down at me, his lips pressing to my temple. "Excuse us boys, but I need to dance with my girlfriend."

Mikey and his friends are already chatting about some bar they want to go to afterward and how there are no hot girls at the wedding.

"Or baby mama," I say.

His free hand covers my stomach. "You're no baby mama," he murmurs. "I've yet to tell you how excited I am, but tonight I want it to be about us. Okay? Please know as scared as I am about being responsible for someone else's life, I'm so happy I knocked you up."

I push away from him, but he grips harder.

"I'm kidding."

"Yeah, because a baby doesn't mean you have me forever, mister."

"Believe me, I know." He chuckles.

We walk back into the dining room. "Sink In" by Amy Spark starts playing. Dean doesn't skip a beat as he weaves us through the tables until our feet are on the makeshift wooden dance floor. He holds his hand out and when I accept, he pulls me into his chest.

Slowly our bodies sway, his strong hand on the small of my back making sure I'm as close as possible. My head falls to his shoulder, our joined hands tucked between our bodies.

The smell of his cologne brings me back to the few months I've gotten to know him again and a feeling of security envelops me. We get lost in each other as we move around the floor.

"I love you," he whispers.

I tilt my head up, my lips landing on his neck. "I love you, too."

When the song ends, all I want is to snatch Dean away from everyone else. I love my cousin, but I don't want to do the bridal dance, or wait for the cake to be cut.

"Ladies and gentlemen, the bride and groom are going to take the dance floor for their first dance," the DJ announces and the dance floor clears.

Beckett and Skylar step onto the floor and she spins into his arms. Dean comes up behind me, his arms around my middle, his hand running up and down my stomach. He's always done that, but I wonder if it means something more now. Has he absorbed the fact that there really is a baby inside me? Have I?

"They make a good couple. He evens her out."

I laugh, my head falling back against his shoulder. "Is that you saying she's uptight?"

"You said it, not me."

For the rest of the night, we dance and mingle. Molly and Caiden join us to become a foursome on the dance floor before I get tired and sit down, watching them instead.

Dean sneaks a look my way. "You okay?" he mouths, and I nod, certain that he'll be just as great with our kids as he is with Molly and Caiden.

"So, it looks like it all worked out." Skylar sits down next to me, a bottle of water in front of her.

"Looking that way."

She stretches her arm out, her hand covering mine. "I'm glad. He's a better man than he was before."

"He is."

"So maybe I'll be coming to your wedding next?" She raises her eyebrows.

"Not for a while. I refuse to get married until after the baby is born just to piss my mom off."

She giggles, sipping down her water. "If and when you need me, I'm there."

"If I carry to term I'll need you next April."

She slides closer to me. "You will and if you don't, I'll be there, too. Think positive, okay? In our training, they teach us to envision the outcome we want. That's what you need to do. I know you'll worry so I won't tell you not to but remember that it's different this time. The doctors are aware of your condition and they're going to watch you closely."

I nod, stealing her water and taking a sip.

"Don't contaminate my water!" she screeches.

"Oh, Beckett will have you knocked up in no time, I'm sure."

She says nothing, and I wonder exactly how soon they plan on having a family.

"The timing has to be right."

"I hear congratulations are in order?" Beckett comes to join us, bending down and kissing my cheek.

"Yes, they are. I was just telling Sky that she needs to hop on board the baby train."

Beckett smiles down at his now wife and raises his eyebrows.

They're having a conversation I'm no part of. I know with her schedule that she needs time to be pregnant, have the baby and get back into shape if she wants to compete at the next Winter Classics. Since they just finished, I'm wondering if this might be the time for them.

We talk about nothing in particular, my eyes veering to the dance floor every once in a while.

After the night draws to a close, Dean holds my hand and leads me out to the parking lot.

"I'd wanted to bring my motorcycle. It's a great night for a ride."

"Yeah, it is."

"But even if I'm a great rider, I'm not risking my two most precious cargo. So, we're going to cab it."

He opens up a door to a cab waiting out front of the building and I slide in.

"Whose place are we going to?" My head falls to his shoulder.

"Just close your eyes and let me handle the details."

I close my eyes and trust him to do exactly as he says.

Chapter Thirty-Four

"Chelsea." Dean's soft voice stirs me awake.

I pick up my head, happy it wasn't a dream —that he came to the wedding and that we're all good again. Then I inspect our surroundings.

"I thought we were going home?"

"I love that word when you say it." He opens up his door and holds his hand out for me.

I step out and he guides me to where I was hours earlier.

"I was just here a few hours ago. It's so much more beautiful at night."

The array of lights illuminating the water spouting out of the fountain with the dark sky and the skyline in the background is breath taking.

"You were?"

"Pictures."

"Great location. Maybe we'll have ours here, too."

I roll my eyes. "I think we have a bigger obstacle first. Not to mention, I kind of liked Elvis in our pictures."

He chuckles and at this late hour, there are only a few

couples milling around the fountain as they head down to the lakefront.

"Why are we here?" I ask, unable to hold back a yawn.

"I wanted to come here because this is where I first felt like we had a future. It's where you finally opened up to me about your life and let me in."

"That's so funny. I was thinking the same thing when I was here earlier."

"You were?" His face lights up with a smile, his dark eyes twinkling in the night like one of the stars above us.

"Yeah, it all kind of shifted for me that night."

He sits me on a park bench, but instead of joining me, he falls to his knee in front of me.

"What are you doing?" I ask, my voice laced with panic. "You don't have to marry me. I'm perfectly okay with having a child out of wedlock. I don't need a full-on commitment."

"Will you please be quiet," he says, pulling a ring out of his jacket pocket.

My ring. The first one he proposed to me with. His great-grandmother's ring.

"I refuse to let you feel obligated." I shake my head.

He rolls his eyes. "You're ruining the mood."

"Wait." I hold my hand up. "Before you continue, tell me if you wanted to do this before you found out about the baby?"

He blows out a big breath and runs a hand through his hair.

"Chelsea, I've wanted this ring back on your finger from the moment you took it off. I got clean for myself, but also to be a better man for you. I sought you out and agreed to work for free for the foundation you work for just to be close to you." He tilts his head. "And to make sure you couldn't get rid of me. I've spent the last few months pushing my way back into your life and you think that I feel *obligated* to marry you?"

My cheeks heat. "Well, when you put it that way..."

"Now, are you going to let me continue?"

"Yes." I smile and straighten my back, almost too antsy to sit still.

"I've loved you from the first time I saw you. It's like my heart knew something my mind wasn't ready for. I would've eaten a dozen of those wings for a date with you that night. If you had said no, I would've tracked you down anyway. I was stupid and young and a complete moron for letting you slip out of my grasp once. But I learn my lessons because you'll never slip away again. I promise to love you more every day, although I can't even fathom it's possible to love you any deeper than I do now. I promise to take care of you no matter how stubborn you get. Most of all I promise that we do this together. One day at a time for the rest of our lives. For richer, for poorer, in sickness and in health. No matter what happens." He glances to my stomach and with a hopeful smile, he holds the ring out to me again. "Will you please be Mrs. Bennett for the second and final time?"

I hold out my left hand. "I'd love nothing more than to be your wife again."

He slips the ring on my finger and I stand up and wrap my arms around his neck. He squeezes me and swings me around the gravel area and as if on cue the center stream of the fountain bursts out of the top. The fountain dwindles down for the night and the other spectators continue on their way.

Dean sets me on my feet and then falls down to his knees once more, his hands molding to my hips.

"I wanted to make sure we were good. Now I want to

take in the fact that I'm going to be a father." He runs his hand along my stomach. "A part of us is in there?"

I nod.

He presses his lips to my belly. "I have a promise to you too, little Bennett. I promise to keep your mom in line."

I lightly smack the back of his head.

He chuckles.

"I promise that I'll love you so fierce you'll be begging to escape me by the time you're eighteen. Don't worry though, I'll make sure your wings are ready for you to soar. Just keep growing, because I think I can speak for your mom and I both. You're already so loved."

He stands to his feet, his hand never leaving my stomach. "Thank you for that, too."

"Dean, what if—"

He shakes his head, sealing my words with a kiss. "Shh... Enjoy the beginning of our happily ever after, Chelsea."

Epilogue

Two Weeks Later

"So, let me get this right, the woman just called you out of the blue. Said she heard about your foundation and she wants to make a sizable donation?" I lean back in my chair, no longer into the pastrami sandwich I thought I was dying for when we walked in.

Hannah forks her salad and shrugs. "I can't very well advertise her company. She has a sex toy company."

Victoria glances around to make sure there are no small kids around since Hannah obviously hadn't thought about that as she lays it all out in the small restaurant with the lunchtime crowd.

"She does? What's the company name?" I ask.

"Hart something. She did the Unicorn Cock thing."

My eyes light up and even Victoria seems more intrigued. "She did? And she knows about RISE?"

"You act like she's your heartthrob and you're thirteen." Hannah slides the lettuce off the fork.

"Tell me you have a vibrator?" I ask, having the courtesy of leaning forward and lowering my voice.

"I tried one once and eh," she shrugs.

"Eh?" Victoria asks, her mouth agape like she can't believe it.

"Sue me if I'm an old school masturbator."

"You're missing out, Han." I lean back. "And the Unicorn Cock one. Holy shit. Dean used it…"

Victoria's eyes look over my shoulder and she shakes her head. I glance to see a kid with his mom waiting for their sandwiches in line.

"Let's just say, there are not many substitutions for Dean, but that comes in second every time."

"Really? A vibrator?" Getting the clue, Hannah whispers. "Now you're piquing my interest."

"I'll buy you one. It saved me during my dry spell until Reed," Victoria says.

Hannah's interest definitely looks piqued now and I can't believe a woman as independent and strong as her, hasn't taken her orgasms more seriously.

"Not like I really have any other options at the moment," she says.

"Hannah Crowley?" a dark-haired woman peeks her head in the middle of our table, whispering like Hannah's name should never be heard.

We all look at the woman who's dressed in a cute tank top and shorts. Tattoos down each of her arms. Her hair short and sassy. Ten shopping bags hanging off her arms.

"Lennon?" Hannah wipes her mouth and stands, putting her hand out.

The woman stretches her arm out and shakes it. "Guilty as charged."

Hannah motions to the empty chair at our table. "Please join us. Do you want a sandwich or anything?"

"Well, those pickles look good." Lennon laughs and we all glance to the jar of full-size pickles floating in juice on top of the counter.

"They're delicious," I comment.

She laughs, and points. "I have a feeling we have a lot in common."

"I take that as a huge compliment since you're the inventor of the Unicorn Cock. Can you tell me about the name?" I lean forward like I'm a keener in school and can't get enough.

She sits back, crossing her legs. "Well, truth be told, it actually came out of my friend Whit's mouth at first when she was dating her now husband. She was drunk and referred to his cock as magical. I still think it's hilarious. Anyway, it turned into a joke with my friends."

"What made you want to invent sex toys?" I ask. I hope I'm not coming off like a desperate fan girl right now, but truth be told I kinda am.

"Let her be," Hannah urges. "Sorry, this is Chelsea and Victoria. They work at RISE as well."

She nods and smiles at both of us. "You guys remind me a lot of me and my friends."

I know I probably look like a complete loon right now because I'm grinning from ear to ear.

"Anyway, I wanted to say how impressed I am with your foundation. My husband is an investment banker and his partner, Drew, was telling me about it. I don't even know how he found you guys, but I really wanted to help. I have a daughter myself, and I try to teach her to be a strong female. So much so that my husband thinks I'm making her twin brother too submissive to her." She laughs. "He just hasn't found his voice yet. Good thing he has an older brother. Brady will show him the ways of the world if he could stop doing the five knuckle shuffle for five minutes. He's fourteen."

All of our heads nod in understanding.

"Anyway, here is the check." She digs into her purse. "I'd love to open up a branch in San Fran. Instead of my company name, we'd do it through my husband's company. That is if you're ever game."

"Expansion already?" I glance to Hannah whose eyes are poised on Lennon.

"I think we could definitely talk more about it. We're still getting on solid ground right now."

Lennon smiles and slides the check across the table. Hannah never looks at it and pushes it Victoria's way. She picks it up, stuffing it in her purse. You'd think we were doing a drug deal here.

"Great. I'm so happy you feel that way," Lennon says, seeming really sincere.

"Would you like to come to our gala in September?" Hannah asks. "It's like our coming out party."

"I do love a good coming out party." She winks.

As the lunch crowd slows down, there are more empty tables available and Lennon glances over the chalkboard menu. "My husband will be here soon. I'd love for you guys to meet him."

"Let me buy you lunch," Hannah says. "What would you like?"

"It's funny because I feel like I should have Santora sausage." She looks at our table. "It's my friend's family company."

We all smile.

Then she stands. "I'll be right back." She heads to the counter, ordering her sandwich or sausage or whatever.

"What are you thinking?" I whisper.

Hannah shrugs. "I don't know. I don't really know her, but she seems professional."

"And wealthy, wait until you see the amount of the check."

We both raise our eyebrows to Victoria.

"What? I'm the bookkeeper, am I not? I saw a bunch of zeros before I put it in my purse."

We laugh.

"Our mission is to reach as many girls as possible. So, I think it's something we should consider." Hannah leans back in her chair. "Now here are three guys who could probably put your Unicorn Cock vibrator to shame, Chelsea."

I turn my head toward the door and in walks Mauro, Cristian, and Luca Bianco, all of them dressed in shorts and t-shirts. Sweaty but probably still smelling entirely edible.

Not as much as Dean though. No one can beat that guy in my books.

"Hey, Bianco brothers," I call out.

They each stop, wide welcoming smiles on their mouths.

"Chelsea, I heard a rumor about you." Luca eyes my left hand. "And it's true, huh? Dean's going to make an honest woman of you?"

"Again?" Cristian asks.

Mauro hits him in the stomach. "Great news." He bends down and kisses my cheek.

"Thanks."

He doesn't pull away right away. "I'll leave the other rumor to myself." He winks telling me his brothers haven't heard that there's a little one holding its own in my belly. So far so good. Knock on wood.

"Thank you for that."

"Luca!" their mom yells and points from behind the counter.

"Seriously, have you not heard about the loser line?" Cristian follows his brother over to his mom. Once he's hugged her, he heads to the back while Mrs. Bianco lectures her youngest son for the millionth time about giving his hookups the deli number.

"Aren't you mackadocious." Lennon looks up to Mauro.

He studies her for a second. "Thank you?"

"Definitely a compliment. I mean you don't hold a candle to my man, but I imagine you'd make a great hero in a romance book." She winks and then sits down in her chair.

"Doesn't the hero always end up falling head over heels for a girl?" Mauro asks.

"Yep," me, Victoria, and Lennon say in unison.

"Yeah, I'm not sure about that then." His hand grips my shoulder. "I need to get to work, just stopped by for a sandwich. Have a great day ladies." He nods.

"Your man?" Lennon asks, and I catch sight of Dean and Reed crossing over from the courthouse, already assuming we'd be here.

"No, that's my man." Dean walks in with a smile on his face as Reed's going on about something. Probably baseball.

"Oh, I do love a briefcake," Lennon says. When we all look at her for an explanation, she says, "You know a beef-cake in a suit?' "Truthfully, I like them in just about anything."

Dean kisses me on the cheek and as usual, his hand runs over my stomach.

Reed grabs a chair and sits next to Victoria, pressing a sweet kiss to her lips. "How's your day?"

"Better now," she says.

I give the introductions, the guys shaking hands with Lennon. "You guys are so sick in love." Lennon's gaze pings around. "Where's your man, Hannah?"

"Oh, I don't need a man." She waves off Lennon's question.

"I agree with that, but a warm body is nice from time to time. My guess is you're next?"

"Yeah, never again," Hannah says.

"Oh, don't worry, everyone knows you save the best for last," Lennon says with another wink.

"There's always something unique with the first," Victoria chimes in.

"Everyone knows the middle one is the best. The first is practice, the third they throw all rules out. The middle is where the gold is." I laugh.

Lennon and Hannah look at one another. "Nah, last is the best."

Just then a guy walks in. Tall, dark wavy hair, piercing hazel eyes, all decked out in a suit. It takes him no time at all for him to find her. Although she can't see him, his smile widens, and he approaches the table, bending down to kiss the back of her neck.

She startles and whips around. "You're lucky I didn't karate chop your nuts!"

He laughs. "After eight years I would hope you'd know my lips from another man's."

"Oh, I know your lips, Mr. Banks."

They share another kiss and it's nice to see a couple together so long still so in love.

"Brady called and Bianca is acting like she's the CEO, telling Evan what to do. Saying he's the mail boy."

Lennon can't fight the smile. "I told you she'll be the youngest female entrepreneur on record."

"With her brother doing all the dirty work."

We all laugh. "They have Santora sausage here. Want one?" she asks her husband as he grabs a chair from a nearby table and drags it over. Seeing the table shrinking, Reed and Jasper pull another table over. The guys go order their food and by the end of lunch, all of our cheeks hurt from spending time with Lennon and Jasper Banks.

LATER THAT NIGHT, we walk into Torrio's. I told them I'd only stay for a little while but after getting the news that our venue for the gala has pulled out for some unknown reason, Hannah needs some company and a few Vespers under her belt.

"I have no idea what to do. It's July. Invitations were being printed which means I have to get them reprinted, but I don't even have an address. Girls, we need to brainstorm."

After our nice lunch, the shit hit the fan for the rest of the afternoon.

"We'll figure something out," Victoria says.

"As if I need anything else bad tonight," she says.

I look over my shoulder, finding the silver fox walking in with a cocky smirk on his lips.

"Ignore him." Victoria squeezes Hannah's forearm.

Hannah takes her drink to her mouth and silver fox takes a seat at a table behind us. Why does he enjoy torturing her?

She rolls her eyes. "I'm sure we'll figure something out." She fluffs it off.

"We'll find a venue. Don't worry." I drink my water with lemon that I'm already growing tired of.

I see Roarke stand and I keep my eye on him as he heads to the bar, waiting patiently for a drink.

Victoria and Hannah start talking about the possibility of pushing back the gala date and having a winter gala instead. Sounds like Hannah's warming to the idea. All the while, my eyes are on the silver fox and my gut churns when I know for certain he's heading toward our table.

"Ms. Crowley, I couldn't help but overhear that you're in need of a venue." He places his drink down and eyes the spot next to me.

I slide over in the booth closer to Victoria. Hannah narrows her eyes at me.

"Thank you," he says in a deep voice.

"Sure," I respond and again Hannah gives me a death look.

"I'm not interested." She sips her drink.

"What if I can get you not only *a* venue, but *the* venue?"

We all wait for the rest of his offer because none of us were born yesterday.

"I'm sure your price is more than we can afford," Hannah says with a saccharine smile.

Hannah is so impressive. So cool. So collected. But I think she may have found her match.

"Oh, Ms. Crowley, you have it all wrong. You know as well as I do that the art of negotiation is simple. I give you something you want, and you give me something I want in return."

She twirls her glass around by the stem. "And what is it that you want, Mr. Baldwin?"

Victoria and I look to Roarke with intrigue.

"You."

The End

Cockamamie Unicorn Ramblings

Let's see, what can we tell you about Afternoon Delight...

We'll start with Chelsea Walsh. Her character was supposed to be similar to Chelsea Handler's character in *This Means War* when we introduced her in Break the Ice. Hence the reason for her name. In Breaking the Ice we wanted her to test Beckett and give him hell for sitting back and not acting on his feelings for Skylar for so long. The kind of character that knocks on the hero or heroine's head saying wake up and see what you're missing out on.

As things often do with us, things changed. We decided midway through that Chelsea would be one of our Divorcee Dating heroines (see Manic Monday). Which meant she had to have been married. So we threw in a quickie marriage in Break the Ice, wiped off our hands and said done. Or so we thought. At this point the hero was not going to be her ex-husband! Uh-oh!

Dean matured from a bad boy to having the stuffy exterior

of tax attorney to being her ex-husband. Originally, at the end of Manic Monday, Victoria got a message from Chelsea saying that she'd messed up again by marrying her ex in Vegas a second time. They were going to be there for Skylar's bachelorette and that would have been perfect because they could have met Lennon and Jasper at a black-jack table (perfect scenario if only it would have worked out). But there were timeline issues and we just couldn't make it work in a way that allowed us to do what we wanted to with Hannah's story in Happy Hour. Needless to say, Chelsea and Dean's story changed—A LOT!

And for any readers wondering about Chelsea and Dean's first marriage. We purposely didn't do any flashback scenes because we wanted their story to be about the here and now…how they've both grown and how Chelsea was finally able to open her heart again at the risk of having it broken again. BUT…that would make PERFECT box set material, don't you think?

That's about all the 411 on Afternoon Delight.

Our usual dream team plus a few new additions who need a round of applause.

Letitia from RBA Designs.

Ellie from Love N Books.

Shawna from Behind the Writer.

Sarah Ferguson and Social Butterfly PR

All the bloggers who continue to make room for our books!

Heather and Angela for being (not so early) readers. One of these days we'll be ahead of the game. LOL

All our early ARC readers.

And of course, all our unicorns. <3 Without you we wouldn't be able to keep doing what we do. This industry becomes more challenging every day, but we push on because we have you in our corner shouting from the rooftops and encouraging other readers to try our work. <3

Be on the lookout for Happy Hour. As with the entire series, our hero, Roarke Baldwin has a lot of ground to make up if he wants to win Hannah Crowley's heart! Should be interesting!

xo,
Piper & Rayne

Also by Piper Rayne

Chicago Law

Smitten by the Best Man

Tempted by my Ex-Husband

Seduced by my Ex's Divorce Attorney

Blue Collar Brothers

Flirting with Fire

Crushing on the Cop

Engaged to the EMT

White Collar Brothers

Sexy Filthy Boss

Dirty Flirty Enemy

Wild Steamy Hook-up

The Rooftop Crew

My Bestie's Ex

A Royal Mistake

The Rival Roomies

Our Star-Crossed Kiss

The Do-Over

A Co-Workers Crush

The Greenes

My Beautiful Neighbor

My Almost Ex

My Vegas Groom

The Greene Family Summer Bash

My Sister's Flirty Friend

My Unexpected Surprise

My Famous Frenemy

The Greene Family Vacation

My Scorned Best Friend

My Fake Fiancé

My Brother's Forbidden Friend

Hockey Hotties

My Lucky #13

The Trouble with #9

Faking it with #41

Sneaking around with #34

Second Shot with #76

Offside with #55

Kingsmen Football Stars

You had your chance, Lee Burrows

You can't kiss the Nanny, Brady Banks

Over my Brother's Dead Body, Chase Andrews

The Baileys

Lessons from a One-Night Stand

Advice from a Jilted Bride

Birth of a Baby Daddy